Elbow Patches and Other Stories

William Miller

Grosvenor House
Publishing Limited

This book is published by
Grosvenor House Publishing Ltd
Link House
140 The Broadway, Tolworth, Surrey, KT6 7HT.
www.grosvenorhousepublishing.co.uk

A CIP record for this book
is available from the British Library

ISBN 978-1-78623-354-7

Contents

A JOB TO KILL FOR

Marcia was a tall, slim woman in her late thirties, who carried with her an air of self-assurance. She did not, in Josephine's judgement, have a logical mind, but she did have a certain wit, which along with her energy and enthusiasm made her, apparently, irresistible to the Men Who Mattered. She was also Sales Manager of the company to which Josephine was giving the best years of her life as Production Manager; and two days hence, one of them would be appointed General Manager, to Lord, Lady or Person it over the other; to be the first among unequals and to be within a talon of a seat on the board.

To say that Josephine was obsessed with securing the top job would have been a masterpiece of understatement. It wasn't just that she coveted the power it would bring, it was also that, over the years, she had come to hate Marcia with a passion almost pathological in its intensity.

Josephine was aware that she couldn't compete in appearance. Her figure was Rubenesque compared with Marcia's classical Greek, nor did she have the woman's style in clothes and accessories. That would have been tolerable had it not been for the condescension, the 'compliments' pointedly made to draw attention, when Josephine's handbag didn't match her shoes, or when her blouse hadn't been ironed properly. Then there was the almost inaudible, impatient, tapping of the pencil during Josephine's presentations to the executive committee; the glazed stare, the flickered glance of amusement when Josephine made a point clumsily. None of these pinpricks were in themselves significant, but endured constantly, they became a knife wound permanently felt between the shoulder blades. So, when Marcia came into the Production office with a sheaf of sales forecasts and said, in a loud voice; 'I like your new hairstyle', Josephine determined that she just couldn't bear the thought of having to congratulate the evil bitch, having to look in her eyes and see the gloating; having to be subordinate. The fact that she hadn't been near a hairdresser for a fortnight was the catalyst that completed the process of crystallisation that had been bubbling under the surface for years. Marcia had to be got rid of.

There was a third contender for the post of General Manager: George the Accountant. Unfortunately, or perhaps, in the circumstances, fortunately, for George, he was a kindly soul with all the personality of a grapefruit, who could not be considered a threat.

It didn't take long to work out a plan. It depended in part on the fact that Marcia had no sense of smell; something that had been revealed once when they had been walking together through the factory. There had been an accidental release of a small quantity of mildly toxic, pungent smelling gas used in the process. Marcia, apparently unaware of anything untoward, had to be pulled clear by Josephine. Initially furious at the rough handling, Marcia had subsequently apologised, thanked Josephine and explained her disability.

The knowledge helped in the construction of a simple, undetectable, murder plan.

Marcia had been with the company for two years when Josephine arrived, and because she was the only other woman on the management ladder, had made a special effort to be helpful to the newcomer, who was intelligent, but apparently, by her appearance, totally lacking in self-esteem. In these early days, Marcia had tried hard to instil in her the importance of not only being, but looking, efficient. At first, Josephine seemed grateful, and for a time they were friends, to the extent that when Marcia decided to buy a bigger house, she sold her flat to Josephine at a very reasonable price.

Over the next few years, however, their relationship, despite Marcia's best efforts, gradually cooled, until a sharp frost was generated whenever they were in the same room. Josephine continued to make no effort to improve her appearance and apparently came to resent even the slightest encouraging comment that Marcia, with the best of intentions, put in her direction.

Then there came the day when Marcia suddenly realised that this dowdy woman, who had all the dress sense of an Eskimo's grandmother, had become a serious rival.

The Men Who Mattered had always paid attention when she, Marcia, appeared, particularly if she was wearing one of her favourite outfits, but gradually she came to realise that they were no longer eating out of her hand. Increasingly, on matters of business, they were paying close attention when Josephine spoke. There was no doubting that her mind was cool, logical and fast, like a stainless-steel rat trap. Furthermore, it had time on its side, for while Marcia had the suspicion that her face and figure were slowly succumbing to the relentless pull of gravity, Josephine's mind continued to burgeon and become too big for its boots.

Too often lately, Marcia's passionate advocacy of new ideas, new product lines, had been blown out of the sky by the elephant gun of Josephine's insensitive production-line logic. Marcia was coming to the belief that, in business, the value of flair and grooming lay somewhere between the ability to lick stamps and the capacity for saying nice things to the canteen manager.

So now she faced, with no equanimity whatsoever, the increasing possibility of becoming second in command to Josephine. She didn't rate George. George was a woolly pullover. But Josephine, good old lumpy Josephine, two years her junior, was a real threat.

For some time, she had been thinking "She'll get the job over my dead body." Now she was rearranging the order of the pronouns.

Dressed in workman's overalls and with her hair completely tucked up under a peaked cap, Josephine, armed with the tools of Marcia's destruction: a screwdriver and a toffee hammer, approached the secluded back door of the small detached bungalow.

With the screwdriver, she carefully prised off the wooden moulding around one of the small glass panels in the door, removed the glass, reached in and turned the key, which she knew would have been conveniently left in the lock. She went through the kitchen to the lounge, paused just long enough to sneer contemptuously at Marcia's taste in furniture, then lifted a small upright chair and returned to the kitchen. She covered the chair seat with a plastic bag she had brought with her, stood on the chair and, using the toffee hammer, carefully broke the glass of the light bulb. Then she lifted the plastic bag, folded it carefully and put it back in one of her overall pockets. Making sure that no slivers of glass remained on the chair, she returned it to the lounge. Next, she replaced the glass door panel and the strips of moulding, tapping the small nails into place with the toffee hammer. Then she turned on one of the gas cooker rings. It lit with a faint popping sound. She turned the pressure down, below out the flame, turned the gas on to a higher setting, smiled, and left the way she had come. It was only as she was closing the door that she realised she wouldn't be able to re-lock it. 'No matter', she thought.

The fact that the door was unlocked would go unnoticed among the general carnage. She gave a quick glance at her watch. The whole thing had taken less than ten minutes and it would take Marcia only a further second to complete the task; for when a light is switched on, the filament becomes incandescent. Exposed to air, it would burn out very quickly, but not so quickly as to fail to ignite a gas-rich atmosphere. There would be a wholly spectacular explosion, and Marcia would leave this world, quite properly, in a blaze of glory.

Josephine got back to her office at ten-thirty. She phoned Marcia's extension, ostensibly to complain about the most recent sales forecasts, but in reality, to create the illusion that she had been in her office working hard. Marcia's secretary answered the call and said that Marcia wasn't in but was expected back around midday.

Marcia was having a busy morning. She went to Marks and Spencer's and bought an outfit as near as possible in style and colour to the one that Josephine had been wearing the previous day. Then she went into a ladies' toilet and spent some time in strict privacy creating a passable counterfeit of Josephine. Her hair was the same colour, so apart from making it look untidy, no effort in that department was necessary. She shuddered a little when she emerged from the cubicle and looked at herself in the long glass, but the padding, the hair and the clothes seemed good enough to get away with anything but a direct face-to-face encounter with a neighbour. She spent a little more time on finishing touches, then made her way to Josephine's flat.

With her, she carried a little green, fluted bottle with a glass stopper encased in a wax seal and labelled 'Poison-Cyanide'. It had belonged to her grandfather, who had been a chemist and something of an eccentric. The bottle had sat on a high shelf above the dresser in her grandparent's house for as long as she could remember. She had been a teenager when she had first asked about it. Her grandfather had smiled and said cryptically: "That's the marriage guidance bottle." When pressed further, he had explained; "I brought it home one evening after your grandmother and I had had our first real row."

I said to her: "If ever you feel our marriage is becoming impossible, if you've had as much of me as you can bear, just open the bottle and sprinkle a little over my food. But be aware that I'll check the seal before I eat."

"And did you ever need to check it?" Marcia had asked.

"Once or twice", he admitted with a wry smile.

"And was the seal ever broken?"

"Only once", her grandfather had replied. "After there had been a particularly unpleasant row over something that I can't even recall now. I noticed that the seal was broken but said nothing. Then your grandmother put my meal in front of me. We looked long and hard into each other's eyes, saying nothing. Then I ate. Shortly afterwards we hugged and made up. The next day I re-sealed the bottle. And the seal has remained intact ever since."

"What a brilliant idea", Marcia had said. "But is it really Cyanide?"

"It would have been pretty pointless otherwise", replied her grandfather. "And after I've gone, I want you to have it. You may want to use it in your marriage. Its mere presence is a powerful reminder of what really matters."

Marcia had never married, and the little bottle had been put away among a case of mementoes. Until recently.

She let herself into the flat with a key she had kept. Fortunately, Josephine hadn't considered necessary to have the lock changed.

Marcia quivered when she saw the vandalism Josephine had wrought on the place. The creature had no taste....

She broke the seal on the bottle and emptied some of the contents into a jar of instant coffee granules, stirring until the power became invisible. Then she sniffed to see if there was any suspicious smell. There was none. The smell of the coffee was obviously strong enough to mask the cyanide. And when Josephine didn't turn up for work, she would play the concerned colleague, go to the flat and remove the coffee and the cup she'd been drinking from. Then she'd say she could get no reply from ringing the doorbell and raise the alarm in a most caring way.

She left as she came, unobserved. It was all so simple.

When she returned to the office there was a message asking her to contact Josephine. "To hell with the bitch", she thought. "She can wait." But it happened that they met at the main door as they were going home.

"I wanted to have a word with you", Josephine said. "I left a message with your secretary."

"Did you?", Marcia replied. "She must have forgotten. But I don't suppose it was so important that it can't wait until tomorrow."

"No, it wasn't", said Josephine. "Tomorrow will suit me quite nicely." She looked at the sky, which was oppressively dark. "Looks like rain", she said. As she spoke, lightning forked across the blackness, followed almost immediately by a deafening roll of thunder. "Curtain up on the last act", she thought. "How apt."

"Since neither of the ladies has arrived", said the Group Managing Director, "I decided to have you in first. Save a bit of time. Particularly with things being at sixes and sevens after last night's thunderstorm. Spectacular, wasn't it?"

"Yes. Yes, it was", said George the accountant.

"You've been with us a long time, George, twenty-four years, isn't it?"

"Twenty-five", George replied.

"Quite", said the managing director. "Just over two years until you retire."

George nodded.

"I'm going to be perfectly honest with you, George."

George's heart sank. He knew what was coming.

"We've got a problem."

George smiled weakly.

"Or rather, two problems. Marcia and Josephine."

George became more interested.

"They are both extremely capable, and apart from the fact that we are unable to make a clear value judgement as to which of them would do this job best, we feel that lately there's been a bit of friction between the two, and that, had we appointed one of them as General Manager, we would have lost the other. Knowing that you are a safe pair of hands, the group board has decided to appoint you, George, in the hope that before you retire, we can, with your help, reconcile the two women and make a fair choice as to your successor. We value your judgement highly, so I hope you will understand... and accept the offer."

George could hardly believe his good fortune. He would take the job, whatever the reason. It was worth it, if only for the difference the extra money would make to his pension.

"Congratulations, George", said the Managing Director, not at all surprised at the speed with which the situation had been accepted. "We know you will do a competent job. We're very pleased."

Marcia and Josephine were not a little troubled when each discovered that the other had arrived as usual. They were completely floored after their respective interviews with the Managing Director.

Late in the afternoon, after much soul searching, Josephine phoned Marcia.

"I think we should have a chat", she said. "What about having a meal together tonight?"

There was a momentary silence, then Marcia replied: "Yes. All right. Let's do that."

They went straight from work to the 'Vespuccio'. It was too early to eat, so they sat in the bar drinking, initially in a somewhat awkward silence.

Eventually Marcia said: "George! Can you really believe it!"

"Oh yes", Josephine replied. "Oh, dear me, yes. I can believe it. He's a man, isn't he?"

"Is he? Yes, I suppose he is. God! It's so unfair! We should have realised... Look Josephine, I know we have had our little differences..."

"Who hasn't", Josephine interrupted.

".... but now we'll have to stick together, you and I."

"Yes. Stick together. Show George up for the prat he really is."

"He can do that without any help from us", said Marcia. "Although I suppose we could give him a nudge in the right direction from time to time."

After several Martinis and much discussion about perfidious men, the years of enmity seemed to melt away, and later, part-way through the meal and most of the way through a bottle of wine, Marcia said:

"If it wasn't for you Josephine, for your friendship, I don't know how I could have taken this."

Josephine felt tears pricking her eyes. "Yes, right", she said. "At least we've got each other."

Later still, over their second liqueur, Marcia said: "You know that thunderstorm last night?"

Josephine nodded.

"The strangest thing", Marcia went on. "When I got home, there was no electricity... Not even any street light. Strangest thing... I eventually groped my way into the kitchen – keep candles in a drawer – I began to feel really dizzy... couldn't get my breath. My legs started to go under me and I fell back against the back door. I must have turned the handle, for the next thing I knew I was lying in the back garden. After a while I recovered, and went back in... and do you know what...?"

"What?" asked Josephine.

"The gas cooker was turned on.... Could a power cut do that?"

Josephine shrugged. "Don't know", she said. "Lightning's powerful stuff. My power was off all night – and this morning. Couldn't even boil a kettle."

"Must have been the lightning", Marcia grumbled. "Put off all the electricity. Turned on the gas. It's just as well I had forgotten to lock the back door. Probably be dead by now."

"I'm ever so pleased you're not", said Josephine. "Need all the friends I can get."

"That's awfully nice of you, Josephine."

"Not at all. Mean every word. You and me are like the Three Musketeers. Onc for all, and all... that stuff. Come on, let's pay the bill and get home."

"Shall I call a taxi, Madam?" asked the head waiter as they made their way unsteadily to the door.

Marcia turned on him.

"Never call a taxi Madam", she said, glassy eyed. "Call a spade a spade, but never a taxi Madam."

The man smiled, shrugged, and turned his back as they tumbled through the door.

"I'm too drunk to drive", said Josephine as they emerged into the night.

"So are you", replied Marcia. "Let's call a taxi Madam."

Giggling, they weaved their way across the car park and after much waving of arms and shouting: "Madam", they finally managed to attract the attention of a cab driver.

"My flat I think", said Josephine. "The night is still young."

In the flat, Marcia collapsed into a deep comfortable arm chair. She looked around as Josephine poured a couple of large gins.

"The old place is looking beautiful, Josephine. "You've improved it so much."

"Not improved. Just changed."

They smiled fondly at each other, sipped their gins and discussed, in a somewhat confused way, the difficulties faced by women in business and the duplicity of men.

When Marcia finally decided it was time to leave, she found she couldn't stand up.

Josephine managed to get to her feet but was swaying gently.

"Stay the night dear", she said. "Just sleep where you are. Save a lot of bother."

"Good idea", mumbled Marcia. Tell you what. Let's have a nightcap. Let's drink to all the men who only have to be there to get promotion. Let's drink to good old George and his woolly pullover."

"OK", agreed Josephine. "Let's toast good old useless George."

Marcia raised her hand imperiously. "In cocoa. Only cocoa good enough for George."

Josephine staggered off to the kitchen. By the time she came back with two mugs, she had to waken Marcia.

"…Y'are…" she said.

Each raised her mug on high, said, "George" then drank.

After the second mouthful, Marcia wrinkled her brows. "Cocoa tastes funny", she said.

Josephine waved her mug in front of her. "Not cocoa", she said. "Couldn't find cocoa. Made coffee instead. Never mind. No harm done. Pretend it's cocoa."

Suddenly clearheaded, Marcia found herself thinking about her grandfather, and hoping, desperately, that he had not been the honest, upright man she had always supposed, but devious, like all the rest…..

A PENNY FOR THE GUY

Bonfire night was the last and most important event on the Scout Troop's Golden Jubilee calendar and as John stood watching the final preparations he thought, not for the first time, how fortunate it was for both the Troop and himself that this special year had fallen within his period as Leader.

He had been able to demonstrate to others what he already knew: That he had a genius for organisation. Even the Parents' Committee, some members of which could be, frankly, a pain in the neck, had gradually stopped trying to take over and had accepted his leadership.

So disputes had faded and there had been virtually no setbacks in the weeks leading up to the big night. The Scouts had collected a vast quantity of combustible material from every available source and had slowly built a real monster of a bonfire, twice-three times bigger than the village had ever seen. They had even acquired fifteen railway sleepers which, although some thought too good to burn, were to be raised vertically and placed around and against the pyramid as the final act of construction.

Earlier, John had watched the lunchtime weather forecast with some trepidation, hoping that the forecaster was not going to place one of the little black rain clouds in a position that would dampen his optimism; but the prediction was for nothing more serious than local fog patches.

As it turned out, it was a perfect November evening. The sky was clear, and a three quarters moon was brushing a water-colour wash of pale light across the busy scene of preparation, adding just a touch of mystery that plain day could not provide. John took no credit for the weather, but he knew it would do his reputation no harm.

As he looked at his watch, he was running the immediate future through his mind.

Nineteen-o-three. Mr Smith due to arrive at nineteen forty-five. (Mr Smith was the local MP who had been persuaded to attend, to say a few words and to light the bonfire.)

Fireworks in place. Panther Patrol to be positioned to Fire when instructed.

Parents group ahead of schedule ..... Tables laid out ..... Sausage rolls and sandwiches ready ..... Kettles being boiled for tea ..... Mr Smith's welcoming party assembled in hut ..... Work on bonfire to be completed by nineteen thirty-five.

"Colin," he shouted. "Andrew!"

Within seconds the two patrol leaders appeared before him. "You've got twenty minutes left. Colin, take Jaguar Patrol and give a hand with the sleepers on the south face. Andrew, get your lot to put two ladders on the north side and put all these odds and ends on top." He pointed to a small heap of material that had been forgotten.

"Off you go. Quick as you can."

"Perfect," he thought. "Everything going like clockwork."

He looked at the bonfire and for the first time noticed an imperfection "I really should have thought of having a Guy on the top." He gave way to a short twinge of irritation at his oversight. "It would have finished it off beautifully. Well, no matter. We'll have to do without."

"Penny for the Guy, mister?"

For a moment, John fancied that the words had come from inside his head. Then he turned abruptly, and found his eyes caught in the gaze of two others. They were grey-blue and uncomfortably intense. A small boy of about ten was staring fixedly up at him. He was holding the handle of an ancient pushchair and was accompanied by a little girl, perhaps two years his junior.

The Guy in the pushchair was only marginally scruffier than its two attendants. It appeared to have been made from hessian sacks stuffed with straw. An old soft hat was pulled down over its crudely shaped head so that the features painted to create its face were only vaguely visible. It was tied tightly to the pushchair with yards of coarse string, lashed in such a way as to maintain it in an upright position. It was crude, yet oddly realistic.

"Not much of a Guy, is it?" John said.

The boy transferred his attention to the object in the pushchair. "Dunno," he replied "disnae look too bad!"

At this point John made an uncharacteristic, unplanned decision.

"Tell you what. I'll buy it from you. I'll give you a pound for it." He only just heard the girl's gasp of surprise and the boy turned back towards him.

"A quid?" He repeated, "A quid?"

John took out his wallet, which he always carried, removed a single note and handed it to the boy, who grasped it eagerly. He turned to show it to his sister whose eyes and mouth were perfect circles. Her hand reached out instinctively, but the boy quickly stuffed the money into his trousers pocket.

John watched the interplay between the two in some amusement, then, stooping, picked up the pushchair.

"What you doin'?" cried the boy.

John stopped, startled at the vehemence in the voice. "I'm taking the Guy ..... You just sold it to me." He retorted.

"Didnae say nothing' aboot the pram!" The disconcerting stare was again fixed firmly on John, who turned and had another look at the Guy. It was obviously inseparable from the pushchair. Both children watched him intently as he hesitated.

"What's so special about the pushchair?" he asked, placing it back on the ground.

The boy shrugged. "Me Mam might want it again."

John looked at the dilapidated object. "I doubt it," he said. "It's pretty old."

The boy stared at him balefully. "So're you," he retorted.

John sighed. "How much?" he asked in a resigned tone.

The children exchanged glances. "Coupla quid."

"Two pounds!" John exploded. "No way!"

This time two pairs of eyes stared unwinkingly. John stared back for a moment or two, then capitulated. "All right," he said. "All right". And he handed over the money.

This time there was no protest as he lifted the pushchair and carried it off, relieved to be away from the children and to become involved again in the last-minute preparations.

Jaguar Patrol was summoned and instructed to use the ladders already in position to place the Guy on top of the bonfire. Brushwood was strategically placed to disguise the pushchair, the ladders were removed, a final railway sleeper was placed vertically at the base, and the bonfire was complete.

John prowled round, inspecting the finished article, making sure that the space for ignition was filled with paraffin-soaked rags and paper. Finally, he pronounced himself satisfied.

"Good work, boys", he said. "Now, get to your final positions."

He paused for a moment and looked upwards. The Guy, from its lofty perch, and now illuminated in soft moonlight, was looking back down at him. Its painted lips, half shadowed under the battered old hat were twisted in a mocking smile. The eyes were staring fixedly into his just like the eyes of the small boy. He became suddenly aware of the cold night air and a faint shiver ran through his body.

Eventually and only five minutes late, Mr Smith the MP arrived and was escorted by the welcoming party to a small raised platform at the front of the bonfire. He made a speech during which he said nothing of any consequence, but in a shorter time than is usual for someone of his calling. He ended by saying that he was sure that everyone was going to have an absolutely splendid evening and that he had better shut up so that the fun could begin.

This was greeted with loud applause and the first batch of fireworks were set off exactly on cue, giving time for a burning torch to be lit and handed to Mr Smith. He first raised it above his head and then, to ragged cheering, applied it to the appropriate point at the base of the bonfire.

A second batch of fireworks disappeared into the night sky, paused in momentary silence, then burst loudly into cascades of brief colour before fading into wisps of grey smoke.

As the initially feeble tongues of flame began their attempt to take hold of the inert bonfire John ushered everyone to safety behind the rope barrier.

He stood watching as the faint glow slowly expanded. Gradually, the tongues of orange energy began to advance, feeding on the dark mass. Then, quite suddenly the whole scene burst into life.

Sheets of flame leapt up into the night and yellow sparks were everywhere mingling with the hubbub of voices that had sprung up in acknowledgement.

The parent's committee were already bringing the tea urns to the tables which had earlier been laid with rows of mugs and plates of food.

John felt smugly satisfied that the whole thing had gone off just as he had planned, even congratulating himself on the decisiveness in his dealings with the two urchins, who had apparently disappeared back into the night as suddenly as they had come.

He turned again towards the bonfire, feeling the warmth of it on his face. He looked at the Guy, thinking how lifelike it was from a distance. For a moment it seemed actually to be moving in the pushchair, but it was only the distorting effect of the warm air as it rose, surrounding the body and the face – and those eyes, which still seemed to be fixed in John's direction.

He glanced away towards the crowd and saw, right at the front, the pair he thought had gone. They were standing hand in hand, ruddy faced in the glow, and evidently enjoying the fiery fate of their erstwhile companion.

He was about to go and have a well-earned mug of tea and a sandwich when he saw a woman suddenly appear behind the two children. She grasped each of them by a shoulder. They turned and flinched when they saw her. The woman, apparently very agitated, was gesticulating wildly and talking rapidly.

After a moment the boy produced something from his pocket and held it out. Even from a distance John realized that it was the money he had given them and as he watched he saw the woman smack the boy hard across the face. The little girl began to cry.

John felt sudden stirrings of proprietorial interest in the children, not unmixed with anger at the person he assumed was their mother, thinking that the children should not have been allowed out on their own at this time of night.

He started towards them, wondering as he went if she thought they had been stealing. As he approached, he could hear the woman's voice, high-pitched and hysterical above the roar and crackle of the bonfire. He reached the little group just as the boy had begun to speak.

"But Freddy wisny any use as a Guy, was he? Widny sit still. We didn't get any money with him, did we?" He turned to his sister, who nodded enthusiastically and began wiping away her tears with the tips of her grimy fingers. "So we stuck him in wi' the straw an' pit a bag over his heid ..... That shut him up, Eh?

Again the little girl nodded in agreement. The boy's eyes glanced towards John, then back to the woman again.

"He took the pram off us. I think he's put it on the bonfire." He raised his arm and pointed dramatically. "Aye, he did. That's it up there."

John looked again at the top of the bonfire. He was mercifully too far away to see the eyes, but the Guy was definitely moving, jerking grotesquely in the midst of the flames .....

John's normally clear thought processes suddenly became like a tangled skein of wool left behind by a playful kitten. "What!" he said. "What.!?..."

Just at the edge of his area of muddled comprehension he saw the woman falling as if in slow motion, to the ground.

He was vaguely aware of heads turning towards him, but all he could see clearly was one of the fire extinguishers that had been placed strategically in case things got out of hand. He turned towards it, but the movement of his legs was restricted, as if he was trying to wade knee-deep through porridge, so that it seemed an agonisingly long time before he got it into his hands. He released the valve and a small jet of foam spurted ridiculously, ineffectively, towards the bonfire. He struggled to get nearer, feeling the intense heat radiating against his face. Then, as he tried to direct the foam more directly towards its target, the Guy's right arm rose heavenwards in a final salute and it disappeared into the heart of the bonfire in a spectacular shower of sparks. An additional fierce blast of heat drove John back and he staggered and fell. The extinguisher flew from his hands and lay, gradually covering itself in a mound of foam. John dragged himself slowly away from the fire that had begun its brief existence as a warm, friendly centrepiece of celebration and was now a roaring, crackling, mocking monster. He felt sick. Sick to death. There was a peculiar dull sensation in the pit of his stomach and across his chest. He began to moan softly.

The attention of the crowd was attracted equally between the woman lying on the grass and John's peculiar behaviour. Those nearest began moving, dividing automatically into two groups, some coming towards John, some towards the woman. The boy, realising that his part in the drama had not been recognised – at least not yet – took his sister's hand and they disappeared within the developing melee.

Once out on the other side of the crowd, they stopped. The boy turned to see if anyone was following, but no-one was.

"Silly old cow!" he said scornfully. "What a fuss grown-ups make, eh? Serves her right for making' us take him ..... Come on better get goin' afore she finds oot we're no' there."

A sudden thought brightened his face. "We'll go to the chipper," he went on. "We got plenty money now, eh? We'll get two bags o' chips. Get one for Freddy, to gie him when we let him out o' the cellar. He'll be howlin' his stupid head of by now. Bag o' chips'll shut him up."

Again the little girl nodded happily and they set off hand in hand towards the chip shop .....

A REAL MAN

David supported the tray between the crook of his left arm and the curved palm of his hand. With his right hand, he turned the key in the lock and pushed open the door.

"It's me, Ada" he called as he went on to the small room that was combined kitchen, dining and living space. Ada was sitting, as always, in the threadbare armchair. Her face and neck reminded him of a tortoise he had had as a child. Her grey cardigan had a spare button at the top and a spare button-hole at the bottom. He laid the tray carefully across the arms of the chair. He had fixed two pieces of wood on the underside of the tray so that it wouldn't slide. He was quite proud of the idea. He might patent it.

Ada lifted the cover from the larger of the two plates and looked suspiciously at the contents.

"What's this?" she asked.

"Spaghetti Bolognese."

"What's in it?"

David sighed. "Mince, spaghetti, tomato, garlic, herbs. It's good for you. I cut the spaghetti into short pieces, to make it easier."

"Waste of good mince", Ada snorted. "Foreign muck."

"You enjoyed it last time."

Ada picked up her fork and stirred. "No I didn't", she said.

"Yes you did. You said so."

Ada glared. "Foreign muck" she repeated.

David disappeared into the bedroom. When he came back, his arms full of discarded clothing, she was eating. He sorted out the garment, put in the powder, set the washing machine to 'mixed fabrics' and switched the machine on. Then he returned to the bedroom and stripped the sheets from the bed. He bundled up the linen and took it back to the living room, where he dumped it on the floor by the washing machine.

Ada had finished the spaghetti Bolognese and was spooning up rhubarb and custard.

"All right then?" he asked.

"Not enough sugar."

David filled the electric kettle and switched it on. Then he began to wash the dirty dishes. As he worked, he was aware of Ada watching his every moment. After a while, she said:

"Why can they no' send a woman? That's no' a man's job."

"They can't get enough women. They have to put up with what they can get." The irony was lost on Ada.

"You're not a real man. You're one of *them,* aren't you? You're a pansy."

He carried on with his work, pretending not to hear.

She said it again, louder this time.

"You're one of them. You're a pansy."

He turned towards her, wet plate in one hand, dishtowel in the other, and asked "What makes you think that, Ada?"

"A man wouldn't do a job like that. Not a real man."

"It's what I do. I'm good at it." And he was. He was demonstrating that now, by not surrendering to provocation. Humouring the client.

"You've got limp wrists", said Ada.

"You mean like this." He put the plate down and extended his arm, hand drooping.

Ada snorted, splattering custard over the tray. "You making tea?" she asked.

"Kettle's nearly boiling"

"My Albert wouldn't have let your sort over the door. Smashed your face in, most likely."

"Real man, then, was he?"

Ada's wrinkles wrinkled into more wrinkles as she smiled. "He wouldn't have ponced about washing clothes and dishes for a living. Never washed a dish in his life. He went out to work. I washed the dishes. But he was good to me."

"Tell me about him", said David.

"Oh, he had his faults. But that was all right. Ye need a man to have faults, so you can nag him. If he didn't have faults you would need to make them up. I nagged him a lot. He put up with it most times, but sometimes he would say 'Shut up Ada', and I would know to stop." There was a silence.

"Is that it?" David asked.

"Is that what?"

"What a real man is?"

Ada snorted. "Only a poofter would ask that. I hadn't even started. You wanting lessons?"

"Not really."

"What do you do?" she asked. "What's it like? I mean. Two men."

David filled the teapot from the kettle and continued washing the dishes.

"I've often wondered", said Ada.

David glanced over his shoulder. "You've been lucky", he said. "Good husband. Children."

"Not want to talk about it then?" Ada persisted.

David sighed quietly. He dried his hands on the dishcloth, poured tea into a mug and took it to her.

"Housework is no longer gender specific", he said, knowing full well that Ada wouldn't understand, then for that reason felt annoyed at himself for saying it.

"He worked hard", Ada said, taking the mug in both hands. "We never had a lot, but we were never really hard up. Aye, just had enough."

“That’s nice”, said David.

“Brought the children up to have respect.”

“That’s nice”, David repeated.

“You’ll not get children out of a man.”

“No”, said David.

“Albert was a real man”, said Ada. Wouldny have got on with the likes of you. Get them to send a woman.”

David lifted a plate from the basin and had a momentary urge to hurl it at the nearest wall.

“Don’t see them much now”, said Ada. “Too far away.” Her eyes took on a clouded look, and she stopped speaking.

“That’s a shame”, said David.

He spent the next hour finishing the washing and ironing and cleaning the flat. As he prepared to leave, he said: “I’m off now Ada. See you on Thursday.”

She didn’t reply. She had forgotten him. She was watching an old film on television.

David had two more clients to visit and he was late getting home. He hadn’t realised he was hungry until he smelled the food as he opened the front door.

“That smells good”, he called from the hall.

“Another ten minutes and it would have smelled burned”, came the reply.

"Sorry I'm late. One of these days."

"That's what you always say."

As he went into the kitchen, Sam was lifting two heaped plates of Irish stew and potatoes.

"What a plateful", David said. "There's enough there to feed a regiment."

"A real man's meal", said Sam. "It's not too much for you, is it?"

"Oh God, not you too", said David angrily. "What made you say that?"

"You *have* had a bad day", said Sam, startled. "I only said it was a real man's meal."

"What's a real man then? Do you know one?"

"What the hell's the matter with you? Wrong time of the month, is it?"

David brought his first down hard on the table. Sam and both the plates jumped. "Shut up", he shouted. "Just shut up!"

They ate in uncomfortable silence, a silence that lasted until the meal was over and the dishes were cleared away. A silence eventually broken by David.

"I'm sorry Sam", he said. "Ada's been rattling my cage. I shouldn't be taking it out on you. I enjoy my job, but what she said brought out something buried deep. Made me wonder. Made me almost ashamed of what I am. What I do."

"What rubbish, David", said Sam. "You're brilliant at your job. Everybody knows that."

David shook himself mentally. "Yes", he said. "Let's forget it. It's a long time since we were hunter-gatherers. And we're still evolving. Sorry again. Fancy a game of gin rummy?"

"OK", Sam smiled, relieved that the storm cloud had passed. "Tell you what. Loser goes down to the off-licence for a half bottle."

David grinned. "Ada would never believe it." He put an arm round Sam's shoulders.

'Believe what?"

"That I'm shacking up with a woman."

"And what a woman", Samantha said, dealing the cards. "I'll show you after you bring in the booze. Pick up your cards and start worrying."

"Best out of three", said David.

ANDY'S TRIAL

Andy was looking at the row of cards in the Job Centre. Looking but not seeing.

Fifteen months, he was thinking, since he had left school. Only one job and that had lasted all of four days. He had learned that he did not have a natural talent for driving a fork-lift truck. But the foreman, who had seemed to be a reasonable man, could have been more understanding. After all, it had only been a little wall..

The only thing, he reflected, at which he had become skilled over the past year, was lying on his back in bed staring at the ceiling.

His eyes slowly began to focus on the cards. 'Part time dishwasher - £30 p.w.; Steeplejack, Time served welder'.

Then his heart leapt in excitement. 'Defence lawyer for GBH case – no previous experience required'. Andy couldn't quite believe it, so he read it again to be sure. Then he glanced quickly around. There were only two others looking at the vacancies, neither of them seeming to be of lawyer material. Nevertheless, he hurried over to the desk.

"Lawyer's joab" he said to the man behind the counter, in a tone of voice he hoped sounded confident. The clerk looked at him dispassionately.

"Ye're gey young", he said. "Ah widny think ye could handle it."

Andy screwed his face into what he fancied was a superior expression.

"Oh, ah'll handle it aw right", he replied. "Ah've seen aw the auld Perry Mason stuff oan the telly."

"Uh-hu", retorted the clerk. "Mebbe so. But for this job ye've got to be able to lie on yer back and stare at the ceiling." A smug expression accompanied the statement.

Andy smiled inwardly. "He thinks he's goat me wae that wan." Aloud he said airily: "Nae bother tae me, mister. Ah've been practising for a year. Ye might say ah'm an expert. Ah kin dae it staunin' oan mah heid. D'ye want me tae show ye?"

"Naw, naw. Ah'll take yer word for it." Now the clerk was looking at him with just a hint of respect in his eyes. Ye'll be telling me next that ye've got 'O' levels in Woodwork an' Geography."

"That's exactly whit ah have got", Andy replied proudly. "And metalwork and'aw."

"Here, that's great!" exclaimed the clerk. "Ah think ye're in wae a chance. Kin ye talk posh?"

"Nae bother", Andy responded, trying really hard. "No bother at all."

"There's only one other wee problem", the clerk went on. "Ye're a bit scruffy looking." He paused for a moment, then produced a slip of paper from under the desk. "Here's your social security cheque for the hire o' a fancy suit. D'ye know where the High Court is?" Andy nodded. Another piece of paper appeared.

"Just give this to the man on the door an' ye'll get in."

Andy, resplendent in a new pin stripe suit and carrying a brief case which contained nothing more legal than a couple of cheese sandwiches, arrived at the door of courtroom six.

"Counsel for the defence", he said to the man who seemed to be guarding the entrance.

"You from the Job Centre?" asked the man.

"Aye", replied Andy. "How did ye know that?"

The man pointed. "The label", he said, opening the door.

Andy looked down and saw a label with the words 'Lawyer's Suit – Property of YTS' stuck to the top pocket of his jacket. He removed it before going through the door.

The courtroom was crowded, but there was an empty seat behind a table in the well of the court. He made his way towards it, acknowledging with a slight inclination of his head the deference shown to him by the common people in the public gallery.

He had only just sat down behind a pile of important looking papers when a voice shouted: "Will yis all stand up!"

As Andy obeyed the injunction, the Judge, an old man in a Santa Claus cloak and a grubby looking wig, appeared through a door and ascended slowly to a seat behind a raised bench which overlooked the whole courtroom.

The Judge sat down and said to no one in particular: "Ah'm fair puffed. They stairs seem tae get steeper every day." Then he produced a hammer with which he banged the bench several times in evident satisfaction.

"Who's fur the persecution?" he asked.

"I am your honour." A thin faced man with a long nose and dark hair carefully plastered over a bald patch rose to his feet.

"Right", said the Judge, waving a hand dismissively. "Who's the defender?"

Andy rose proudly to his feet. "Me, yer Lordship", he said.

The Judge peered at him over a pair of rimless spectacles that were perched on the end of his nose.

"Ah'm not a Lordship, son", he said. "No' yet. But here, ah fair like yer suit."

The thin faced man fairly leapt from his seat. "Objection!" he shouted. "You never said you liked my suit."

"Shut up", said the Judge without rancour. "Objection overruled. Yours doesny fit ye properly."

The thin faced man grimaced and sat down, muttering to himself.

Nothing seemed to be happening after this minor outburst, so Andy, seizing the initiative, rose, put his thumbs in his waistcoat pockets and began to speak.

"Ladies and Gentlemen of the Jury", he began, "Ah wid just like fir tae say..."

The judge banged his hammer. "It's no' your turn yet, son", he said.

Andy bowed his head. "Sorry yer honour. Ah huvny done much lawerin' afore."

"That's all right, son. Nae need tae apologise. We all understand." The judge pointed his hammer. "Mr Weasel gets the first shot."

The thin faced man looked at Andy with a condescending smile on his face. "Call the injured party of the first part", he said loudly.

Andy sensed trouble. His adversary had a posher voice than the Judge.

"The injured pairty", came a disembodied voice. The call was repeated several times, each call being fainter than the last. "Jist like in the films", thought Andy.

Eventually the injured party appeared in the witness box. He was over six feet tall and heavily built. He had large ears and a flattened nose.

Andy couldn't help himself. "Whit a dial", he shouted.

The Judge struck his bench with the hammer.

"Ye canny say things like that son", he pronounced. "No' here onywey."

The prosecution counsel, who had been standing impatiently waiting to start, addressed the man in the witness box.

"Will you please tell us your name", he asked.

Andy was taken aback. "That's ridiculous", he said. "You canny be much o' a lawyer if ye don't even know yer client's name."

"Do you know his name?" Mr Weasel asked pointedly

"Naw... But..."

"Well don't get smart with me!"

"Gentlemen! Gentlemen!" The Judge was wielding his mallet energetically. He addressed Andy.

"Ah know you're just startin' son, but did they no' give ye a book o' rules at the Job Centre?"

Andy shook his head.

"Gie him a book, Fred".

A small blue pamphlet was placed on Andy's table. He opened it and read:

1. Speak proper
2. Wait your turn
3. Don't be rude to people
4. Be nice to the Judge and he'll be nice to you.

Andy thought this to be very similar to the things his mother would say to him, but he was grateful to the Judge and much more confident now that he had the complete guide to behaviour in court. The Judge was smiling and nodding towards Andy. "OK now?" he asked. Then, to the thin faced man: "Right. Get on with it."

"Would you tell the court what your name is?" Mr Weasel asked of the witness.

"Cornelius Sandpaper", replied the man.

Andy forgot the rule book.

"Please yer honour", he called. "Ah think that's a sody name."

“A whit?” asked the Judge.

“A sody name – a nom de ploom.”

The Judge sorted through some papers. “Naw”, he said eventually. “It’s right enough. That’s his name.”

“Goad Almighty” Andy gasped.

The Judge frowned and signalled to Andy to turn the leaflet over.

5. No swearing.

“Sorry, yer honour.”

Mr Weasel, who had sat down during the interchange, stood up again.

“Mr Sandpaper”, he said. “Will you tell the court what happened at the scene of the crime.”

Andy jumped up.

“Objection”, he cried. “We havny asser… asser… made oot that a crime was committed.”

The Judge smiled benignly. “Oh, helluva good son. Ye’re learning’ real quick.”

Andy felt himself blushing. “Thanks very much”, he said and sat down quickly.

His adversary scowled. “Wid you tell the court”, he asked the injured party. “exactly what happened.”

The injured party cleared his throat. “Ah wis walkin’ through this supermarket….”

“Whit supermarket?” asked Andy standing up again.

“Aw wait a minute. Wait a minute. It’s my turn. Ye’ll have to get him to shut up, Uncle George.”

The Judge’s face turned purple.

“Don’t call me Uncle George will ye no’ Alistair, or ah’ll need tae have anither word with yer mother.”

Mr Weasel looked suitably abashed as the Judge turned to Andy. “Son.” He said. “Ye’ll need tae keep yer mouth shut until it’s your turn. Sit doon, will ye!”

Andy sat.

“Please continue, Mr Sandpaper”, the Prosecution Counsel instructed his client.

“Ah wis jist walkin’ through this supermarket, lookin’ fur a six pack o’ export”, the injured party explained. “When this auld biddy hit me oan the heid wae a tin o’ baked beans.”

“What old biddy?” prompted Mr Weasel. “Can ye point her out?”

The injured party indicated an elderly woman who was standing between two policemen.

“Aw here! Definitely objection this time yer honour!” Andy shouted, leaping to his feet. “That’s ma granny.”

The Judge brought down his hammer so fast that it almost flew from his grasp. “Steady on, son”, he said. “Now then, Alist… Mr Weasel. Whit hae ye got tae say about that?”

The person so addressed stood up straight and looked down his long nose at Andy.

"It's not german to the issue", he retorted.

The Judge nodded his head and looked sorrowfully at Andy.

"Ah'm afraid he's got you there, son."

Andy sank back into his chair. Weasel face smirked and continued his questioning:

"Can you tell us what the motive was for this crime?"

Mr Sandpaper considered.

"Malice Aforethought", he said.

"Wait a minute", Andy cried. "Wait a minute! Where did this Alice ..eh..Thingumy come frae?"

Once again the Judge raised his gavel, but this time held it just above the bench and waggled it about.

"Look son", he said firmly. "Ye'll need tae get yersel' sorted oot inside that fancy suit or ye'll be getting yer books."

Andy subsided, feeling confused. "It's no fair", he muttered. "He shouldny be allowed tae bring strange wimmin intae the court withoot... withoot..."

"My learned friend is labouring under a misapprehension", said Mr Weasel. "My learned friend is just showing aff.. off.. his poor education."

"Don't get personal, Alistair", said the Judge. "Onywey, it's no' true. The boy's got 'O' levels in Woodwork an' Geography. Mair than you've got. Huv ye ony mair questions fur the witness?"

"Jist the one", Mr Weasel replied sulkily, turning to his client. "Are ye quite sure it was the defendant that beaned ye?"

"Aye", said Mr Sandpaper. "Ah'm positive."

There was a pause before the Judge asked: "That it, then?"

"Yes, your honour. You can ask my learned friend to cross examine."

"Ony time ye bloody want", said Andy glaring at the Weasel.

"Language! Language!" called the Judge, holding up a copy of the pamphlet. "Remember where yis are."

Andy stood up and stared long and hard at the injured party. Then in an offhand manner he asked: "Whit size of tin wis it?"

Mr Sandpaper seemed baffled. Mr Weasel jumped to his feet with an objection. "What difference does it make what size of tin it was?"

Andy gave him a scornful glance. "Ye widny be askin' that if it hud been you that got hit."

There was laughter in court and the Judge murmured: "Good fur you son."

"Ah'll ask ye again. Whit size o' tin wis it?"

"Ah'm no sure", the injured party replied, "But ah think it wis wan o' they meteoric wans."

"Ye mean metric", Andy corrected.

"Ah suppose so... It wis goin' at a helluva speed."

Andy gave him a withering stare.

"Did ye actually see mah granny... ah mean the accused, fling it?"

"No' in so many words", replied Mr Sandpaper.

"Well then", Andy continued, feeling very much in control of the situation. "Well then. Ah pit it to ye that the hale thing is a fabrication of tissues!"

"Good fur you, wee Andy", shouted his Granny, clapping her hands. "Ah didny know ye had aw they big words in ye."

The Judge looked over his specs.

"My dear wumman", he said patiently. "Will ye kindly shut yer geggie. This is a court of law. Accused persons that speak oot o'turn get the heavies pit on tae them."

The old lady bowed her head "Sorry, yer highness", she said.

Andy was a bit peeved. "Ye shouldny speak tae mah Granny like that", he complained.

"Watch it son", said the Judge. "Don't let that fancy suit go tae yer heid."

Andy resumed his cross examination, returning his thumbs to his waistcoat pockets. He rather liked the pose.

"Now then, mah good man." He repeated the phrase to give it full effect. "Now then, mah good man. Whit makes ye think it was the accused that hit ye wae the metric beans?"

"It couldny of been anybuddy else."

"How no?"

"There was just the two of us therr."

"Aha!" shouted Andy, loudly, making Mr Sandpaper and those asleep in the public gallery jump. "So there wis nae other witnesses?"

"Naw. There wis just the baith o' us. Ah wis jist reachin'... jist reachin' fur..."

As he hesitated there was a sudden stir from the dock and Andy's Granny shrieked: "He wis efter mah boady!"

There was uproar in the courtroom and the Judge went absolutely daft with his gavel. Someone was shouting "Order in Court" repeatedly, trying to be heard above the clamour.

Eventually, order was restored. The Judge turned to the accused person and said: "This is just a common assault case. It isny Burke and Hare."

The comment took a moment or two to sink in.

"You cheeky auld bugger!" Andy's Granny shouted.

There was a startled silence.

The Judge shook his head sorrowfully. "Listen, dearie", he said. "Ah'm the Judge. Ah can say whit a like. But you canny say whit you like. If you call me names again, ah'll huv ye fur bein' contemptible."

The accused said no more but covered her mouth with her hand and stuck her tongue out.

"Uncle George!" shouted the prosecuting counsel. "She stuck her tongue out."

"Don't be a clipe, Alistair", retorted the Judge firmly.

"Yer honour", Andy interjected. "Ye'll huv tae forgive the accused. She's usually at the bingo at this time."

"I understand son." The Judge smiled. "Carry on."

Andy turned back towards the injured party.

"Ah think ye better explain yersel', pie face", he said menacingly.

Mr Weasel, who was becoming extremely fed up at the Judge's lenient treatment of Andy, rose to his feet.

"Aw, come on, Uncle George. You canny let him say things like that to my client. It's his granny that's on trial."

"Listen Alistair", said the Judge through clenched teeth. "Ah'm no gonny tell you again! Forget the Uncle George stuff or ah'll dae something nasty tae yer credentials!" He turned to Andy. "Ah tell't his mother he wid never make a lawyer, but naebuddy ever listens tae me."

"Ah dae, yer honour", said Andy

"So ye dae, son", said the Judge. "So ye dae."

"Crawler!" weasel face shouted.

"Jist ignore him son,", the Judge said. "Carry on. Ye're dain' marvellous."

Andy, swelling with pride, returned to the attack with renewed vigour. "Ah pit it tae ye", he exclaimed. "That on the 9th o'April this year ye wir in a supermarket, trying tae interefere wae mah granny's boady, an' she just defended hersel' wae a tin o'Heinz's beans."

"Listen sonny", retorted the injured party. "Ah widnae interfere wae yer granny's boady if it wis aboot tae step under a bus. Ah wis reachin' over fur a six pack when mah airm must've brushed against her chist."

"Aha!" cried Andy. "So ye admit it!"

"Ah'm admittin' nothin'. Maybe it wis her chist that brushed against mah airm. Whitever wey ye pit it, it wisny much o' a thrill. An' the next think ah know, ah wis unconscious."

"Serve ye bliddy well right", said Andy.

"Language, language", admonished the Judge, not for the first time.

"Whit happened then?" Andy asked.

"Ye mean efter ah come tae mah senses?"

"Ah don't think you've ever came tae yer senses", said Andy pointedly.

"Ye're probably right", Cornelius Sandpaper replied slyly. "Your granny's damaged me fur life."

Andy realised that he had made a mistake and tried to rectify it. "Naw she husny", he retorted fiercely. "Your heid wis full o'broken boattles long afore mah granny goat near it – or didny, as the case may be. An even if she did – an' ah think she didny, by the way – she was jist protectin' her honour."

The Judge, whose eyelids had been drooping, thought he was being spoken to. "Whit?" he asked, "Whit is it?"

“No’ you, yer honour. Her honour, yer honour.”

The Judge looked at Andy with a dazed expression.

“Look”, he said. “Ah’m gettin’ a sair heid wae aw this evidence. Ah think we’ll chuck it an’ get on wae the closin’ speeches. You kin huv the first go Alis... eh, Mr Weasel.”

The prosecuting counsel rose to his feet, the light of battle in his eyes.

“Ladies and gentlemen o’ the jury”, he began. “Yous have all heard evidence that my client was the object of an unprovoked attack delivered by the enemy of society you see in the dock. Don’t be deceived by her white hair and bad feet. My client, Mr Sandpaper, who is a kind and gentle man...” Here the injured party went all coy and grinned self-consciously, showing a row of yellow, uneven teeth....”My client was struck down in the flower o’ his youth by a septuagenarian hooligan...”

“Ah’m only sixty fower”, Andy’s Granny shouted, revealing both age and erudition.

Mr Weasel ignored the interruption. “Mr Sandpaper”, he went on, “Was walloped for no good reason. Mugged in a supermarket in broad daylight by the defendin’ counsel’s granny. Ladies and gentlemen, yous have a duty to our fair land of Scotland, for to prevent it degenerating down the drain into anarchy...”

“That’s in Italy, is it no’?” thought Andy, but he remained silent.

“So I ask yous, ladies and gentlemen, to deliver the maximum sentence for this Heinz’s crime.” He spread his arms wide in a gesture of appeal. “In the name of justice”, he concluded. “I rest my case.”

The Judge had a look of pleased surprise on his face. "Here that wis quite good Alistair", he said. "There's mebbe hope fur ye yet." He turned towards Andy. "Your turn noo. Aff ye go."

"Friends", Andy began. "And fellow members of the working class..." Out of the corner of an eye he saw the judge shaking his head in warning. Perhaps some of the jury thought they were not working class. He couldn't understand that, for he was enjoying the novelty. He changed tack. "Friends. Yous are all intelligent people." That was obviously better. Some of the jury were smiling. "You will therefore understand that mah... That the accused grey haired old person wis in the supermarket desperately tryin' fur tae make her pension go far enough tae cover luxuries like food... Trying fur tae stretch her widow's mite..."

"Don't tell lies, Andy", called his Grandmother sharply. "Yer Grandad's still alive.. Well, jist aboot."

"Sorry granny", Andy apologised. "Ah'm dain' mah best."

"Aye, so ye are son. Ye're a good boy."

Andy determined to do even better.

"This poor auld woman", he went on. "This poor auld woman who hus been a granny tae me aw mah life..." Here he thought he could see tears steal into the eyes of several of the jury, so he resolved to repeat himself.

"This poor auld woman..."

"Here. Chuck it Andy. Ah'm no' that auld."

"... Who hus been a granny tae me aw mah days, wis wonderin' whit she could buy wae her last fifty pence and had just picked up a tin o'beans, when this big ugly guy..."

"Ye're nae ile paintin' yeresel'," interjected the injured party.

"...When this ugly big guy went for her."

"Went fir her whit?" asked the Judge.

"Jist.. went for her", Andy explained. "She turnt roon an' saw this big gorilla tryin' tae take unfair advantage. So she did what anybuddy's granny wid dae. She belted him wan oan the bean wae the beans." (Andy had added this in the hope of getting a smile from the jury, but he didn't get one). 'Don't tell me they've got nae sense o'humour', he thought. "So, ah pit it tae ye, that the prosecution's case is a load o'tripe, thrown up as a smokescreen fur tae hide the identity o' the real criminal, who is standing there lookin' as if butter widny melt in his boots. Ah wid ask yis as decent citizens fur tae throw this case oot the windae!"

On that emphatic note Andy sat down, feeling well pleased with himself. He got a round of applause from his Granny.

The Judge looked over the top of his specs. "Is that it?" he asked.

Andy nodded.

"Noo it's mah turn", said the Judge, hitching his gown about his neck.

"Ah'm the heid bummer in here, so ah get the last word. Ah huv tae sum up the evidence, as they say." He looked at the jury.

"You're no allowed tae ask questions, so pay attention. If it gets too technical fur ye, that's your tough luck." He took a deep breath. "Oan the one hand", he said. "He." Indicating his nephew, “Says the auld wumman done it.” There was a muffled sound from the accused person. “Oan the ither hand, he”, pointing to Andy. “Says she acted in self-defence. So ladies and gentlemen, it’s make yer minds up time... And don’t take all day, fur ah’m needin’ mah dinner.”

As the jury filed out, a low murmur of voices filled the courtroom, no doubt debating the verdict. Andy, although sure he had done enough to get his granny off, was nervous. Mr Weasel was surreptitiously picking his nose. The Judge was still in his seat and had got out a needle and thread and was apparently darning a hole in his gown.

Someone in the public gallery began to sing ‘Flower of Scotland’, but stopped when struck across the head by an usher wielding a rolled-up copy of the Sun.

After a seemingly endless wait, the jury returned. When asked for the verdict, the foreman replied:

“We find the accused white haired old person guilty, notwithstanding her bad feet; but ask that the sentence considers the effect o’inflation on the price o’beans.”

Andy’s heart sank, but he leapt to his feet.

“Objection, yer honour”, he shouted.

The Judge sighed. “Ye canny object tae the verdict son. It wis all done fair and square. Onywey, ye got the len’o’ a nice suit oot o’ it, didn’t ye?”

“But whit aboot mah granny?”

The Judge sighed again. “Ach, this is the bit ah hate”, he said. He reached under his desk and produced a black cap which he placed on his head. “Ah sentence the prisoner tae be incarcerated in the nearest jile and fur tae dae sixty years slightly hard labour.”

“Yer honour”, Andy protested. “She’s sixty-five the now. She’ll never make it!”

“Well”, replied the Judge. “She’ll jist huv tae dae the best she can. We’ll no’ take it personal if she kicks the bucket afore her time’s oot.”

The accused person burst into tears.

“Ah never done it, yer honour”, she sobbed. “Honest ah never.”

The judge looked at her and his expression softened. He removed the black cap.

“Ach”, he said. “Ye can call me a softy if ye like, but ah canny go through with this.”

“Objection!” shouted Mr Weasel.

“Shut yer face, Alistair”, the Judge shouted back. “However,” he continued in a quieter tone and looking at Andy’s granny. “Ah canny let ye aff scot free.” He drummed his fingers on the bench. “Tell ye what. Ah’ll make it three days in a nice wee cell. There’s nae carpets, so ye’ll not need tae take yer hoover.”

Andy’s Granny beamed. “Oh, yer honour”, she simpered. “Ye’re an awful nice yer honour.”

The Judge smiled, embarrassed. “Ach, away wi’ ye. Ah’m not all that nice.”

“Yes ye are. Ah quite fancy ye.”

The Judge's face went beetroot red. "Two days not even slightly hard labour", he said.

"Wid knittin' socks be all right?", asked Andy's Granny.

"Perfect", replied the judge. "Could ah take ye oot tae dinner on Friday?"

'Ye're on", cried Andy's Granny as she was led away between the two policemen.

Andy was becoming confused. For a moment he began to think he was dreaming.

"Hey, wait a minute", he called. "Whit aboot Grandad?"

His Grandmother's voice came faintly from the recesses of the court buildings.

"You'll need tae get yer Grandad's dinner ready for him yersel'. Ah'll no have the time what with all this knittin'."

Andy sighed. He hoped he wouldn't burn the mince. His Grandad got real crabbit when he burnt the mince.

AUNTY'S GONE

I saw this play on the telly. It was called 'Aunty's Gone' by Sophie Cockles. At least, I think that was it. The title wasn't all that clear. I doubt I'd have made it out, even with my specs on.

Anyway, it was about this lassie Eponymous whose father had married his mother. Not *her* mother, *his* mother! Whit d'you think about that! I don't think they needed to mention it. It wasn't german to the plot. And anyway, it's not a thing to be talking about when people over sixty might be watching.

Anyway, this lassie, whose mother was also her grannie, had two brothers and a sister, and one of the brothers, called Polly Nices, was a bit of a terrorist – no wonder, with a name like that. Well, Polly got himself wasted and the lassie went fur to scrape him off the pavement and give him a decent Christian burial. But for some reason, the King – he was called Pram or Crayon – I can't remember which – had issued an edict that terrorists had not to be scraped off pavements and thought that her doing so was a bit of a liberty, so he had her incarcerated in the nearest jail.

Now, it turned out that the King's son fancied the lassie and wanted to marry her, so he went to ask his old man why he had locked her up jist for being nice to her brother, and him dead and all. So you can imagine his astonishment when King Thingumy told him he wis going to put the poor lassie in a cave and plaster up the door so she couldny get out.

The boy had started the conversation by telling his father what a great King he was and how much he loved him, but when he heard this he changed his mind and tellt him he wis a rotten old scunner. Then he said if he wid just let the lassie go, he wid be awfy fond of him again.

But his old man said: "No,no. I've made up my mind and if I change it, everbody'll say I'm not worth the money I'm printed on!"

The son says "No you're wrong. If you don't let her go, everybody'll say you're a rotten auld scunner."

But the father's a real hard man and he says: "I don't care if you fancy her. She's for the cave and that's that."

Well, whit can the boy do? He gives the King the two fingers and storms off, slamming the door behind him; and it wasn't half a big door, I'm telling you. Well actually, when I think about it, it *wis* half of a big door. Twenty feet high and six feet wide. This was no wee semi-detached castle the old guy had. The next thing that happened wis this even older guy comes in, looking like he's been to a heavy party, and he tells Pram or Crayon, or whatever his name was, that in his considered opinion, he is acting like a rotten old scunner and will come to a sticky end. This even older guy is called Sooth Sayer, or something like that. (It wasn't Leo Sayer, I know that, for there was no singing and dancing in this play. It was just all talk).

Well anyway, King Pram seems to take this message very hard. "Aw, even older guy", he says. "Whit makes you think that?"

"Well", said the even older guy. "I was cooking this chicken and thinking about you, and instead of the chicken going nice and brown, it went all slobbery and nearly put the fire out.

Then, blow me, its gall bladder exploded, which is a very bad omen indeed."

"Behave yourself, Sooth", says Pram. "I've never heard such a load of rubbish in all my life." (I must say this was the only time I agreed with Pram. I would have said the same thing myself).

"All right", says the even older guy. "All right. Suit yourself, then. But don't come running to me when you're diving about, wailing and gnashing your teeth."

"Away and raffle yourself", says Pram. "Why should I listen you. You can't even cook a chicken."

You can tell the even older guy doesn't take kindly to this, for he's cooked more chickens than Pram's had hot dinners, but he doesn't rush out and slam the door, for he's blind. (There's a lot of blind people in this story. Even the lassie's old man went blind).

Anyway, the even older guy, seeing that King Pram wasn't impressed with exploding gall bladders, gets his boy to lead him away.

There was this funny thing – funny peculiar. When the boy first brings him in, he's saying to anyone that will listen that they've only got two eyes between them and I mind thinkin' 'that's one each' – but it wasn't. So away the pair o' them go with whatever eyes they've got and when they disappear, Pram sends for the lassie.

Well, when she arrives, he tells her what he's got lined up, and how it hurts him more than she'll ever know. Then *she* tells him he's a rotten auld scunner. Everybody's tellin' him this, but he's that sure of himself that he just batters on regardless.

So that's what happens. The poor lassie, who has never done anybody a bad turn in all her life – (even countin' her father, who wis called Eddie Puss... daft names they all had!) The poor lassie gets walled up in a cave.

You don't actually see this happening, but there's a crowd of guys hanging about that keep you in the picture. All through the play they're saying things. One minute they're telling Pram he's magic, the next, they're saying he's a bum. No wonder he was all mixed up and useless.

Now, I'm not sure how it happened. Maybe these guys talked him round, but the next thing we know, Pram has done a U-turn and has decided to let the lassie go free. So away he goes to dig her out with his bare hands, even if it dirties all his fingernails.

Then, a while later – well it was right away on the TV, but it was supposed to be a while later, another bloke comes in with a beard, and starts telling the crowd of guys that is still hanging about, that there's been a hitch in the arrangements.

And King Pram's wife (I think this must be the aunty of the title), who just happens to be pressing her ear to the keyhole at the time, hears a bit of what was bein' said and gets quite agitated.

"Speak up", she shouts, opening the door.

"Holy Moses!" says the guy with the beard. "I didn't want you to hear this, but since you were listening anyway, you might as well hear the whole can of worms along with the rest of them... I have for to tell you" he goes on "That your son's bit o' stuff has topped herself, her not being too keen about being incarcerated in a cave. Your man arrived to dig her out just in time to be too late. Then your boy arrives and goes absolutely spare and tries for to stab your husband, but I think he takes after his father, for he makes a right dog's breakfast of the whole thing and kills himself instead. There was blood everywhere, so there was! All over the walls and his fiancée. What a mess it was! I'm helluva sorry for to be telling you this, Mrs Pram, but you did ask, and I have to speak the truth, for I am an honest man, even if ah'm not always as tactful as I might be."

I could see the old dame wis trying to take all this in. She wasn't the only one – for you never saw any of it, and you had to take the beard's word that he wis a truthful man.

But eventually, the old wifie turns on her heels and walks out, which seems to worry this bunch of guys in the background. I think they were used to her giving them the verbals and couldn't understand her disappearing with her mouth shut.

However, before we had time to worry about her, King Pram bursts in, looking real fed up, but before he can speak the bunch o' guys say: "Here Pram, you'd better away and take a look at your old lady. We think she's not herself."

Well would you believe it! She had snuffed it as well! This must be where they got the title 'Aunty's Gone'. I think I could have thought of a better one.

Anyway, Pram was left staring into space an' muttering to himsel', "Maybe everybody wis right. Maybe I am a rotten old scunner. One thing's for sure. Old Sooth Sayer's chicken was talking turkey."

And all the guys in the background were speaking among themselves and sayin' "Aye, there's no doobt. He is a rotten old scunner, but ach, nobody's perfect."

I tell you, it wis real sad. The whole thing wis just like a Greek Tragedy!

BLOWING IN THE WIND

I was walking along the sea front; just me, the seagulls and the wind when I heard the voice calling.

"Ian!"

That was all, yet for all the years that had passed I knew instantly who it was.

I turned and coming up behind me was David Smith, his face wrinkled in a smile.

"It is you!" he shook my hand vigorously.

"I don't believe it", he went on. "I was standing by the shelter and I said to myself "Good God. That's Ian Armstrong."

He hadn't really changed. A bit older looking, but instantly recognisable.

"What are you doing here?" he asked.

"Walking", I replied, rather coolly.

"Still the same old Ian. No discount for old friends."

"I live here", I relented.

"Here?" he echoed. "Dear me! You must be older than I thought."

"Two years younger than you"

"So you are. But why here?"

"I like it."

"And Rosemary?"

"Rosemary's dead."

"Oh! Sorry to hear that." He wasn't really.

"How about you?" I asked

"Me? You see it all. Footloose and fancy free." That was no surprise.

"Marjorie?"

"Don't know. Haven't seen or heard of her in ten or fifteen years." That was no surprise either.

"Good God! Ian Armstrong!" he said again. "How long has it been?"

"About twenty-five years." I replied. I remembered quite clearly the last time I'd seen him.

The wind was beginning to chill me.

"I would like to continue my walk", I said. "It's rather cold standing here."

"What? Yes. Right. Look, what about retreating to the nearest pub? We could chat about old times over a pint. How about it?"

“I drink very little nowadays”, I said pointedly.

“Well, we’ll chat over my pint then”, David countered.

No, he hadn’t changed. I used to think he would only notice disapproval if he was physically attacked. He never seemed to be in possession of any faculty that told him to back off. Or perhaps he was and merely ignored it. I envied him in a way. Insensitivity must give rise to a remarkably untroubled spirit. It could also persuade others to do things that they really didn’t intend.

“All right”, I said in proof of this and we turned and walked back towards the town.

In the event, I bought him a pint and had one myself.

“I took early retirement”, I explained as we sat down with our drinks. “With Rosemary dead and the children off living their own lives, there didn’t seem much point in continuing. Nobody to work for. So I took the handshake and the pension and went.”

“But I mean! This place!” He said, circling his hand to encompass the town.

“I told you. I like it. What’s wrong with it?”

“It’s full of geriatrics”, he protested. “It’s like a cemetery annexe. I can’t believe you would want to live here.”

“But I do. I’ve bought a small house with a view across the bay and a garden that gives me pleasure.”

“Good God man! You sound as if you’re ninety! You’re only what?”

"Like I said before. Two years younger than you."

"So you're sixty. Plenty of mileage in you yet. And what do you do for excitement?"

I shrugged. "Watch the wilder seas beating on the promenade. Watch the flowers grow."

"And go to whist drives and local dramatic society productions?"

"What's wrong with that?", I asked.

David Smith snorted in disbelief.

"It's existing! Not living! Just waiting for someone to close your eyelids and draw the curtains."

I smiled.

"Death comes whether we wait on it or not."

"Come on Ian. You know what I mean."

"I'm quite content", I said. "I don't need your notion of excitement to chase away the shadows. I've got four grandchildren now. My family visits when they can. One of them will close my eyelids when the time comes."

"Content", he countered. "An admirable word. Not happy. Not really living. Content."

"The majority of the human race would settle for content."

"Not me", he said. "I'm still living."

"And what exactly does 'living' mean?" I asked.

"Christ! Everyone knows what living means. Something new every day. No ruts. Stress I think they call it." He grinned and took a long drink from his glass. "Always looking for something better…"

"I'll settle for content", I said.

"Suit yourself, but I hate to see an old friend …. content."

I had an uneasy feeling that he was going to try to do something about it.

"What about your family?" I asked, to change the subject. "You and Marjory had two boys the last I heard."

"As far as I know, that's the full set", he answered. "There may be others, but I've had no official word from any quarter."

"You don't see them?"

"Not if I see them first."

"And it doesn't bother you. Not seeing them?"

"Why should it? Does it bother you?"

"Does what bother me?"

"Not seeing your family."

"But I do see them", I protested.

David smiled cynically. I became defensive.

"They visit when they can."

"Families only visit when they want something." Words running into sands of lost relationships, experiences not understood. I changed the subject again.

"You asked me what I was doing here", I said. "What are you doing here?"

"Cherchez la femme", he replied with a silly grin on his face. "La femme riche."

"Femmes in general or one in particular?" I asked, falling in with his fatuous phrase.

"Oh particular", he replied. "Very particular."

"And she lives here?"

"Hell, no!" I wouldn't be interested in any woman who actually lived here." Just one of his insensitive little jokes. "No, she's on holiday with a friend."

He saw me looking quizzically.

"A woman friend", he explained. "She said not to follow her. She wanted time to think."

"About what?" I asked naively.

He laughed. "She's resisting my advances."

"What a sensible woman", I thought. Aloud I said:

"So why don't you give her time?"

"Christ Ian, don't you know anything about women?"

"Enough to believe that if one asks to be left alone, she probably means it."

"Nonsense. If a woman told you she found you attractive, wouldn't you be intrigued, flattered?"

"That eventuality is unlikely to arise", I replied. "But if it did, my response would depend on whether or not I found her attractive."

"Not entirely", he countered. "Attraction is seldom immediate. You'd still be interested. I'll give you ten to one she's wondering if I'll show up in the hotel foyer or waiting for the phone to ring. She'll be disappointed if I don't get in touch one way or another. It may just annoy her if I do, but it will annoy her more if I don't."

This was typical David logic.

"What if she genuinely doesn't like you?"

"You haven't been listening. No-one will totally dislike someone who professes an interest."

I suppose there's some truth in this, for I didn't have a strong desire for his company, but he seemed to want mine, and I was going along with it.

"I wish you luck", I said. "Where are you staying?"

"I haven't got anything fixed yet. Some cheap hotel, I suppose." There was a silence and I knew he was waiting for an offer. He didn't get it. Not that it was going to make much difference.

"How about giving an old friend somewhere to lay his head?" he asked.

I could think of lots of places. Here was the reason for his interest in me. He was so predictable. Only David would have the nerve to presume on an acquaintanceship that had been dead for almost twenty-five years; that had died in somewhat unfortunate circumstances.

"No. Look David, I'm sorry. I'm too used to being on my own."

"You wouldn't say that if I was young, blonde and female."

"I'm sorry David..."

"I'm quiet and I'm housetrained", he interrupted. "You'll hardly know I'm there."

I doubted that.

"Tell you what, I'll take you out for a meal at the best hotel you have around here."

I sighed inwardly.

"How long are you staying?" I asked.

He exploited the sign of weakness.

"Oh. Only one night. Two at the outside."

That probably meant about a week. I could just about cope with that.

"Oh, very well", I said reluctantly. "Twenty pounds bed and breakfast."

That caught him off guard just for a moment. Then he laughed.

"You haven't changed, have you? You nearly had me believing that."

I had nearly believed it myself. He drained his glass.

“What’s your address? I’ll have to collect my bags from the station.”

I wrote the address on a page torn from my diary.

“I’ll get a taxi. The driver will know where it is. See you in about an hour.” With that he was off. He hadn’t even said ‘thanks’. He was almost certainly going to an hotel to cancel his booking.

I finished my drink and walked home. He arrived about four o’clock.

“Here I am then”, he said dumping a large suitcase in the hall.

I showed him to one of the spare bedrooms.

“Nice”, he said, pushing the flat of his hand into the surface of the bed. “Very comfortable.”

I left him and went to the kitchen to prepare a meal. As I worked, I thought about the last time I’d seen him and wondered at my weakness in letting him stay. He had borrowed a hundred pounds, which was a lot of money in those days, promising to repay it within a month. About a week later he vanished. Left his job and disappeared. There were rumours that he had been gambling; that he had been running around with some woman; that he owed money all round; that he had been sacked for incompetence. Whatever the reason, he had just cut and run. He had taken his family with him, which was a point in his favour, although his concern for them had obviously waned in the years that had followed.

Later in the evening he said:

"That was an excellent meal, Ian. How did you learn to cook like that?"

"Necessity", I replied.

"I envy you in a way", he said. "You're solid. Sort of like a tree." Then he laughed. "But that wouldn't do for me. I don't like roots. Life's not for roots. Life's for blowing in the wind." He was a great one for clichés.

After the meal we retired to the lounge and over several whiskies recalled mutual youthful escapades until it was late. I couldn't help thinking how odd it was that although my guard was up continuously I had allowed him back into my life.

I had never really trusted him even all these years ago. When I had lent him the hundred pounds I had doubted that I would get it back. Now I had given him free board and lodgings, saving him a few hundred more no doubt. By the time we decided to go to bed I was feeling guilty about evaluating our relationship in terms of money, while still being annoyed at his presumption.

In the morning I had a hangover and was less understanding. I prepared breakfast and ungraciously fended off David's attempts at conversation. I wanted to be on my own. It was eleven o'clock before I achieved it. David said he was going out to find his lady. He said he would be back in the late afternoon. When he left, I took a couple of aspirin and tidied up the previous evening's litter. In the event, he didn't return until after ten. I had made dinner for both of us, eaten half of it and thrown out the other half. I had returned to my mood of the morning.

"Great news Ian", he said. "The eagle has landed."

"What?"

"Tomorrow night, dinner a quatre."

"What?!"

"You, me, Davida and Margaret."

"Davida?"

He laughed. "Isn't fate wonderful? David and Davida."

He'd obviously had a few drinks. I scowled at him.

"Enjoy your fantasies. I'm going to bed."

He laughed again, and I left him, hoping that whatever wind he was blowing in would soon carry him away.

The following morning over eggs, bacon and sausage, he said:

"It's odd how we form long term attachments to certain people. I've always valued our friendship."

That was preposterous enough to be ignored.

"What were you trying to say last night?" I asked

"Ah he replied. I've arranged to inject a little excitement into your life. I've found you a woman."

"If I wanted a woman, I'd find one for myself."

He forked a piece of bacon into his mouth, inclined his head and said:

"No you wouldn't. You're too wrapped up in the cling film of what you have. You're content for God's sake. So I've done it for you. Be grateful."

"And this is an act of pure benefaction?"

"You know me better than that", he said with surprising candour. "I need you. But my necessity is your opportunity."

"And if I said I wasn't interested?"

He smiled.

"Oh, you're interested", he said.

He was right. I wasn't interested in finding a woman, but I was interested in the thought. A blind date wasn't in the usual fabric of a sixty-year-old life. So it was a little excitement. To see what the lady was like. To find out what he was up to.

"Very well', I said. 'I'll go along with it."

He didn't comment. It was obvious that he had been sure of my reaction. I didn't ask why he needed me. I suspected that it was in the hope that Margaret's attention would be engaged elsewhere whilst he ingratiated himself with Davida.

"By the way", he said that evening just before we left the house. "Davida prefers Vi. She dislikes her full name. So call her Vi, will you?"

"By all means", I said. "Anything else?"

"No, just be your normal sober, upright self."

'Boring self' was what he meant. He wanted a touchstone.

It was a mild dry evening. We walked down to the seafront. Apparently, the women were staying at the Bay Hotel. That was the best there was around here.

"Vi's the more voluptuous of the two." David explained as we walked. "She looks as if her blouse is stuffed with banknotes." He grinned. "Nothing more erotic than a woman who looks as if her blouse is stuffed with banknotes. Margaret's a bit skinny."

Thus, Margaret was dismissed. I began to picture the female equivalent of Laurel and Hardy.

"Mrs Brown and Mrs Pearson", David said to the desk clerk. "They may be in their room."

"Oh. Yes sir; no sir. Mrs Brown said to tell you they would meet you in the lounge. To your left sir." The clerk indicated with his arm.

Vi was slimmer than my expectation and Margaret more rounded. Two perfectly normal women in their late fifties.

"Vi", David was saying "This is Ian. Ian, this is Margaret."

I was aware of grey-green eyes.

"Hello Margaret."

We held each other's hands briefly, casually.

"So you are Ian Armstrong", Vi said. "I've heard so much about you."

I wondered if this was merely a platitude and my eyes flickered towards David, but he was smiling at Vi.

I ordered a round of drinks. I felt uncomfortable. I always felt uncomfortable in the presence of new people. I wasn't good at small talk. Fortunately, with David present, there were no awkward silences.

"You ladies are looking very attractive tonight", he was saying.

"Knowing you, I expected something more flattering", Vi countered.

Perhaps she had his measure.

David smiled. "That would put me at too much of a disadvantage", he said. "Be content with very attractive."

"I believe you live here, Mr Armstrong." The grey-green eyes again.

"Ian", I said "Yes. I do."

"It's a lovely little place, I envy you."

"David was telling us you're a stockbroker", said Vi.

"Was", I said. "Was a stockbroker. I'm retired."

"Retired?' she repeated, surprise in her voice. "You're retired?"

"Yes."

David laughed. "You won't get much out of Ian. He's not the talkative type."

Give a dog a bad name. I smiled and went along with the advance publicity.

Later, after an excellent meal, for which, unexpectedly, David insisted on paying, he enquired of Margaret and I if we would object if Vi and he took a stroll by themselves in the late evening twilight.

I noticed a quick glance passing from Vi to Margaret. However, we concurred politely, and they went off, leaving Margaret and me at the dinner table, which was by now cleared of everything except four wine glasses.

I was more relaxed by this time, so I raised my glass and said: "Here's to being on our own."

Margaret smiled and copied my gesture. I noticed the curve of her lips as she drank, and it occurred to me that it was the first time I had been alone with a woman since Rosemary had died. I hadn't sought the experience, but here it was, and I was enjoying it.

"Let's go through to the lounge", I said.

I was aware of her perfume and of the movement of her body as she preceded me and was momentarily disconcerted by a small stirring of desire.

I bought two brandies and tool them to the table where she sat.

As she wrapped her right hand around the brandy glass, her eyes caught mine and she smiled.

"I've enjoyed this evening", she said.

"Yes. So have I." I wanted to say more, to take advantage of the moment, but couldn't find the words. After a short silence she said:

"You and David are close friends." A statement that was really a question.

"I haven't seen him for twenty-five years", I replied. "We met by accident a couple of days ago."

"But you are friends?" she persisted.

"To be perfectly honest, no. An acquaintance, but no, we're not really friends."

Her expression changed slightly, and her attractive eyes seemed to become more grey than green.

"He's rather laying siege to Vi", she said. "I just wonder what he's up to."

"You suspect his intentions may not be honourable?"

She gave a short snort of laughter.

"Good God", she said. "I don't remember when I last heard that phrase – if ever!"

"It wasn't meant too seriously", I replied

"I realise that.... But he's not interested in her physically. I can tell."

"He may just be looking for feminine companionship. He's been away from his wife for some time."

"He's divorced then?"

I didn't know the answer to that. It occurred to me then that I knew nothing other than what he had told me, and that was precious little. For all I knew, chasing women was what he meant by 'blowing in the wind'.

"I can only assume that he is", I said.

"Hmm..." Margaret looked into her glass.

"So you suspect his motives. If it's not sex, it's money?"

"That's what I suspect"

"Vi's wealthy then?"

"She's not Croesus, but I think she's pretty comfortable. She's paying for this holiday for both of us. She doesn't need to count the pennies."

"Obviously I don't know her as well as you", I said. "But she seems to be a fairly intelligent woman. How would David get her to part with money?"

"I don't know." Margaret smiled apologetically. "I'm probably being neurotic. She seems quite taken with him, but there's something about him I don't trust."

'Sensible woman!' I thought.

"Have you known Vi long?" I asked.

"It's rather like you and David", she replied. "I knew her many years ago but hadn't seen her until we met by accident last April and got talking; sort of renewed our old friendship. Then one day she asked me if I would like to come with her on holiday. Her treat. At first, I refused. I didn't like the idea... too like charity. I'm a widow living on a small pension of my husband's – but she was quite insistent. So eventually I agreed." She sighed. "I still feel a bit uneasy about it though."

"Why should you", I said. "If she enjoys your company and if she can afford it, why not?"

"Why not, indeed", Margaret said doubtfully.

"Forget David and Vi", I said. "How about having dinner with me again tomorrow night? My place. My cooking. Eight o'clock."

To my delight and surprise, she accepted the invitation immediately and with apparent pleasure.

We were still talking when David and Vi returned.

Later, when David and I began our walk home, the sky was clear, and the moon was up. The familiar buildings and streets were mellowed in the soft light. I was experiencing some sort of metamorphosis. David was right. I had been merely existing. Or perhaps it was just the effect of the alcohol.

"That was a very pleasant evening, David", I said. "Thanks."

"I told you I'd found you a woman", he replied.

"Perhaps. Yes, perhaps you have. I enjoyed her company."

"There you are then. Happy to be of service."

Maybe he wasn't such a bad sort. Maybe his heart was in the right place. "How about you and Vi?" I asked.

He frowned. And I realised then that he had seemed rather subdued since he and Vi had returned from their walk.

"Don't know exactly. I'm not sure how she feels about me."

"What do you want of her?" I asked, remembering what Margaret had said. It occurred to me to ask if he was divorced, but I reckoned that it was really none of my business. Both he and Vi were more than mature enough to handle that sort of thing between them; and I had told Margaret that he had been married.

“What does a man of my age want with a woman?” David replied. “Companionship, some signs of affection. Softness.”

I laughed. “What happened to blouses stuffed with banknotes?”

“Joke!” he protested. “Just a joke. I really like her.”

Maybe he did. Maybe we all misjudged him.

He didn’t get up for breakfast the following morning. He was still in bed at 10.30 when the telephone rang. It was Margaret.

“Is David there?” she asked.

“He’s in bed. I’ll call him.”

“No. No, it’s you I want. I just wanted to know if David was around. Within listening distance.”

“Why?”

“Vi wants to talk to you.”

“To me?”

“Yes.”

“About what?”

“David.”

“David?”

“Yes. But she doesn’t want him to know. Can you come down to the hotel within the next half hour?”

"Yes, I suppose so. But what...?"

"I don't know. Will you come?"

"Yes of course. I'll be down shortly."

"Thanks Ian. I'll see you tonight."

I left a note for David:

Going out to see a friend. Expect to be back soon, but if not, I'm entertaining Margaret at home tonight. Make yourself scarce and I'll be forever in your debt.

Yours, Ian.

I didn't expect that whatever Vi was after would take long, but I wanted to take some time shopping so that the meal would be special. Then I would need time for preparation and cooking. It would suit me very well if he was out before I got back.

Vi was sitting in the entrance lounge of the hotel when I arrived. She rose to meet me as I came through the door.

"Thanks so much for coming, Ian", she said. "Look. Do you mind if we get out of here? My car's in the car park."

"How about driving along the coast to the next village?"

"Ryemouth?"

"Yes. Although it doesn't really matter where. I hope you don't mind. I feel so guilty, but I don't want to take the chance of David seeing us together."

"That's all right", I said. I wondered what the hell he'd been up to. As we drove to Ryemouth we talked about everything except David. It was almost midday before we arrived.

"Shall we talk over a meal?" I asked.

"Yes. That's fine. But could we choose somewhere quiet?"

We walked along the front until we saw a rather drab looking hotel.

"Let's try here", I said. "It doesn't look like the hub of the universe. Anyway, it's just after twelve. Most dining rooms are quiet this early."

In the event the dining room was deserted. I asked the waiter to bring a couple of sherries and said that I would let him know when we wanted to see the menu.

Vi fidgeted nervously with her glass before she spoke.

"I couldn't think who else to speak to", she said. "You know David, and ...you're a stockbroker."

"It's about money then?"

"Yes, but about David too. I've grown very fond of him and I want to please him... but."

"But what?"

"He's wanting me to invest in this company. He's got money in it himself. He says it's enlisted or something."

"An unlisted company."

"Yes. That's it. I just wondered if it would be a wise thing to do?"

I sighed inwardly. I had never really believed that people actually fell for this sort of thing. I had to choose my words carefully.

"How much did he suggest?" I asked.

"No specific amount. Well – he said it wouldn't be worth investing less than £20,000. He said it could be worth half a million in a few years."

"What sort of company is it?"

"Pharmaceuticals", she replied. "They've got some new product in development – some genetic thing – that will completely transform the treatment of diabetes. No more injections. They're doing clinical trials now and it's very promising."

"Any investment is a risk", I explained. "But that sort of thing is high risk. David might be right. You may make a lot of money. On the other hand, you may lose it all. High risk investment is fine if you can afford it. Can you afford to lose £20,000?"

She grimaced. "Who would want to lose £20,000?" she said. "But I suppose that I would still be able to survive."

"What other investments do you have?" I asked.

To my surprise she opened her handbag and handed me a folded sheet of paper. On it was a list of her investments. Some British Blue Chip, some gilts, but mostly unit trusts. American, European, British, Far East, Japan. A mixture of income and growth. The number of shares was shown against each. I made a quick calculation based on what I could remember of the current values. Probably about a hundred and fifty thousand.

"That's an excellent portfolio", I said. "Very solid. I wouldn't change anything."

Vi turned down the corners of her mouth

"David's so insistent", she said. "I'm sure he sincerely believes I'll make a lot of money."

"That may be so. But you have to decide if you're willing to lose £20,000 just to please David. Really think about it. When you've got the answer to that your decision will be made."

I beckoned the waiter and we started lunch.

It was a surprisingly good lunch. Between courses we continued talking.

"Did David suggest you give the money to him?"

She looked up, startled. "Do you have reason to distrust him?" she said.

I avoided answering directly. "If I told you that David's proposal was sound, would you trust me to invest the money for you?"

She considered for a few seconds and then said "You're a retired stockbroker. Yes, I would trust you."

"Then you would be very unwise", I said. "You don't know me from Adam. In this sort of situation, never, never, under any circumstance give your money to an individual. I can't stress that too emphatically. Don't even consider it. Go to an accredited broker."

I asked Vi to give me the name of the company David wanted her to invest in and I said I would get a friend in the city to make enquiries. I would have been suspicious that the company existed only in David's imagination had it not been for one unsettling thought. Vi had known I'd been a stockbroker. Only David could have told her that, and he must have considered the possibility that she might ask my advice. Why had he told her?

"I'm so glad we've had this talk", said Vi. "You've been so helpful. I can't tell you how grateful I am."

It was after two when we left the hotel.

Vi suggested a short stroll along the front before we got back into the car.

"That was a rather large lunch", she said. "I need a little exercise."

I wasn't keen on the idea. I explained that I was entertaining Margaret and that I had some shopping to do.

"Yes. Margaret said she was seeing you again tonight", said Vi. "I'm so pleased that you two like each other. She's been on her own too long. But why not do your shopping here? I'll come with you. Kill two birds with one stone. Your shopping. My exercise." That was sensible. I agreed.

It was almost five before we got back. Vi insisted on driving me home before going back to the hotel. I was grateful and said so.

"Be nice to her", she said as I got out of the car with my plastic carrier bag. "She deserves it."

David wasn't in. He had scribbled an addendum to my note.

"Your wish is my command. Just remember you owe me. I found her for you." I crumpled the sheet of paper and threw it in the bucket. I didn't want Margaret to come across it accidentally. David's words made her seem like a piece of Stilton he had discovered in a supermarket.

I forgot about David and set about preparing dinner, which was to be shrimp in avocado, fillet steak en croute and a fresh fruit salad in a light rum sugar syrup. I just had time to shower and change before she arrived.

She was looking very attractive in a green silk dress. She had had her hair done and had spent some time on make-up that accentuated her fine eyes. I was flattered.

I had a bottle of good red wine to go with the steak, and we ate, not talking much.

When I brought in the coffee, Margaret said:

"That was superb, Ian. Have you always been interested in cooking?"

"I suppose I have", I replied. "I used to make the occasional meal when Rosemary was alive. Then, after she died, it became a necessity and I decided that I may as well make a proper job of it. It helps to occupy the time. But it's not the same – cooking for myself."

"Tell me", she invited. "About you and Rosemary and your children."

So I did. I suppose it was the first time that someone was interested, so I rather overdid it, but to her eternal credit there was never a glazed stare nor a stifled yawn.

I eventually relented and said:

"Forgive me. You must be bored stiff."

"Not at all", she replied. "I wouldn't have asked had I not been interested."

"And long suffering", I smiled. "Go on then, your turn."

Margaret told me that she had one child, a daughter who was married and living in Canada, whom she hoped to visit when she'd saved enough for the air fare. But it wasn't the bare facts of her past life that were the real interest, it was that in talking, attitudes, interests, sympathies, prejudices are revealed, and I could find nothing in her mind or personality that seemed in conflict with my own.

That she felt the same way, she apparently signalled by taking my arm as I walked her to the hotel.

That evening breathed real life into our relationship; changed it from two into three dimensions.

When I got home I washed the dishes that I had refused to allow Margaret to touch. By the time I had cleared everything away it was almost midnight. David wasn't back, but I was tired, so I left the door unlocked and went to bed.

There was still no sign of him when I got up next morning. That gave me the opportunity to phone an ex colleague who promised to look into the company in which David had proposed that Vi should invest.

I thought no more about him until Margaret phoned just after lunch.

"I'm worried about Vi", she said. "I haven't seen her since late yesterday afternoon. Her bed hasn't been slept in."

"That probably explains it", I said. "David hasn't been home either. I wouldn't worry. They've probably gone off somewhere together."

"Why would they do that?"

"I could make an educated guess."

"I told you before Ian. I'm sure he's not interested in her in that way."

"She seems interested in him", I said.

"That's what worries me. She's going to get hurt."

It hadn't been my intention to see Margaret that day; I didn't want to appear to be pushing things, but I said: "Look. Do you want me to come down there?"

She hesitated, then replied: "No. No. it's all right Ian. I'm okay. Just an overheated imagination."

"I'll come tomorrow then. We'll have lunch."

"Yes. Fine. I'll look forward to that. Until tomorrow then?"

"Until tomorrow."

The following day, Margaret was more relaxed. Vi had left a note for her with the desk clerk to the effect that she was going off for a few days and apologising for the suddenness of her departure. It didn't say much else and there was no mention of David, but it was fairly obvious that they had gone off together. The fact that David had vanished without explanation was quite in character.

The good thing, the positive thing, was that Margaret and I were together every day and growing ever closer.

However, after eight days had elapsed, Margaret had been concerned.

"I can't understand why Vi hasn't been in touch", she said. "You would think a phone call or card wouldn't have been too much trouble."

I tried to reassure her. "They're probably enjoying themselves too much to notice time passing", I said. "Or maybe Vi's idea of a few days differs from yours."

Another couple of days passed and Margaret said she was becoming really worried. Over lunch we discussed whether or not we should go to the police. Our conclusion was that we were being neurotic. That was Saturday. We decided to wait until the following Monday. On Monday, nothing had changed. We waited until Tuesday, then we decided, for Margaret's sake, to go to the police. They were polite, but didn't as we had expected, take it very seriously. They took a description of David and Vi and said if they 'heard of anything' they would let us know, but we were sure that this was mere window dressing just to get rid of us.

I had got to the stage where, like the police, I wasn't much concerned with David and Vi. Two people in late middle age had gone off together. So what?

And I had found a woman who, although not another Rosemary, seemed to chime as I chimed, something that I wouldn't have thought possible before David came on the scene.

So I suppose, as he had put it, that I owed him.

Then my old colleague phoned me back, apologising for the delay, to tell me that David's pharmaceutical company did exist, and was trying to develop a new drug. It was a very small company, undercapitalised and apparently in some difficulty financially. I didn't tell Margaret. I didn't know if she was aware of this complication, and I didn't want to worry her unnecessarily.

Two weeks to the day after David and Vi had disappeared, and I was walking with Margaret along the seafront, something occurred to me. Something that I should have thought of earlier.

"What about your hotel bill?" I asked.

"What?" She turned towards me and her eyes told me everything.

"It's all right", she said. "It's perfectly all right."

"You said that Vi was paying for your holiday."

"Yes. Of course she is... will."

She made her way to a bench and sat down, looking out towards the sea.

"Have they said anything about payment?"

She didn't answer, but she was as stiff as a board.

"They have, haven't they?" I persisted gently.

"No. It's all right. There's no problem."

"Tell me Margaret. I want to know."

Her body began to shake quietly, and I did what I had been waiting to do for some time. I put arm around her shoulders.

"Tell me", I repeated.

There was a long silence before she admitted the truth.

"They gave me our bill last week. I said to wait until Vi came back. Yesterday the manager came to my room. He was very polite, but he gave me another bill, up to date, and said that he had to insist on payment within the next few days. I didn't know what to do. They may call the police."

"I doubt that", I said reassuringly. "How much is it?"

"Two thousand three hundred and something", Margaret replied. "We – I've been there for about five weeks and Vi obviously hadn't paid anything to account."

I took her hand. "Don't worry', I said. "Will you permit me to have a word with the Manager? I'll sort something out."

"Oh Ian, do you think you could? Persuade him to wait until Vi returns."

"Yes I'm sure I can." I didn't say that I had decided to pay the account. If Vi came back, I'd be refunded. If not, I could afford it. So that's what I did. I took Margaret back to the hotel, saw her off to the room then went to the reception desk and paid the bill.

The following morning, having been aware when I wrote the cheque that there wasn't quite enough in my current account to cover it, I prepared to go to the bank and transfer money from my high interest account.

I unlocked my writing bureau and opened the top right-hand drawer where I kept the passbook. It wasn't there. I looked through the drawer again without success and suddenly I knew why David had gone, and that he wasn't coming back. I looked through all the other drawers, not for the passbook, for I always kept it in the top right-hand drawer, but to see if anything else was missing. My share certificates were all still there, but my passport and a small collection of gold coins were gone. The coins were worth perhaps a thousand pounds, but I had over eighty thousand pounds in my high interest account. For a moment I panicked. I couldn't remember the account number and I was in the bank so infrequently that I wasn't sure if any of the staff would recognise me. I always drew what cash I needed from the auto-dispenser and my pension and dividends were transferred directly into my current account. I took the passbook in only once a year, in November, to get the interest added. Then I remembered the annual statements, showing interest for tax purposes, which fortunately were still there. I breathed a sigh of relief and wondered what to do first. Phone the police? Phone Margaret? I decided there was no point in contacting either until I was in possession of all the facts. So I went to the bank, where I was relieved to discover that the manager remembered me from when I had opened my account almost five years previously. Thank God for people with good memories. I gave him a brief explanation of my problem and he keyed my high interest account number into the computer. After a few interminable seconds he looked up and said:

"The balance is eighteen thousand, two hundred and forty." He keyed again. "There have been several withdrawals in the last two weeks. Amounts varying from four to seven thousand. All from different branches in the London area."

"How is that possible?" I asked.

"It's simple. Whoever has the passbook has a sample of your signature."

"But surely you would make checks?"

"Only to see if the signature looks right and find if there were sufficient funds to cover the withdrawals. He has been clever enough not to try and clear the account in one transaction."

"So what do we do now?"

"Transfer the balance immediately into a new account. We'll circulate all branches so that if he tries again we'll catch him. I'm sorry Mr Armstrong, but that's the best we can do."

To his credit, he managed to refrain from commenting on my carelessness.

I requested the transfer of three thousand into my current account and left him to organise things while I went to the police station.

I had to wait for some time before a policeman answered my repeated assaults on the bell push. I reflected wryly that in a small seaside village I was probably fortunate to find anyone in at all. I asked to see a senior officer.

"There's only me and the detective sir", he said. "And he's got someone with him. I'll tell him you're waiting, but it will be about ten minutes before he can see you."

"Can I make a phone call?" I asked just as he was about to disappear again.

He nodded and lifted a telephone from a table and placed it in front of me.

I called the hotel and asked for Margaret. At first they thought she had gone out, but eventually contacted her.

"Hello?"

"Margaret. It's me. Look, I've discovered why David has gone."

"Ian. I've been trying to contact you all morning. Did you pay the hotel bill?"

"Yes I did. Margaret, I..."

"You really shouldn't have done that. I'll pay you back."

"I'm sure you will. Don't worry about it."

"But I do worry about it. I'm very grateful, but I'll pay you back."

"Margaret. Did you hear what I said. I know why David has gone."

"And Vi? What about Vi?"

"I think he must have persuaded her to go with him. He suddenly found he could afford it."

I did my best to keep an ironic intonation from my voice.

"Look", I said. "I'll have to go. I'll explain later." I wanted to tell her the whole story face to face.

"You sound strange", Margaret said. "Is something troubling you?"

"No, not really", I lied.

"When will I see you?"

"About seven. We'll have dinner then."

"Good. I'll see you then."

I said goodbye and hung up. It was about thirty minutes before the detective appeared. He led me to a small, bare office with a table and three chairs. We sat down, and I told him everything I thought relevant. Of my chance meeting with David, of his pursuit of Vi and of my earlier suspicions of his motives.

"Now that I've had time to think", I said "David must have taken the passbook while I was with Vi, discussing her business affairs."

"Have you considered the possibility that they were in it together?" asked the detective.

"Oh, I wouldn't think so. They didn't really know each other until...."

My voice trailed away, and the detective gave a wry smile. I realised that they could have known each other for years, for all I knew.

"Didn't you think it odd when they both disappeared at the same time?"

"Not really. Unexpected perhaps. But, knowing David.... Anyway. I did report it – their disappearance."

"You did?"

"Yes, I came in here. But no-one seemed interested. Of course, I didn't know about the passbook and the coins, then."

The detective looked slightly discomfited, but only for a moment. "They've been rather clever", he said. "Diverting your attention towards the woman, making you think he was after her money. Then she gets you away for the day while he goes carefully through your possessions."

"But surely they took a chance with the passbook? These separate withdrawals. I could have noticed it was gone the day after they left."

"One look at the book would have told him you only used it once a year", said the detective. "That's probably why he took it. The coins were slightly riskier, but only slightly. By the way, why did you look for it?"

"I had a large amount of money to pay unexpectedly", I explained. "My current account wouldn't have covered it, so I needed to transfer cash."

"Well now", said the detective. "They won't have expected that. They'll probably try another withdrawal. If so, we'll stand a good chance of catching them."

"Do you think that's likely? Catching them in the act?" I asked.

"Depends on how alert the bank people are", the detective replied. "There's a fair chance."

After some form filling, I left, feeling slightly better than I had when I arrived. It would be nice to think that Vi's shabby treatment of Margaret would be the reason they were caught.

Margaret and I had dinner at the Bay Hotel, although neither of us felt much like eating. I explained the whole situation of her.

"Oh, Ian", she said. "How awful for you."

"At least there appears to be some chance of catching them now; if they try to make another withdrawal."

Her eyes were clouded and troubled. "I can't believe that Vi has anything to do with it", she said.

"Well, that's only the police theory", I replied. "I don't see that David needed an accomplice. He could have taken the passbook at any time. He would have plenty of opportunity. I knew he was untrustworthy in a minor way. But not this. Not outright theft."

She leaned over and took my hands in hers. "You're far too trusting", she said. "I told you there was something not right about him, although it was Vi that concerned me, not you."

"If Vi is involved", I said "She won't be back. Have you thought about that?"

She smiled brightly. Too brightly. "There's no need to worry over me. You've got enough on your plate. I can sort myself out. Besides, Vi will be back. I'm sure of it."

I looked directly at her, and she lowered her eyes, indicating to me that she wasn't sure at all. I gripped her hands tight.

"Just remember I'm around", I said. "Don't hesitate to lean on me. I may have lost money, but I've found you."

She looked up again, her face suddenly flushed red.

"God, you're a nice man", she said. "I wish I had met you a long time ago."

"We were both married then", I said pointedly.

She smiled and sat more upright, her back against the back of her chair.

"Yes", she said. "Yes, we were, weren't we?"

I didn't pursue that line of conversation further. We talked for another hour, inconsequentially, avoiding what was on both our minds.

I had difficulty finding sleep that night. Despite all that had happened, it was these words of Margaret's that kept coming back into my mind. I kept finding different intonations, different interpretations in that simple phrase: 'Yes we were, weren't we?'

The next morning, I went down to the bank to find if there had been any developments. I could have phoned, but I wanted the walk. I find walking therapeutic, and it helps me to think. I was thinking about Margaret. What my next step should be. In the event the bank had no news, and I was no clearer about Margaret.

I got home about eleven-thirty. As I opened the front door there was a smell of frying bacon. Puzzled, I called out:

"Who's there?"

David appeared from the kitchen.

"Oh. There you are, he said. "I wondered where you had got to. I couldn't wait any longer. I was starving. I got in through a window you'd left open. Would you like some bacon and egg?"

My intellect told me he would not have come back if he had stolen my money. My emotions ignored the thought. "Never mind bacon and egg", I shouted. "Where's my bloody money?"

"Money? What money? You're surely not talking about that few quid I borrowed all those years ago?"

So he did remember.

"My money. The passbook. The coins!"

"Calm down Ian", he said. "Hold on a minute. Let me rescue my breakfast. I've been waiting for it long enough."

He disappeared into the kitchen and came back shortly with a plate in one hand and a fork in the other. By this time, I was sitting in the lounge. I'd had more excitement than my legs could bear. Talk about blowing in the wind!

"Sure you don't want some of this?" he asked, moving the plate towards me. "It's first class bacon. Where'd you get it?"

I nearly knocked the plate out of his hand.

"Forget the bacon", I said with commendable restraint. "I want the passbook, the coins and the money."

"I honestly don't know what you're talking about", he replied, eating with obvious enjoyment.

He was quite unbelievable.

“Where the hell have you been? The police are looking for you.”

That got his attention.

“The police? Looking for me?”

“I told them that you have stolen sixty-five thousand pounds.” It seemed pointless to mention the coins again.

“Thanks a bunch. Sixty-five thousand pounds?! From you?”

Then, incredible as it seems, I ended up doing the explaining.

“So you see”, I concluded. “What else is there to think?”

“I didn’t think you’d be bothered about me and Vi going off like that”, he said. “Anyway, it was her idea. We’ve had rather a nice time, the pair of us.”

“Why didn’t you leave a note, for God’s sake?”

“We did. Well, Vi did. She left a note for Margaret.”

“Yes, I know that, but it didn’t mention you”

“That’s hardly my fault, old man.”

“And where’s Vi now?”

“Back at the hotel. She dropped me off on the way.”

“You’ll have to go to the police”, I said. “You’ll have to explain to them what’s happened. If you are innocent, you’ll have to persuade them, not me.”

"You didn't really believe I'd taken your money, did you?" He looked rather hurt.

"Of course I bloody did. I still do. What else is there to think?"

It took a little time to persuade him to come to the police station with me, but he eventually realised that there was no alternative.

I think he was given a hard time by the detective. I saw him come out of the interview looking white and being shepherded into some other room. I'm not normally vindictive, but I was rather pleased. The detective eventually reappeared and spoke to me.

"I've asked Mr Smith to stay here for the time being", he said. "We'll have to interview Mrs Brown. I suggest you go home and wait until you hear from us."

"Has he admitted the theft?" I asked.

"He denies all knowledge of it", he replied. "But if you don't mind I'll send a PC home with you to search his belongings and to take fingerprints from your desk."

The policeman was very thorough. He dusted the desk and lifted fingerprints which he said might all be mine. He found nothing incriminating in David's belongings.

"We didn't think he would have brought anything back here", he said before he left. "But if I've missed anything, you'll no doubt find it yourself, eventually."

After he had gone, I went through David's stuff myself, then packed everything into his suitcase and brought it to the front door. If the police released him, even if he was presumed innocent, I wasn't having him under my roof another night.

Then I remembered Margaret. I cursed myself. In all the excitement I had no thought of the effect that Vi being taken to the police station would have on her.

I telephoned the hotel and after an interminable wait, eventually got through to her. I had expected her to be upset, but her anger took me by surprise.

"How could you do this to us Ian! The police have taken Vi away, and they are searching both our rooms. I would have thought that you would have warned us. But perhaps you didn't want to; perhaps you expect them to find something! I feel so humiliated. So..so..dirty!" I could hear the tears behind the words.

"Margaret", I said. "Please understand. None of this was my idea. I don't suspect you of anything."

"And Vi. What about Vi?"

I sighed. "I don't know about Vi. The police..."

"Did you know they were coming here?"

"Well yes... They said they wanted to interview Vi..."

"And you didn't think to phone me?"

"Not right away, no.. I wasn't thinking straight. I'm pretty upset myself. I didn't seek any of this. Look, I'll come down to the hotel right away."

"No. There's no point, Ian. When they've finished searching the rooms I'm going down to the police station to find out what's happening to Vi. She must be devastated."

"I'm sure she will be", I said. "I'm so sorry this has happened. I'll go with you..."

There was a click and the line went dead. I was left feeling stupid and inadequate. I realised that it was inexcusable of me not to have phoned Margaret earlier. I went through to the kitchen and made myself a cup of tea. Later, as I sat with the tea, my mind going round in circles, my feelings of guilt began to be replaced by anger.

Here I was, having been robbed of sixty-five thousand pounds, trying to explain, apologising to everyone in sight! Damn David Smith!

I don't know how long I sat, wondering what to do next, trying to make up my mind if Margaret's attitude had been understandable in the circumstances, or just a bit insensitive. Probably a bit of both. I had just begun to feel a little calmer and had decided to go back down to the police station when the doorbell rang.

It was David. I stood looking at him for a moment, then, without speaking held the door wider to allow him in. I noticed his glance taking in his suitcase. We both went through to the lounge and I motioned to him to sit down.

He forced a smile.

"Completely innocent, old man", he said.

I couldn't think of anything to say in reply to that. Anything civil. Eventually I asked him if he would like a cup of tea. He said yes. I had another myself. Then I asked: "Is Vi still down there?"

"No", he replied. "She's been released. Margaret was waiting for her. They went off together. She was in a bit of a state.

Well, they both were. I tried to speak to her, but she wasn't having any. They just went off – back to the hotel, I suppose." He drank from his cup, seemingly quite relaxed in the company of someone who had accused him of theft.

"David", I said. "You'll have to go. I assume you saw your case in the hallway."

He raised his eyebrows. "You don't believe me", he said. "You still think I took your money."

"I don't know what to believe", I replied. "But surely you can understand how I feel."

He dismissed my feelings with a shrug of his shoulders. "There's something you should know", he said. "Remember the day you left me the note. Asking me to make myself scarce. The day Vi and I went off together?"

I nodded.

"Half an hour after you'd gone", he went on, "Margaret came by and told me that Vi wanted to see me at lunchtime - at Retborough – in the hotel we stayed at later. I had to leave almost immediately to catch a bus that would get me there on time. When I arrived, there was a message saying that Vi had been delayed and would I mind waiting. She didn't actually arrive until after six." He stopped speaking as if waiting on a comment from me.

"What about it", I obliged.

"Margaret was still here when I left. She said she was going to prepare a meal to surprise you. I thought nothing of it at the time but now it all fits into place. She would have had plenty of time to do what she needed to do. You have to admire them.

They fill your head with ideas about me ripping off Vi. Vi makes eyes at me, Margaret makes eyes at you. Then, that day, Vi gets you out of the way, Margaret gets me out of the way and just about cleans you out. She gives the stuff to Vi, who takes it off, with me in tow – a prize red herring, while Margaret stays behind to keep an eye on you. What you did wrong was to pay the hotel bill before they had got the last eighteen thousand. Margaret must be kicking herself for overdoing the poor widow bit. Then you tell her the passbook is missing, she tells Vi, Vi brings me back. Bloody cheeky. Bloody brilliant."

I stared at him coldly. It sounded very plausible, but I didn't want to believe it. "Did you tell this to the police?" I asked.

"Of course," he said. "They seemed to think I was the only suspect. But you see, I wasn't."

"Did they interrogate Margaret?"

"I don't know, Ian. I suppose they did, but I was under lock and key at the time. Didn't have much time to think about others."

He never did.

"Your hypothesis doesn't stand scrutiny", I said. "Why, if she is involved, would Vi come back here – with you – and risk arrest?"

"Double bluff, old man. Act the innocent. Probably got everything safely hidden away. No evidence."

"The same could be said for you", I pointed out.

He considered this for a moment, then said: "Yes, I suppose it could. But it wouldn't be true."

I asked him if the police had instructed him to stay in town, and when he said "No", I got up, went to the telephone and called the local taxi company.

As he left, he offered his hand and said: "Perhaps we'll meet again, Ian." No: "Sorry for all that's happened." No: "Thanks for putting me up."

I ignored his hand and instead gave him an insincere, watery smile. "I don't think so, David", I said.

He got into the taxi, and without a backward glance, was gone.

It took me half an hour to pluck up the courage to go and see Margaret. I didn't want to face her anger – I'm not good at handling conflict – but I had to see her again. To smooth her ruffled feathers. To tell her I wanted her to stay. To be with me.

The hotel receptionist said: "I'm sorry sir. Mrs Pearson and Mrs Brown have gone. They left about an hour ago. Mrs Pearson left you a note."

My dear Ian,

Forgive me, I was unforgivably rude on the telephone. You are a dear and special man, but after what has happened I just want to get away from here. Vi wants to get home and try to forget the whole thing.

I said I wished I had known you years ago. I really meant it.

With Love,

Margaret.

The job of the police is to catch criminals. They are not much interested in victims. That was the impression I got as I waited in vain all of the next day for a call from them. Then I suddenly remembered something that David had said to me, something I realised could be important. I went down to see the detective.

He was long on theory and short on conclusions. It was not, he said, a casual theft. He was quite sure it was either David, Vi, or Margaret, or any two of them, or all three working together.

Unfortunately, he had no evidence to hold anyone. They had found no large amount of money in their possession, no gold coins, no fingerprints on or in my desk, no sudden influx of money into any bank account. Yes, they had checked accounts – those that they knew of. Yes, they had taken their fingerprints. I pointed out that since the money had been cashed in London and I had been seeing Margaret every day at that time, she couldn't have been involved. He said that would only be true if she was acting alone. It was quite possible that there was another, yet unknown accomplice, working with any or all of them.

Then I told him what I had remembered. What David had said after he came back from being interrogated, when he was laying the blame on Vi and Margaret. "What you did wrong", he had said to me, "Was to pay Margaret's hotel bill before they had got the last eighteen thousand."

"How did he know", I asked the detective, "That there was eighteen thousand left in the account?"

I had hoped that this would give new impetus to the investigation. Instead the detective thought for a moment, then looking uncomfortable, said "We may have mentioned this at some time during the interview."

Immediately I knew that 'We may have' meant 'We almost certainly did'. It would be written large in the transcript of the interrogation.

He finally assured me that the investigation was 'still being given a high priority' and that they would be in touch whenever they had anything further to report.

I left with the clear picture of a folder being placed in a 'pending' file and slowly gathering dust.

That was just over two months ago. I had said to David that I was 'content' and I suppose I still am. Nothing much could affect me after surviving the awful storm of Rosemary's death, and now as then, in the quiet waters I thought I'd never reach. I reckon that to lose sixty-five thousand pounds and still be able to live comfortably must be some sort of blessing. There won't be as much to leave to my family, but they're pretty well off anyway, so what the hell.

Last night there was a thunderstorm, I sat at my window and watched the lightning flickering across the bay. It was quite spectacular. Tonight, I'm playing bridge. Next week my daughter and her family are coming to visit.

And maybe, one day, Margaret will turn up again, and when I look into her grey-green eyes I will know she was an innocent dupe in the whole affair.

I'd like that.

CAT AND MOUSE

Yellow light from street lamps reflected wetly on the deserted suburban pavement and filtered into a large garden through the shadow haunted leaves of an overgrown laurel hedge. Persistent mist-like drizzle was drifting across the faint light and disappearing where high rhododendrons guarded the totality of darkness at the far edge of a sodden lawn. The light caught the green eyes of a cat as it disappeared into the interior of the bushes. There came a tiny agonised cry of a field mouse, then the night returned to silence.

Where the garden ended, a square Victorian villa, sooty grey stood, solid and dominating, its unlit windows staring blindly into the night. Inside a woman sat in a deep comfortable armchair, half-filled glass by her left hand and a telephone on a little table by her right. She was perhaps forty, elegantly dressed in a fine wool suit. Manicured fingers lay on the arm rests of the chair. She was waiting, in darkness, for the telephone to ring, for the darkness matched her mood. When it did ring, the sharp slivers of sound pierced her body. The pain of it made her move instinctively and before she was fully aware, the receiver was pressed to her ear.

"Yes!" she said sharply, "Yes?"

There was no reply.

"Hello?" she said more urgently. "Is that the hospital?"

There was a silence before the telephone spoke.

"No. This is not the hospital."

Then there was a click and a contended purr, which continued until she replaced the handset. She sat back in the chair, her mood disturbed. She lifted the glass by her left hand and drank.

When next the telephone rang, she moved more slowly. Carefully she lifted the instrument and listened, saying nothing. The telephone echoed her silence. She held it for some moments, then replaced it on its base. Within seconds it rang again.

"Who is this?" Her voice was crisp.

"It is I", said the telephone, and purred.

She looked at it, as if by doing so she would identify the caller. Somewhere in the emptiness of the house a clock chimed eleven, and when it stopped, the silence flooded back. Her eyes were so attuned to the dark that through the open doorway she could see the outline of the staircase; black on deeper black stained with smudges of grey at the full extremity of the dying light from the street lamps. She pressed the flat of one hand into her stomach then brought it down over her lap, smoothing out the faint wrinkles in the soft textured wool of her dress. Taking comfort from the feel of it, she took another sip from the glass and sat back in the chair, waiting for the telephone to ring again. When it did, she had almost fallen asleep.

"Be patient", said the telephone. "I am coming."

"Who is this?" She almost screamed the words.

The telephone chuckled; then purred.

Far off in the weeping night, a siren wailed. In the garden the cat played with the field mouse. It had no desire to kill, to tear it apart, for it was not hungry. This was just a game, just a bit of practice.

The woman felt sweat beading her brow, and again the telephone rang.

"Get off the line!" she screamed "I'm waiting for a call from the hospital!"

"Hello", said the telephone "Hello?"

"Sorry!" she said "Sorry! I thought... Is that?....This is Mrs Somerville. Dr. Somerville's wife."

"Yes. Queen's Hospital here. I was asked to contact you. We thought you may be worried."

"Is... Is everything all right then?"

The fatuousness of the question struck her as soon as she had spoken.

"Yes. Your husband is holding his own. We hope to have something to tell you very soon. We'll be in touch immediately if anything..." The female voice tailed away.

"Thank you. Thank you so much." Mrs Somerville smiled into the darkness and put the telephone down... It rang again almost immediately.

"Lovely lady", it said silkily; and purred.

The cat was becoming bored with its prey. It licked a paw and brushed it over one of its ears. Then the mouse twitched, and the cat's body stiffened, boredom gone.

Mrs Somerville flicked a light switch and the room leapt out of darkness, solid and comforting. And again the telephone rang. This time she didn't answer it. She went into the kitchen and by the time she had filled the kettle, it had stopped ringing. She sighed in relief and dropped two tea bags into the teapot.

In the garden, the cat rolled the mouse over. The creature's eyes flickered momentarily into life, then closed again.

Mrs Somerville took the mug of tea back to her chair in the lounge and as she sat down the telephone rang. When she lifted it the voice spoke immediately. It sounded slightly different this time.

"You the violin and I the bow." It said.

She gasped and was infuriated that her hand shook.

"Ah", said the telephone softly. "I shall come."

On impulse she went round the house, switching on every light. The cat's eyes flickered and were diverted as the light spilled out into the garden, so that it didn't notice the body of the field mouse quiver.

'I should go to the hospital. Go and wait there.' But the thought came too late. Suddenly she couldn't bring herself to leave the brightly lit house and go out through the overgrown garden and into the lonely street. She had no car. The car was parked by the side of a road many miles away. Earlier she had forgotten it as the trauma developed. She had taken a taxi home from the hospital…..'A taxi!' As the thought occurred, she almost shouted her relief. There was a directory lying on the floor below the telephone. She found a large advertisement for a car hire company and the dialling tone was comforting, reassuring. Then it stopped; there was a double click and the voice was back on the line.

"Don't be so impatient!" It sounded faintly amused. "I am coming!"

The handset dropped and spun on the end of the cord. "Soon", she heard faintly. Then it began to purr.

The cat's eyes turned away from the lighted windows and regarded the field mouse without much interest. It extended a paw and very gently laid it on the still warm body of its prey. The fast thready throb emanating from the little creature vibrated through the paw into the cat's awareness and the shining claws slowly unsheathed.

Mrs Somerville extended her beautifully manicured hand, lifted the receiver from where it hung and laid it on the little table. She would wait thirty minutes and then try to contact the hospital. She went back to the kitchen. From the teapot, she poured more tea. From a drawer, she removed a carving knife. Then she returned to the chair and laid the knife on the table, beside the telephone.

The cat turned away from the field mouse and made its way through four gardens before stopping and crying plaintively before a closed kitchen door. Several moments elapsed before the door opened and a voice said: "Poor pussy! Look at you. You're a poor bedraggled puss."

The cat entered, paused disdainfully before a plate of food, then continued on into the warm, carpeted interior of the room beyond.

Four houses back, all the lights went out.

Mrs Somerville screamed. She grasped the handle of the carving knife so tightly that her fingernails pierced the skin on the palm of her hand.

Out in the garden, just beyond the shelter of the rhododendrons, there issued from the mouth of the field mouse, a tiny trickle of bright red blood which stained a patch of grey fur on its lower jaw. It remained bright red only for a moment, before it began to be diluted and washed away by the gentle but relentless drizzle.

CLOSE ENCOUNTER OF THE FOURTH KIND

"We ar-ra pea-pol! We ar-ra pea-pol!"

The sound, part sung, part shouted, rose in a small pool of frosty breath and drifted off into the darkness beyond the yellow pool of light from the street lamp. Wee Davie was very very happy.

Although it was not unknown for him to be in such a boisterous condition, it was a fairly infrequent occurrence. In this case it had been triggered by a marvellous football match a few hours earlier, in which, Scotland had been victorious over much fancied European opponents. The intervening time had been spent in a pub, celebrating the unexpected victory.

"We ar-ra peo-pol!"

He turned away from the street and began making his way across a dark, derelict area of ground. As the light from the street lamps faded, he recalled that he had promised his wife he would come straight home after the final whistle. His conscience flickered briefly into life.

"Sadie'll murder me", he thought. "Her mother was comin' round the night." He pictured Sadie's mother, a formidable lady, and the tiny flame of conscience spluttered and went out.

"We ar-ra pea-pol!"

He walked with careful deliberation through clumps of rank grass and across patches of rubble until he found himself on an area of flat concrete, at which point, he stumbled and fell.

He rolled on to his back and saw the clear starlit sky and a brilliantly bright, perfectly circular moon.

"Hey moon!" he shouted. "Did ye see the match the night?"

The moon didn't answer but it occurred to Davie that it was becoming bigger and brighter and whiter.

He tried to rise to his feet.

"Hey!" he called as he struggled to get up. "Ye're no half a braw moonlicht nicht the nicht.. an' that."

The white moonglow enveloped him and he felt as if… although at first he couldn't be sure.. as if his feet had left the ground.

"Hey moon!" he shouted. "Ye're no half dain' yer stuff!"

"Hey!" 'Hey' was one of his favourite words when he was drunk.

"Hey! Ma feet arny touchin' the grun." By this time, he had become fairly sure about this. "Hullo rerr", he bellowed, stretching his arms wide. "Ah'm a seagull! Keep yer bunnets oan." Then the bright glow and the impression of flying faded to be replaced first by an impression and then by a certainty, that he was once again standing on a solid surface.

"Ah wis jist beginning tae enjoy masel", he said to no-one in particular.

He looked around him. He was standing on what seemed like a white marble floor in an all white circular room with no furniture except for a dark-coloured, comfortable looking chair exactly in the centre.

Two thoughts came to him. One, that police cells were improving, and two, that chairs were for sitting on. He weaved his way across the room and sat down. As he did so, the sides of the chair seemed to close gently about him, in a vaguely comforting way.

Moments later, another glowing light began to develop in front of him and from the heart of it came a voice. "Greetings, my friend."

Davie stiffened. "Hey wait a minute Jimmy. Ur you English?"

"No, I am not English. I am not even of your planet. I speak to you in my own tongue, which our technology translates instantaneously into the language appropriate to your terrestrial location."

"That's aw right, then", said Davie. "Ye jist sounded a bit English."

He raised a hand in front of his face, shielding his eyes as he tried to peer into the light. "Ah wish ye wid show yersel', Jimmy. Ah'm no in the habbit o'talkin' tae hundred-watt bulbs."

"We are not like you..." the voice began.

"Ah'm sure ye're no", interrupted Davie. "We ar-ra people."

"...Such is the difference", the voice continued. "That my appearance may cause you distress."

"Don't you worry aboot me, Jimmy. Ah've saw some weird sights in mah time. Ah even seen the mother-in-law withoot her teeth. Ye canny be worse than that."

There was a pause before the voice spoke again. "You are a very relaxed individual. Perhaps you will be able to cope with my appearance. We shall experiment."

The glow began to fade and as it did, the outline of the speaker gradually revealed itself. First, a vaguely human shape, but longer and thinner. Legs, feet, arms and hands of a kind, but – and here Davie blinked in disbelief, no head. It was only when the background light had gone completely that Davie saw the creature's eyes. They were yellow in colour and spaced well apart on its upper trunk – just below where the collarbone would be in a man. Between and slightly below the eyes was an oddly shaped orifice which Davie took to be its mouth. The creature was dressed overall in tight fitting grey material.

Davie stared for several seconds, then he began to laugh. He laughed until he was sore. Eventually he controlled himself sufficiently to speak.

"Ah'll tell ye somethin' son. Ye're nae Mel Gibson!"

"Your reaction surprises me", the alien said. "But I did not understand your remark."

"Jist a wee joke", said Davie. "But tell me. Dae the birds fancy ye?"

"Birds?"

"Birds…dames…females"

"I am the equivalent of what in your species is classified female. And yes, if I interpreted your question correctly, I suppose I am considered fairly becoming among my people."

"I bet ye're a wee smasher", said Davie, fascinated by the outlandish being. He looked at the eyes below the shoulders. "Ye must have an awfy job getting a semmit tae fit ye. D'ye mind if ah come ower fur a closer look?" He tried to get to his feet but found that the chair had his lower body and buttocks in a firm grip.

"Hey! Whit's goin' on? Ah canny get up!"

"Do not be alarmed. We are making a physiometric and medical audit of your body. It will do you no harm, but we have to restrain you until it is complete. We apologise for the inconvenience. Insofar as closer contact is concerned, that is impossible. There is an invisible screen between us – something like your glass. This is necessary because your atmosphere is poisonous to us, as ours would be to you."

Davie relaxed. "Whit a pity hen. Ah wis gony ask ye fur a dance."

"Some of your speech is incomprehensible. Our language data is obviously incomplete."

"Don't worry hen. It's jist patter. Gie's a wee smile."

"How do you name yourself?" the alien enquired.

Davie was puzzled for a moment.

"Eh? Oh. Aye... eh.. Davie McBride. Whit's yours hen?"

"Prurrrl. I am named Prurrrl."

"Aye..well..right.. Wid it upset ye if ah jist keep callin' ye hen?"

"If that is your wish I do not object." There was a pause.

"From the information we are gathering from you it would appear that you are under the influence of a powerful drug of some kind."

"No' me, hen."

"You have not been taking drugs?"

"Naw. Jist a wee bevvy."

"Bevvy?"

"Aye. Don't tell me your lot canny get a bevvy? ... Hey!" A sudden thought struck Davie. "Can ye get oor telly? The big match highlights'll be on the night."

There was another pause – longer this time – before Prurrl spoke again.

"Who is the greatest man in your country?"

In his mind's eye, Davie saw a football rocketing into the net, just beyond the despairing fingers of the opposition goalie. "Ally McGubbin." He said, without hesitation.

"Has he much influence with your people?"

"Influence? He's the greatest thing since sliced breid."

"Is he all-powerful?"

"Just gie him the sniff o'a chance and they canny stop him. Powerful's no in it. The best left fit in the country." Davie paused, then corrected himself. "In the world!" he concluded emphatically.

"I think", said Prurrl slowly. "That the influence of the bevvy is making communication more difficult than it might otherwise have been. However, I must tell you of our purpose here."

"Fire away hen. Ah'm all ears... Nae offence intended, by the way."

"I am of a chosen group. We call ourselves 'The Watchers'."

"Hey. That's a great name fur a group. Whit instrument d'ye play?"

Prurrl continued, ignoring the interruption. "Our task is to patrol the Galaxy and monitor the progress of developing species and cultures, offering non-violent help or guidance only when absolutely necessary. We are, to put it bluntly, worried about your planet."

"*You're* worried", said Davie. "Ye want to try livin' here. And if ye want tae help, ye could maybe pit a word tae the Cooncil aboot getting' us a better hoose. They'll no listen tae me."

"It is our opinion", Prurrl went on, "That your technological ability is advancing much faster than your emotional development. This can be very dangerous for continuation of the species."

"Ye needny worry aboot me hen", said Davie. "Ah canny even mend a fuse."

"It is not you as an individual that worries us, Davie McBride. It is your humankind as a whole. But we believe that individual, personal contact better serves our purpose, and hope that those who meet us will understand that we wish only to help. We shall give you a message to take to the Ally

McGubbins of your world.. It contains also, a warning to those who oppress and manipulate and subjugate. You will see this message appear before you, as if in mid air. In fact it will be printed on your side of the screen. It will be your task to see that it gets to the person you believe to have most power over your life. When it is complete, please remove it and take it with you... And now we must part. Goodbye, Davie McBride. It has been a pleasure and a privilege to meet you."

Davie had not really followed all that had been said, but he felt that he had made a new friend.

"Yer patter's brilliant", he commented with genuine affection.

The glow around Prurrl reappeared and began to intensify. She raised a long bony arm in salute and began to fade into the light.

"Cheerio hen", Davie shouted. "Awrra best an' that!"

In front of him a printed sheet began to materialise and simultaneously the chair relaxed its grip.

He stood up and removed the message from the screen. He stuffed it into his pocket and wondered what to do next. Then suddenly he was in bright moonlight and flying again.

"Aw hey!" he shouted. "Hey!"

He felt his feet make gently contact with the ground and there was the distant smell of a fish and chip shop.

He stood for a moment and looked up into the night sky. The moon was small and far away. He sighed and turned towards home. When he arrived at his door, he paused and ran a finger nervously round the inside of his collar and rang the bell.

The door was opened by a small, blonde, plump woman.

"Davie McBride! D'ye know whit time it is?"

"Aw Sadie. Ah'm helluva sorry hen. Ye'll never believe whit happened."

"Ah know bluddy fine what happened. Ye got drunk!"

"Naw, naw hen. Aye, ah suppose so, but that wisny whit happened. See, it's important. Therr wis the moon shinin' and it got bigger an' brighter an' it wisny the moon"

"God almighty. You've got the DT's."

"Naw, naw. Ah wis flyin' and there wis this dame ah hud tae talk tae..."

"Dame? Whit dame?"

"Well ah thought it wis a fella at first, but she says she wis a wumman an' that but she wasny. She wis mair a sort o'a... thing. But really nice. Friendly ye know..."

"Friendly", said Sadie fiercely, "Ah'll gie ye friendly! Don't stand there babblin' on the doorstep, the neighbours'll hear ye." She grasped Davie's arm and began pulling him inside. "Mah Mammy's here the night. Ah tell't ye she was comin'. She'll be tellin' me again ah shouldny've married ye. Can ye no' do somethin' sensible just for once!"

Davie turned to have a last look at the sky. There was no moon, but he fancied that one star was brighter than the rest. He smiled as he remembered the friendly alien and recalled vaguely something of what she had said. "Those who oppress and manipulate and subjugate."

He turned to Sadie. "Wherr's yer Mammie?"

"In the back room."

He reached into his pocket.

"Well, Ah've got a message furrur!"

COCKTAIL PARTY

Why did I come? I'm terrified of parties. I'm no good at small talk. But here I am, back to the wall, glass in hand and a fixed smile on my face. So why did I come? I could think of less stressful places to seek a meaningful relationship. Perhaps I'm a masochist. No, I'm a Presbyterian. Same thing, when you come to think on it.

God! This wine is disgusting. Bouquet more cat than grape. So why am I drinking it? Because it's my defence. Gives me something to do with my hands. I'll have another. It may be vile, but it eases the stress. And it's free. I'm not drinking it because it's free, but it helps. I'm not like George over there. He's got a gold medal for freeloading. In a class by himself. Good old mean, arrogant, short-sighted George. And he's chatting up a woman. Why does that not surprise me. Wait a bit, I thought. That's not a woman. That's Arabella. Now isn't that interesting. The only two people I know are talking together. I know them, but they don't know each other. That's why she's talking to him. No woman who knew George would talk to him without a chaperone. I feel sorry for Arabella. No, to be honest, I don't give a damn. They're laughing at one of George's jokes. Usually it's just George who laughs. God! She must be really thick. That's the one about the farmer's daughter and the commercial traveller. I can tell by the way his hands are moving. Arabella had better be careful of those hands.

Standing beside this tray of drinks is very convenient. I may not have much bottle, but I've got plenty of glasses. Hah!

That's a good one. Must remember that one. No, rather forget that one. This one tastes a bit better. Maybe they've had the cats neutered.

I believe I'm turning into a cynic, whatever that is. What's a cynic? I know... A cynic is what you wash dishes in.... Don't be silly, a cynic is a small swan. No, that's a cygnet. Can't be. A cygnet is a kind of ring with your initials on. Who cares anyway. I think I'll have another drink. Why? Because I can still see George.

What's this? The tall, attractive woman is looking in my direction. Perhaps she thinks she knows me. Be composed. Look down at the floor for a moment. Oh, my God! I forgot to polish my shoes! What a time to discover I'm a slob. No, no. I'm not really a slob. Just a bit forgetful. No, I've got a good memory. Mind you, I'd forgotten what a slob I am.

Perhaps I should know that woman's name. What if she comes over and says: "Well, hello Robert", then waits for me to reciprocate. What an embarrassment. I never could reciprocate. I didn't take the lessons. That's the worst of a classical education. Too much Latin prose and not enough reciprocation. So, I'll have to say: "Sorry, dear lady. My name's Andrew. I'm not the person you first thought of. I'm someone you thought I wasn't."

Oops! Is it my imagination, or is the wall beginning to slide up my back? I'm going to make a fool of myself. No, I'm not. Have another quick drink. Legs straight. Fix your eyes on an object that isn't moving. Difficult. Diff-e-cult. "No, no. Dear Lady. My name isn't Andrew. I can't remember exactly what it is, but it's a word of one syllabub, beginning with me. I was educated at a school for the sons of indignant gentlefolk. No, no! Not indignant. Indigenous. Ingenious, even. No, I've got it. Indigent. That's it. Indigent. That's it. Indignant. So, you see, I am not so drunk as to render myself unanimous. In fact, I'll just have another one of these delicious drinks."

Oops again! Drink one, spill one. Knit one, purl one. This is probably the best party I was ever at, but I wish someone would talk to me. Preferably you, lovely lady. Someone who can appreciate my Jen-ne-sois… My ginny….thingy….

Isn't this funny! I feel so much better. Much more in command, as if I've grown a foot! Oh no! Can't allow that to happen. I've only got shoes for two feet. I can't go round with two muddy shoes and a naked foot.

George, you're a wart. Yes, a wart. Wart it in my power... the giftie gie us. There's an idea! Maybe if I began to sing, someone would come over and talk to me. Even if only to tell me to shut up!

Legs straight, Eric… Who's Eric? Who let Eric in? Ignore him, Andrew, you're going to grow two feet. No, I'm not! I can't afford the shoes. Legs straight. I say, isn't this wallpaper expansive. Expensive even. Axminster wallpaper. Let's call it a carpet. The wallpaper's a carpet. Where's that little grub George?

My dear lady! How kind of you to notice. Cradle me in your lovely arms. Ah! Sinful blissfulness. Blissful sinfulness! I shall remember this moment until the cows come home. Or perhaps I shall remember the cows until you come home… What soft hands you have, Grandmama!

But, love of my life, a beautiful lady like you should not need to stoop so low as to pick up a drunk man at a party!

DAFFODILS

He first noticed her at just after eleven in the morning when he looked down from his window high above the street. She was sitting on the pavement side of a low concrete wall on which the park railings were supported. Laid against the wall by her side were bunches of daffodils, bright yellow, like a splash of sunlight against the dark grey of the pavement. It occurred to him that she was not dressed very sensibly for the time of year, for although the small patches of white fluffy cloud moving slowly across a blue sky seemed to indicate a pleasant enough day, he knew from his earlier excursion to get his rolls and newspaper that the light northerly breeze felt as if it was carrying ice crystals straight from the Arctic.

He watched for several minutes as she sat motionless beside the flowers. She had the figure of a boy, flat chested and thin, and was dressed in a light coloured half-sleeved top and a long skirt of some thin paisley-patterned material that came almost to her feet. An unexpected feeling of nostalgia came upon him and some moments passed before he realised the cause. Had she had her hair bobbed and been wearing a cloche hat, she could have come straight from an Aubrey Beardsley print. She looked like an insubstantial wraith from the nineteen twenties, that a sudden gust of wind might lift into the air and carry twisting and turning gracefully over the trees and out of sight.

His reverie was interrupted by Mabel, his marmalade cat, who jumped on to the windowsill, demanding immediate attention.

"OK, OK", he said. "Let me guess. You're wanting fed." Mabel gave a chirruping sound and followed him across the room.

"A tin of cat food on legs, that's all I mean to you, isn't it?"

The cat didn't deign to answer.

Occasionally he looked down to the street, and each time the girl sat as if she had never moved, but although he didn't once see her making a sale, the flowers were diminishing in quantity. Then when he looked out just before one o'clock she had gone. He felt a tinge of regret that he hadn't seen her go and, absurdly, pictured her as he had imagined earlier, drifting wraith-like over the trees and into the park.

He made his lunch and watched the television news with Mabel draped across his lap. Just after two, the girl was back with a new lot of daffodils.

Now he was more attentive and did see a woman buying a couple of bunches. The girl was still there at 5 o'clock, now with only one bunch left. The tenement building from which he watched now cast a long shadow across the street and into the park. "She must be absolutely frozen" he thought and immediately determined to buy that last bunch and release her from her discomfort. Throwing on his heavy windcheater, he almost ran down the stairs, lest she should have gone before he reached the street.

To his relief, she was still there.

"How much?" he asked, nodding towards the daffodils.

"A pound", she replied.

The voice disappointed him. Foolish old man that he was, he had expected ethereal tones. The reality was slightly coarse and sharp-edged.

"Aren't you frozen?" he asked as he sought the money from a trouser pocket.

"A bit", she replied, and as if to make the point, crossed her arms in front of her and began rubbing the sleeves of her blouse on either side of her body.

"You'll be able to get off home, now", he said.

"Home?" she said, as if wondering what the word meant.

"You do have a home to go to?" he asked.

"Yes... well, no. Not exactly." She replied. "You don't happen to know if there's a youth hostel or a 'Y' about here, do you?"

"No, I'm sorry, I don't."

She shrugged and began to get to her feet, lifting a small back-pack that she had put on the wall and had been sitting on. "Oh well, never mind. I'll find something."

He felt a sudden, overwhelming need to help.

"Look", he blurted out. "I've got a telephone and a yellow pages. Why don't you come up to my flat and we'll get something sorted out for you."

He could see that she was immediately on her guard, and he realised, so was he.

"No", she said. "I'd rather not." She began to move away.

"I'm sorry", he said. "I do apologise for startling you." God! Why was he apologising? Why not let her go? Forget the whole thing. "I just wanted to help", he continued. "It would only take a few minutes. You'd be perfectly safe, you know."

She hesitated, stopped and turned and said "Well, all right. Thank you. If it won't be too much bother."

"It won't be any bother", he said, relieved that the awkward moment had passed. As they began to climb the stairs, he said "I'm afraid you'll need to go at my pace. It's the top flat and I'm a pensioner. Not quite so energetic as I once was. But the climb keeps me fit." Not wishing to appear too decrepit, he moved more quickly than was his custom, and had to stop on the second floor landing to get his breath back. He tried to make it appear that he had stopped as if a thought had come to him.

"Whilst you are looking through the yellow pages, we'll make you a bowl of hot soup to help you on your way. How about it?"

She picked up the word as she had known she would. "We?" she asked.

"Mabel and I." He said this deliberately and again knew what she would be thinking. "Mabel's not much use at cooking, but she'll make you welcome. She's quite friendly as long as she gets her own way."

He saw the look of puzzlement cross the girl's face and he smiled and said, "Mabel's my cat."

The girl laughed. It was an enchanting laugh, quite unlike her speaking voice. And it transformed her thin, sharp-nosed face. She didn't say anything in reply, but her laughter had wiped away the last vestiges of tension between them and he took her silence as acceptance of the offer.

Once inside his flat, he sat her down on one of the big leather covered armchairs and fetched the yellow pages. He removed two plastic containers from the freezer and set them to defrost in the microwave. Mabel had appeared and then disappeared almost immediately when they had come in, and was no doubt in some hidden vantage point, allowing time for her suspicion of the intruder to dissipate.

He re-crossed the room to where the girl was sitting. "I've been a bit slow to introduce myself", he said, extending his hand. "I'm Peter."

She took his hand in a strong grip that belied her fragile appearance. "Catherine", she said. "Kate", then went back to her search through the book. Peter sat down in the other armchair.

"You on your travels, then", he asked. "Back packing?"

She gave him a long, rather distant stare, then returned her attention to the yellow pages.

He found himself apologising again, simultaneously feeling rather irritated at her seeming rudeness. "Sorry", he said. "None of my business."

"It's ok", she replied. "I've got a backpack, so I suppose you could call it backpacking."

"What else might you call it?" Peter persisted.

She gave a sigh of resignation. Leaving the book open on her lap, she said "I'm looking for work." Then, pre-empting the next question, continued. “I haven’t run away from home, if that’s what you were thinking.”

“I admit I did wonder.”

She didn’t seem disposed to offer any more information, so Peter didn’t probe any further. The microwave pinged, indicating the soup was defrosted, so he rose and decanted the contents of the cartons into two deep bowls and set them to full heat. He cut slices from a crusty loaf, and by the time he had set the table, the soup was ready.

They ate in silence. Kate, obviously hungry, had accounted for most of the bread and had finished her soup before Peter was halfway through his. He looked up from his plate and asked: “Would you like something else? An omelette or something?”

“I wouldn’t mind some more soup, if you have any.”

“No problem”, he said, rising and putting another container in the microwave. “Always plenty of soup. Home-made.”

Later, when he had made a pot of tea and Kate was finishing the soup and what was left of the bread, he had another try at making conversation.

“You sold a good few bunches of daffodils today, didn’t you?” he said.

“Twenty”, she replied.

“I felt for you, having to sit in the cold all day. I don’t suppose there’s a lot of profit in daffodils.”

She looked up and smiled. “The soup had obviously improved her mood. “More than you think”, she said. “I pinched them from the park.”

Peter gave a surprised laugh. "That's one way to do it", he said.

"The only way', she replied. "I didn't have any money."

Peter considered her in silence as she scraped the last vestiges of soup from the bowl. She couldn't be much older than seventeen or eighteen, yet she had a way of speaking and an assurance about her that belied her years.

As she pushed the empty bowl away, she said "That was really good." There was a pause before she added unexpectedly and artlessly "I'm going to be rich one day."

"I wouldn't be surprised, if you make the same profit from all your enterprises", Peter said.

Kate stood up and went back to the armchair. "I'm going to try", she said, picking up the yellow pages again.

Peter left her to it. He cleared the table, washed and dried the few dirty dishes and fed Mabel, who had reappeared as he went into the small kitchen.

"Found anything yet?" he asked later as he returned to the living room. There was no reply. Kate was fast asleep.

Two hours later, she was still sleeping.

After some thought, he decided not to waken her. Instead, he brought a quilted bedcover and draped it gently across the arms of the chair, covering her lower body and legs. He had pinned a note to the cover which said: 'I have made up the bed in the spare room – the door on the left. There's a lock on the door, and the bed will be more comfortable than the chair. See you in the morning'. Then he turned out the lights and went to bed himself. He had a small television set there, which he watched for about an hour before he too, fell asleep.

When he arose the next morning, Kate was no longer in the armchair. Mabel was somewhere crying for attention, rather petulantly, he thought. It took him a little while to locate her. She was outside the front door. He let her in and went immediately to the spare bedroom. Kate had gone. There was no sign that she had slept in the bed, although she could have made up the covers before leaving. He looked around to see if she had left a note but found nothing. He felt an enormous sense of disappointment. A simple 'Thank you' would have made all the difference. Later, he thought that a good deed should be reward enough in itself, without the need for thanks, but it didn't seem to work like that. He had been intrigued by the girl. Their lives had met only fleetingly, but he wished they had parted on a more positive note.

About ten days later, a fat envelope came through the letter box. To his astonishment it contained his savings passbook. He used the passbook so infrequently that he hadn't even noticed it was missing. A slip of paper had been stuck to the front cover. On it was written one word: 'Sorry'.

When he looked inside, he discovered that £3000, half of what he had, had been withdrawn. How she had managed it, he didn't know, but she had.

Hurt, anger and puzzlement chased each other around his mind. How could anyone be so low as to steal from someone giving them shelter? On the other hand, she hadn't asked for shelter. And why hadn't she taken the lot when she had the opportunity? Perhaps, he thought, that showed some sort of conscience.

When he had got over his initial confusion, he reported the theft to the police. They were very attentive. Noted the postmark on the envelope, which was local but covered a large area, got a description of the girl, took the one word note as a record of her handwriting and as many other details as Peter could supply. The result of their enquiries, was, as he had suspected, precisely nothing.

In succeeding months, he found the whole episode impossible to get out of his mind, but as months rolled into years, the memory, as is the way of most things, was less frequently recalled and began to fade into the background of the business of living.

He was sitting at breakfast one morning just over four years later when the doorbell rang. It was a delivery man with a large bunch of daffodils and a small recorded delivery parcel.

"Are you sure these are for me?" he asked.

In confirmation, the man showed him the documentation and asked him to sign that the delivery had been made.

He took the daffodils to the sink and laid them on the draining board, then opened the parcel and withdrew a newspaper cutting. 'Girl from Council Home Makes Good' said the headline. The article was accompanied by a photograph that he only just recognised as that of the girl he had tried to help. Obviously older, looking very sophisticated and dressed in a very smart business suit. 'Kate Brown, reared in a council home after being abandoned at birth', the article continued, 'has overcome many obstacles to win the Queen's Award for Industry as owner of a company which, in three years has progressed from making and selling sandwiches to getting a foothold in corporate catering. Her clients include some of the biggest companies in the financial and industrial markets and she says her last years' turnover was just short of £1 million. She attributes her incredible success, founded on an initial investment of £2000, to sheer hard work and determination'. There was much in similar vein and the article concluded: 'Ms Brown, whose first attempt at making money was selling daffodils in the street, is still only 21, and her achievement will, we are sure, inspire many more of our young people to make good'.

There were two other items in the envelope. One was a brief note, which said 'Forgive me. This is not hush money, but a genuine attempt to right a wrong which has been on my conscience all these years. For all our encounter was brief, my judgement is that you are not a vindictive man and I am confident that our secret will be safe with you. Your 'investment' has beaten the FTSE index by a large margin. Yours, Kate Brown'. The other was a banker's draft for £10,000.

DANCE IN THE OLD FASHIONED WAY

DANCE IN THE OLD FASHIONED WAY - RADIO BROADCAST, RADIO 4, TUESDAY 6th AUGUST 1985
Thirty Minute Theatre, 11:00am
Jimmy Chisolm as Willie
Joanna Keddie as Marilyn
Two parents recall their fine romance in a Scottish Ballroom; a courtship full of humour, charm and wobbly knees.
Directed by James Runcie

'Is that her away oot?'

'Aye'

'She might have come in and said she was goin''

'Ye canny blame her. You'd just start askin' her where she was awa' tae, tellin' her no' to be late back'

'What's wrang wi' that, she's just a wean! God almighty. I'm her faither, I worry aboot her'.

'Aye. I suppose you dae. But she's no' a wean ony mair, she's a young woman'.

'Aye, and that's what worries me. She's got a woman's body, and a wean's heid. Ah tell ye all those young fellas today, they're just waitin' their chance'.

‘Just like me when I was her age, all thae fellas, just waitin’ to pounce’.

‘That was different, you had me to look aifter ye’.

‘Aye. That’s what my old man used to worry about. Didnae fancy you much. Still doesn’t come to that’.

‘Daft old bugger. He’s away with the fairies... I was.... Hey, where’s she away to, onyway?’

‘Off to the Palais, with her pal’

‘Which wan? No’ that wee blond eejit doon the road?’

‘Aye’

‘I don’t know how you can just sit there, knitting. Have you seen the clothes that yin wears? Doesn’t leave much to the imagination – all tarted up on the outside and nae drawers’

‘Left something to your imagination, hasn’t she?’

‘Well that’s what I mean. That’s what I mean! Weans! God! The older they get, the worse it gets. Did you tell her when to get hame?’

‘Yes, she said she’d be back before midnight’.

‘She bloody well better be home before midnight, or I’ll have something to say. Would your old woman have let you stay out tae all hours?’

‘Ah well....’.

'Aye, no, ah bet she wouldny. We'd have got thumped. Aye, it's changed days. Changed bloody days'.

'I really like your hairdo, Marilyn, where did you get it done?'

'Deirdre's'.

'Oh, Deirdre's! Aye, she's good. Really artistic. Tries to get a style to match your face'.

'I wonder what she does for Ina Brodie!'

'Oh come oan, Jessie; Ina's all right'.

'Oh yes Modom, I'll part yer hair like this, o'er yer neb; and comb it doon like this, so's naebody can see yer face. Oh, that's bloody marvellous, you look like Veronica Lake '.

'Mair like Veronica Puddin.'

'Don't be so rotten, Jessie, Ina's nice. She's a good soul, so she is'.

'Wi a face like yon she'd need to be. Oh here, I must show you ma frock, I just got it yesterday. Stop a minute, I'll unbutton my coat and show you. Well, do you like it?'

'Oh, eh, aye, Jessie, it's really nice!'

'You don't like it, do you?'

'Aye, ah do! Ah really like it. It's just...'

'Just what?'

‘Well it’s a nice colour and that, but the tap’s awfy low is it no? There’s no much of it, is there?’

‘That’s what the fellas like! They’ll look doon in between, and I’ll say ‘What you looking at’, and they’ll say ‘nuthin’… It’s nice, that!’

‘Did yer maw and yer faither no say nothing aboot yer frock? I couldn’y wear onythin’ like that, the old man’d go barmy’.

‘They never notice nothin’. I could go out in ma skuddy and they wouldny notice. So long as I’m no botherin’ them…’

‘You’re lucky. You want to hear my old man… ‘Whit ye dain? Where ye goin’? When’ll ye be back?’ He’s a pain in the neck’.

‘Oh hear, I hope Andy McBride’s there the night. He’s really sexy, so he is’.

‘Andy McBride? He’s just a big bum, nothing between his ears but broken bottles. I wouldn’y hae him on a sandwich’.

‘You’re just jealous because he danced wi me a couple of times last week’.

‘Jealous? Me? You must be joking. I wouldn’y dance with him if he was the last guy on earth’.

‘If he was the last guy on earth you would just have to join the queue with the rest of us!’

‘No ah wouldn’y’.

‘You would dance with him, don’t kid yersel’

‘Well he isnae, and ah wouldn’y’.

‘Oh here, look! There’s a lot of fellas goin’ in the night’.

‘There’s that wee bloke with the smelly breath. Keep your eyes open and if we see him comin’ over we can make a dive for the lavvies’.

‘Here’s the money for ma ticket. Gies your coat and ah’ll take it to the cloakroom’.

‘Swap ye tickets, Jessie’.

‘Here, you know what my horoscope said the day?’

‘No, whit?’

‘Romance is in the air’

‘Aw..’

‘New claithes you’ve bought will make you attractive to someone you’ve never seen afore’.

‘Aw, you’re lucky. Mine was something like ‘problems rear their ugly heid, don’t do onything you might regret later’.

‘It’s a load of tripe, innit? Horoscopes…’

‘It’s funny I bought this new frock, but…’

‘Aye’

‘Ye comin’ in?’

‘Aye’.

‘Ah think it’s going to be a good night tonight!’

'You're gettin' lifted plenty the night, Jessie!'

'It's the frock! Ah telt ye! That bloke had a wee feel at ma bum. Ah put his arm up, but he just put his hand right back doon again! Ah think ah've got him goin'. His name's Davy. You want to see his eyes, he makes you feel funny the way he looks at ye'.

'I think he's got you goin' an' all!'

'Maybe he has, maybe he husny. Ah bet ye he gets me up for the next yin; he's ower there wi' his pals, lookin' at us'.

'What are they laughin' at?'

'Ah don't know – they're just havin' a good time, like me! You enjoyin' yersel?'

'Aye, it's all right'.

'Ye havny been up as much as me, haven't ye no?

'Oh it's just...'

''Wan o' those nights, aint it.'

'Oh here, there's another guy staring at me'

'Well...'

'Don't look the noo, he's over by the door, leaning on a pillar. Oh, ah don't fancy him. Looks a bit like ma Aunt Mary's dug; ah think it's the hair and the ears... Oh Jeez, he's comin' o'er. Ah'm away to sort ma face, ye comin?'

'No, ah'm okay.'

‘Get rid of him will you, afore ah come back. If he’s efter me, tell him ah’ve got B.O. or something. See ye later’.

‘Lo rerr..’

‘Hello’.

‘Y’a’right?’

‘Yeah, ah’m a’right’.

‘S’no bad here, in’t it?

‘Aye. No bad. Good music’

‘Ye come yersel?’

‘No. wi’ ma pal’

‘Wi yer pal?’

‘Aye’

‘Where is she then?’

‘Away to the lavvy’

‘Oh, the lavvy?’

‘Aye’

‘That her you were talkin’ to?’

‘Aye that’s her.’

‘It’s no bad here, in’t it no?’

'Aye, no bad'

'Ah huvn'y seen ye here afore'.

'Huven't ye no?'

'No'

'Ah come here a lot'

'Same here. Funny ah've no seen you afore'.

'Aye, funny'.

'Seen ye earlier the night, but...'

'Did ye, that's nice. Ah never seen you'.

'Eh – are ye, 'In The Mood?'

'Aye, maybe ah am.'

'Ye comin' then?'

'So whit's this then, a tango?'

'No, it's a quickstep'.

'So how does that go again? Is that slow, slow, quick, quick, slow an' aw' that stuff?'

'Aye. Somethin' like that..'

'Ye see, ah'm no' yer fancy dancin' type. Ah'm more yer strong, silent, leaning on the wall watchin' type'

'You were just kiddin' us weren't you? You can dance okay'.

'Ah well, it's great what you learn leanin' on a wall... Hey - ah like yer shoes. What's the yellow bit?

'It's plastic. So's the green and red. It's all plastic'.

'Oh. You've got nice wee feet'.

'Size three'

'Mine's are eights. Big feet'.

'No big for a man'.

'Feet's important'.

'Eh?'

'Feet. Feet's important. Mah old man says it's 'important ah stawn' on ma own two feet'

'What's yer name?'

'Willie. Whit's yours?'

'Marilyn'

'Marilyn? Aw, that's a great name. Here, yer second name's not Monroe, is it?'

'Naw, worse luck'

'Aw. It's just like ah thought you looked a bit like Davy Monroe. That's a guy I know'.

'Funnee'

'Och, it's just a bit of patter.'

'Well, patter aff..'

'No, no, ah really think ye're a looker'.

'Oh, thanks for the vote. Ye're no so bad yerself'.

'Eh? Oh, no, no me. Ah'm ugly. Ma faimily's famous for uglies'.

'Gerrof. You're quite good looking. If it wisnae for the spots'

'Eh? No, that's no spots. That's plukes. My faimily's famous for plukes'.

'It's nothin' to do with yer faimily. The trouble is, ye've never known a wummen'.

'Aw don't gies it; ah've know plenty of wimmen'

'Naw, naw. Like it says in the Bible. When you KNOW a wummen. Well, you know'.

'Know whit?'

'Ach, ye know. Don't tell me you don't know'.

'Ye've lost me, Marilyn, I don't know what ye're talkin' aboot'.

'What ah mean is, have ye ever made a wumman happy?'

'Happy? Aye.'

'How?'

'Well, when I brung hame ma first pay packet, ma Mammy wis happy'.

'You are very neeve'.

'Neeve?'

'Innocent. You don't know nothing'.

'Ah know plenty'.

'Like whit, for instance?'

'Yer pal's a long time in the lavvy, for instance'.

'Well, she's very particular wi' her appearance'.

'Mair like her disappearance'.

'She aye likes to dae her makeup right'

'Makeup? In the lavvy? Ah thought she was away fur a pee'

'God – you are neeve! You don't know nothin' aboot wimmen!'

'Ah know plenty aboot wimmen!'

'Like whit?'

'Well… like… They're different fae men…'

'God, Ah can see you've lived!'

'Och. See you, you're.. you're very… very…'

'Very whit? Good looking?'

'Naw…. Aye, ah mean. Aye. Aye' ye're a'right. But…'

'But whit?'

'You're very sarcastic.'

'Sarcastic?'

'Aye.'

'Oh, have ah upset ye?'

'Upset? Me? Naw. Ah'm used tae sarcastics; ma faimily is famous fur sarcastics'.

'Your faimily's famous for a helluva lot, in't it?'

'Aye. They're famous for bein' famous for a helluva lot, too'

'Would ye like to tango with an expert?'

'I wouldn'y mind, d'ye know one?'

'There ye go, hurtin' ma feelings again. Ah tell ye sumthin', ye huvny lived till ye've danced a tango wi' me. I just thought I'd warn ye - plenty of dames have fought tae the death fur the chance'.

'Oh! Well there's no many of them aboot the night'

'What d'ye expect, they're a'deid!'

'Dee-dee, dee-dee, dee-dee-dee-dee...'

'As a singer ye make a great dancer!'

'Oh never mind the patter, just watch oot, ah'm goin' intae ma fancy steps noo. Hang on tight, here we go'.

'Oh here, mind ma feet'.

'Here we go, watch it noo, here's the old three-four... '

'Dee-dee, dee-dee, dee-dee-dee-dee..'

'That's really good, ah'm impressed'.

'Oh, ah bet... Here, ye managed to follow me quite well there. Are ye sure ye huvn'y danced wi' me afore?'

'No, ah don't think so. Ah'd huv remembered yer big heid'.

'Oh see you Marilyn, ye're a good laugh, right enough. Pity ye canny dance, but'.

'I'd dance you aff yer feet ony time!'

'Oh that'd be right...'

'Ah need to be getting' hame after this yin, Willie; ah've got tae be hame afore midnight'.

'Ach. Ah wish ye didn'y, Marilyn..'

'So dae ah, but ah huv tae'.

'What happens if ye don't? Do ye turn intae a pumpkin?'

'It's no funny. Ah'm really enjoyin' masel'...'

'Aye, me an' aw... Listen, can ah walk ye haim?'

'Aye, if ye like.'

‘Where d’ye live?’

‘Partick’

‘PARTICK?’

‘Whit’s up?

‘Oh, nothin. Nothin’ hen, really’

‘Where d’you live?’

‘Pollockshaws’.

‘Aye, ah see what you mean…’

‘You wantin’ to walk me hame?’

‘Aye. Oh aye, nae bother. Whit aboot yer pal?’

‘Jessie? She’s all right, ah seen her up dancin’ a wee while ago’.

‘Marilyn. I want tae tell ye sumthin’. Eh, ye’ve got nice, eh…’

‘Nice whit?…’

‘Nice haunds’.

‘Ach. See you? Ye’re aff her heid. Nabody’s noticed ma haunds afore’.

‘So? Whit’s wrang wi that?’

‘Well, nothin’. You’re just no real’.

‘Oh ah’m real a’right… Ma faimily’s..’

'....Famous for bein' real.... You walkin' me hame, then?'

'Aye. Ah said ah would'.

'See you at the door then, gie's a couple of minutes, ah'll need tae tell Jessie ah'm away'.

'Oh right then, okay. Ah'll see ye at the door, then'.

'Jessie?'

'Hello Marilyn'.

'Whit's up?'

'Nothin. Ah'm okay'.

'Jessie, that fella ah was dancin' with, he's wantin' to walk me hame, d'ye mind?'

'Mind? No me. Please yersel'.

'He's a good laugh. His name's Willie. What aboot your bloke; the one with the eyes, Davy? Ah seen ye dancin' with him a wee while ago'.

'Aye, ah was. He's away oot wi' his pals.'

'Is he comin' back?'

'Oh, no him, they're awa tae the boozer. Ach, he wisny up tae much, onyway'.

'I see. Do you want tae come wi' us?'

'Ye're jokin'! ...'oh, by the way Willie, I'd like ye tae meet ma pal Jessie. Jessie Gooseberry..' Naw, naw, one's company, two's a crowd. Ah'll be a'right. I think ye were right aboot this frock...'

'Naw, naw Jessie, that's the nicest frock you've ever had. It's really nice, so it is. You know, if you hadny gone away yon time, Willie would probably have wanted to dance wi' you instead of me!'

'Aye. Mebbe.'

'Well. You a'right then?'

'Ah'm a'right. Away ye go, Marilyn, ye're crampin' ma style. There's another fella o'er there gien me the eye. Shove aff, will ye. See ye next week'.

'Aye, okay Jessie, see ye next week'.

'See they doors, they're awfy stiff'.

'Stiff? Naw, they're easy'.

'See you, ye're quite strong'.

'Aye, ma faimly's famous fur....

'Ha ha ha'

'What you laughin' at?'

'Yer patter's rotten'.

'Well, why ye laughin', then?'

'Ah just feel like it'.

'It's awfy quiet oot here'.

'Aye. After the racket in there'.

'Aye'.

'Aye'.

'D'ye like yellow street lights?'

'Eh?'

'Yellow street lights. D'ye like them?'

'I suppose so. They're a'right'.

'Ah think they're real romantic, yellow street lights'.

'Ah never thought aboot it; they're just lights.'

'See you, ye've nae soul. Yellow street lights send me'.

'Send you where? Up the pole?'

'D'ye mind if ah put ma airm round ye?'

'Depends on where ye put it...'

'Like... Here, for instance?'

'That's nice. What about a wee bit higher?'

'H-higher?'

'Higher, aye'.

‘Like here?’

‘Aye. That’s nice.’

‘Are ye comfy?’

‘Aye.’

‘What d’ye work at, Willie?’

‘Ah’m learnin’ tae be a jiner. Apprentice. Ah’m goin’ tae be the best jiner in Scotland!’

‘Ma old man’s a jiner an all. He makes coffins fur the Co-op’.

‘Coffins? Yuch..’

‘Well, somebody’s got ta dae it. He likes it. Says ‘onybody getting’ intae wan o’his boxes has a heid start in the field’...’

‘Seems an awfy waste, all that work, just tae stick it in the grund’.

‘Oh, no, no. He disnae think o’ it like that. He just wants tae dae a good job fur his customers. He must be bloody good, an ‘aw’.

‘How?’

‘Nayb’dy’s ever complained!’

‘Is he a’right yer old man? D’ye get on wi’ him?’

‘Aye. He’s a’right. A bit o’a bampot sometimes. Ah wouldnae put him oot o’the hoose fur it, but.’

'You're a bit o'a bampot yersel.'

'Aw hey, no, no me! I'm your strong, silent, un-bammy type'.

'Whit's that? A fight?'

'Naw. Naw, it's just some guys bevvied up and shoutin' the odds. Nae need tae be feart wi' me here'.

'Would ye fight tae the death fur me, Willie?'

'Eh?'

'I mean, if there was a crowd of guys efter ma body an' that, would ye staun up and protect me tae the last drop o' yer blood? Would ye?'

'Well, it depends... Ah mean, aye. Aye, ah suppose so'.

'What do you mean, 'you suppose so?''

'Well... I suppose so...'

'Jesus Christ. Ah seen ye on yer white horse wi' a sword, protectin' me against the rampagin' hoardes'.

'Jesus Christ just had a donkey'.

'You religious?'

'No, no me'.

'Ah jist wondered'.

'See the moon?'

'Aye, ah see it'.

'Smashin', in't'it?'

'Aye.'

'Ye ever seen the moon through trees?'

'Naw. Canny mind. Mebbe ah huv'.

'Aw, it's smashin', the branches an' that against the moon; it makes ye think o' how you're important somehow'.

'Important?'

'Aye. Well, to be able to see it, like'.

'What's important aboot that?'

'Well, it canny see you..'

'Mebbe wouldny think much o'the view if it could...'

'Aye, ah suppose so. But...'

'But whit?'

'This is nice, but. Walkin' doon the road thegither, the moon shinin' an' that'.

'Aye Willie, it's nice'.

'D'you ever think aboot things, an...eh....stuff like that?'

'Things?'

'Aye. Like life'.

'Life?'

'Aye, Life an' that..'

'No really, except....'

'Except whit?'

'Well, ma granny. She's really auld, an' a'wrinkles an' that. I'd hate fur tae be auld'

'Ye will be wan day'.

'Aye. Ah suppose so. Kinda frightens me, but.'

'Frightens ye?'

'Aye. Bein' auld an' that'.

'Ach. Ye've a lang way tae go afore ye're auld. How old are ye anyway?'

'Seventeen'.

Seventeen! Ye're jist young'.

'Ah'm nineteen'.

'Are ye? God, it would be great tae be nineteen. Wish ah wis nineteen'.

'Ah well'.

'Experience. Ye must have a lot of experience'.

'Ay....well...'

'Tell me aboot it'.

'Aboot whit?'

'Your experience of life an' that.'

'Whit would ye like to know?'

'Well, if ah were tae follow ye tae the ends o' the earth, what would ah huv tae put up wi' an' that?'

'Ah'm no goin' tae the ends o' the earth. Ah'm jist goin' tae Partick!'

'Aw.. An' you said ah hud nae soul...'

'Wid ye? Like tae follow me tae the ends o' the earth?'

'Ah'm no really sure. Depends what happens when we got there!'

'Would ye mind if ah kissed ye?'

'No, no really. Oh, Willie'.

'Oh Marilyn, you've got soft lips, no sloppy. Just nice.'

'Kiss me again Willie. Ye're hurtin' me, ye're squeezin' too tight!'

'Oh, ah'm sorry! Here, ye're getting' me a'worked up.. Here listen, what aboot..... would ye like fur tae... sorty well, eh...'

'Naw'.

'Eh?'

Naw. Ye're not on!'

'Not on whit?'

'You know whit ah'm sayin!'

'No, ah don't!'

'Ah know whit ye're askin', ye're NOT on!'

'Ah wis only goin' tae ask ye if would come out wi' me again themorrow night!'

'Oh!'

'Aye. Oh...'

'Well...'

'Well whit?'

'Well, a'right then'.

'Good. Here, are we nearly there?'

'Nearly wherr?'

'Yer hoose.'

'Aye, nearly. Two streets an' roun' the corner'.

'Yer folks be in bed?'

'Bed? No them, they'll be waitin' up fur me. Aye, ah bet ye'll see the old man keekin' oot the curtains afore ye go'.

'Well, if they worry about you that's good'.

'Good? It's a pain in the neck. God, ah would hate tae be like them, sittin' in the hoose. Ye would think they would go oot themselves sometimes, but they never. They never have fun, like me. Aye sittin' in the hoose'.

'Did ye enjoy yersel' the night, Marilyn?'

'Oh aye, Willie, it was great! Ah think you're a really nice guy'.

'Do ye?'

'Aye, ah really think so. Can ah ask ye a question?'

'Well, ye canny ask me an answer..'

'Funnee... Would ye – would ye, take advantage if ye got the chance? Would ye take me intae yer airms an' carry me away an'... eh... possess me an that?'

'Ye mean, would ah huv... like... relations wi' ye?'

'Naw, nothin' tae dae wi' relations. Would ye huv me like, as a wumman?'

'Well ah wudny huv ye like a man, that's fur sure. Ah like ye the way ye are...'

'You know bloody fine whit ah mean'.

'Aye, ah know whit ye mean'.

'Well, then!'

'Well then whit?'

'Are ye gonny answer ma question?'

'No. Ah refuse tae answer on the grounds that it might incinerate me'.

'Ach. Ye're jist like a'the rest. Men!'

'Ah'd hope so'.

'Aye, Alright then, have it yer own way, ah'm away in'.

'Aw, but Marilyn!'

'Aye?'

'C'mere! ... I wid like fur tae take advantage o'ye... Well, onyway, just a wee bit'.

'What's that supposed tae mean?'

'C'mere an' ah'll show ye'.

'Oh Willie. Ye've got lovely haunds. Kiss me there again. Ye're makin' ma legs go all funny....'

'There she's back at last. God! She's got a fella wi' her! They're aw fankled up. What are they up to doon there?'

'Would you get away frae the windae, they'll see ye!'

'Ah bloody hope they dae; they shouldny be dain' that in the street!'

'Would you come away frae there. You'd think she was the first lassie to come hame wi' a fella. Whit aboot the first night you seen me hame?'

‘Ah well, that wis different’.

‘How wis it different? You were a’ower me, so ye were, an’ ah wasn’t exactly fightin’ ye off. D’ye mind?’

‘Aye. Ah mind fine. Ah brung ye hame frae the Palais. Ye were there wi’ Jessie thingywy – eh – her wi’ the six weans an’ the bad back. She was a right we goer in thae days, wisn’t she? Ah can still see that tight red frock she had on that night’.

‘Ye can, can ye? An’ what wis ah wearin’?’

‘You? Em... You had on thon yellow dress wi’ the flooers’.

‘That was the one ah bought for oor honeymoon. It was a green wan!’

‘Oh aye, aye. So it was. Green. Aye, aye, that’s right. Green. Ah’ll tell ye somethin’ but’.

‘Whit?’

‘Ye’re real sexy when ye’re mad’.

‘There’s nae answer tae that. Would ah be even sexier if ah thumped ye?’

‘Naw, naw, no really. Ach. They were the days, weren’t they no? Things were different when we wis that age..’

‘Aye, things wis different. Things is aye different when ye’re young’.

‘Naw, naw, what ah mean is, they discos – they shuffle aboot a’night, no even lookin’ at one another – an’ then they come oot an’ they start wrestlin’ in the street! It’s no right, so it’s not. But we had a bit mair respect’.

'Respect? Ye're jokin'.. Whit's respect got tae dae wi' it? The music's mebbe different nooadays, but it's still the same old dance!'

'Aye, aye, well you could be right. Hey, listen to that on the wireless... hmm, hmm, hmm, hmm.. D'ye fancy a slow foxtrot wi' an expert?'

'Ah wouldn'y mind, if ye can find wan'.

'Nae cracks. Just staun' up, step furrurt an' press yer body ontae mine. I'll show ye dancin'. Discos! Kid's stuff. Haud on tae yer corsets...'

'Ah'm no wearin' corsets!'

'Ye were aye wan fur livin' dangerously, weren't ye?'

'Oh Willie, ye're a nutter'.

'Did ah never tell ye Marilyn? Ma family's famous for bein' nutters.....'

Romantic antics

Thirty-Minute Theatre: Dance in the Old-Fashioned Way Tuesday 11.0 am Radio 4

WILLIAM MILLER (right), author of Dance in the Old-Fashioned Way, is a senior engineer in a company making agricultural chemicals, whose first written work was published in *Mavor & Coulson's Apprentices' Magazine*. And until quite recently he confined his urge to write to valedictory doggerel upon the retirement of colleagues.

Then, two years ago, his sci-fi spoof *Close Encounters of the Fourth Kind* was broadcast as a Radio 4 *Morning Story*, and now the Scottish Arts Council has accepted another short story of his for publication in its *New Writing* series.

Dance in the Old-Fashioned Way is Miller's first attempt at drama, and at the centre of the play is a dialogue between Willie and Marilyn, Glasgow teenagers of the 50s, whose romance blossoms one evening in the faded splendour of the local palais. Miller's challenge was to give voice to the inarticulate in a convincing way, and he succeeds by distilling the remembered language of his own youth in Glasgow.

Willie, played by Jimmy Chisholm, plumbs the depths of gaucheness as the left-footed Romeo, while Marilyn, portrayed beautifully by Joanna Keddie, struggles to equate her ill-formed and grandiose notions of romantic love with what is actually taking place:

Marilyn: Wid ye take advantage of me if ye got the chance? Wid ye take me intae yer arms and carry me aff? Wid ye ... possess me, and that?

Willie: Ye mean, would I have, like, relations with ye?

Marilyn: Naw! It's nothing tae dae with relations!

The story is a simple one, where the father, played by Roy Hanlon, and the mother, played by Ellen McIntosh, view their daughter's visits to the disco with some trepidation. 'She's got the body of a woman and the head of a wean,' says Marilyn's father.

This leads to a trip back to their own courting days, when, it turns out, things weren't so different after all.

Writing is a hobby for Miller, who has no intention of trying to make a living from it. A voracious reader all his life, he jotted down ideas and plots in spare moments, but it wasn't until he took a creative writing course that he learned to impose a framework of discipline on his writing that has since paid dividends. He sees humour as his forte, and recalls how, in his schooldays, it was outlawed from 'composition'. Writing was a serious thing, practised by others.

The author insists there is nothing autobiographical about the story, only the time and place, and he wants it to be taken as light entertainment. He was concerned with an accurate evocation of the past, not its critical examination. Innocence is perhaps the theme of the play: how we lose it, and how there was less of it to lose than we thought in the first place. DOUGLAS YOUNG

ENCOUNTER

The overcast of heavy cloud was nudging the day into evening as the man walked through the main street of the village.

He looked neither to the right nor to the left but, with eyes downcast, saw only the cold grey concrete of the pavement.

The guilt that he had carried for so many years was no longer a burden. Instead, it was a miasma, gathered around him and through him; a fog emanating from the dark places of his mind, obscuring feelings as if they had never been.

He sensed, rather than saw, people moving past. He wondered if they, like him, had purpose; for now purpose alone stood erect and beckoning across the wide featureless plain that passed for life.

As he walked, he noticed a streak of mud on one of his shoes, and wondered if he should stop and wipe it off. But he continued to walk until the loneliness of human activity gave way first to the loneliness of empty streets, and then to a lonely place at the top of a flight of stone steps.

The steps led downwards towards a river, and as he descended he could see, beyond the grassy bank, the powerful body of water in spate; writhing and twisting sinuously like a great swollen brown snake.

As he approached the river's edge, the low overcast of cloud began to weep. He looked at the whirlpools and eddies, forming, disappearing and reforming endlessly; and the river spoke to him, sighing and whispering, like a lover pleading.

His heart began to quicken at the thought of consummation, when suddenly and unexpectedly, his attention was diverted. At first he did not know why, but soon realised that there had been a sound, not of the river, coming from somewhere nearby.

He listened, and it came again. It was the sound of sobbing, coming from a patch of long seeded grasses downstream from where he stood. Life flickered briefly across his eyes and he turned and began walking again. He had gone about twenty paces when he came across a small boy lying face down among the long grass. It was he who was sobbing.

The man spoke. "Why are you crying?" he asked.

The boy, startled, turned a tear stained face towards him but did not reply.

"Tell me." Said the man.

The boy pushed himself reluctantly to his knees, then slowly stood up.

"Why are you crying?" the man repeated.

The child's eyes looked downwards.

"I wasn't crying", he said.

"Yes you were", said the man firmly. "Tell me why."

"It... My rabbit...it..."

The man stood quietly as the boy tried to find words.

"It...my dog. Ruff... My rabbit... Blackie.... It was all... Ruff killed Blackie. I let him out and Ruff started barking – and now he's all – he's all blood. Ruff killed him. I don't like Ruff any more."

And again he wept.

The man, emotionless for so long, felt a sudden painful twinge of sympathy.

"Boy", he said, "It's in the nature of dogs to kill rabbits."

"But he shouldn't", sobbed the child. "Blackie was friendly... He didn't do Ruff any harm. I shouldn't have let him out. It was all my fault."

"Fault?" said the man, "Fault? Is it a fault to love your rabbit and your dog?"

"No... but.."

"Well then", continued the man, "You needn't feel guilty. Your dog wanted you to be proud of him. He doesn't know right and wrong like you. He only knows happy and sad. Go home and scratch his head and tell him he's a good dog." He reached into his pocket and took out some coins. It was all the money he had.

"Here", he said "You can buy another rabbit."

The boy looked at the money on the outstretched palm and then into the man's face. Recognising what he saw in the child's eyes, the man spoke again.

"Don't be afraid! Take the money and go. Give Ruff a big hug – and buy another rabbit."

At once reluctant and eager the boy stretched out his hand. His father and mother both, had warned him never to accept money from a stranger.

The man's eyes were staring at him, hypnotically.

He reached out and took the money, then felt the sudden fierce grip of a strong hand on his wrist. Terror rose, restricting his throat and stifling and impending scream.

The man spoke harshly.

"Remember", he said "Give Ruff a big hug."

As the grip on his wrist was released, the boy spun away and ran on trembling legs across the bank and up towards the street. Reaching the top of the steps, he turned, half expecting to see the man following him. But he was alone. He put his hand into his pocket and touched the money. The coins still retained some of the warmth the man had given them.

His eyes searched the river bank, but he could see nothing except the tall grasses, bowing now under the light drizzle of rain. He listened, but there was no sound.

Except for the river whispering.

GARIBALDIS

When the doorbell rang, Archie McDougall pushed himself out of his armchair, switched off the television and moved slowly towards the door. He was only halfway across the room when the bell rang again.

"Ah'm comin'! Ah'm comin'!", he shouted. Then he called: "Who's there?"

"It's me Grandad."

"Grandad? That's my name. You must be an impostor."

"It's Andrew!" The young voice sounded slightly exasperated.

Archie opened the door a few inches and peered out. "Whit's the password," he whispered.

"I don't know. You didn't tell me."

"Didn't tell ye? Ye stand there tryin' to impersonate a Grandad and you don't know the password?"

"Grandad!!" The exasperation was quite evident now.

Archie smiled and opened the door wide. "Sorry, Son. Jist mah wee joke. Come away in."

The boy held out a small package. "I brought you some biscuits," he said.

"Thanks very much," Archie said. "My, my. Garibaldis! Did yer mother send them?"

"No. I bought them with my pocket money. I get extra now. They're to have with your cup of tea."

"That's real thoughtful." Aye, well. Garibaldis! My, my. I havny seen them for ages."

"Don't you like them?"

"Oh aye. I like them fine. It's jist ah'm mair a sort of Jaffa Cake man maself. But ...... Garibaldis is a rare treat. Tell ye what. Ah'll put on the kettle an' we'll hae a fly cup ..... Wid ye prefer a mug?"

"A mug please, Grandad."

"That's the style. Ah like a mug masel. Cups is for Jessies."

The boy watched as Archie prepared the tea and got out the mugs and carefully tore the paper off one end of the packet of biscuits.

"Grandad", he asked suddenly. "Did you used to be famous?"

The old man paused as he stood the biscuits upright on the draining board of the sink.

"Whit d'ye mean, used to be? I'm famous for being famous."

"The teacher was talking about famous people today and she asked if we knew any ..... And I said you."

"Whit did she say to that?"

"She just sort of smiled as if she didn't believe me and asked someone else."

"Well, there you are then," Archie said. "Ye can never tell with teachers. They're no' on the same wavelength as the rest o' us. Why did you say I was famous?"

"Well, because of all the things you did in the second World War."

"Oh, aye, that," said Archie, pouring boiling water into the teapot.

"What was the most important thing you did in the war, Grandad?"

"Turning up."

"How do you mean?"

Archie poured tea into two mugs and handed one to the boy. "Well, if I hadn't turned up, our side would have been the one short, and the Nazis would have beat us."

"The teacher told us about the Nazis in our History lesson. She said they were evil."

"Aye, well. They werny exactly the sort o' people ye would like living next door. Hitler and Gobbles and all that lot. But they didny scare me ….. Here's your Garibaldi. It's a long time since I had a Garibaldi." Archie raised his mug. "Cheers", he said.

"Cheers", Andrew replied.

They both sipped carefully at the hot tea and ate their biscuits.

"Grandad?"

The old man groaned in mock resignation. "What now?" he asked.

"Did you ask your grandad a lot of questions when you were a boy?"

"I never got the chance."

"Why not?"

"They were baith deid."

"Oh."

"So you see, I didn't have a grandad to keep me right. Mind you, it saved a lot of money on Garibaldis."

"Did they have Garibaldis when you were a boy?"

"Here. Watch it. You're gettin' cheeky like your dad."

"I've just remembered," said Andrew. "Dad said he would come up some time next week, if he can manage it. He said to say he was sorry he hadn't managed up for a while."

"Ach. He does no' bad. He's a busy man."

"Did you tell Dad your war stories?"

"Oh aye. Plenty of times. But he grew out o' them, just like his short troosers."

"Dad doesn't tell any of them to me, Grandad."

"Well, he wouldny. They're my stories."

"The last time you said you would tell me a story about the soldier who got a letter from Hitler."

"Right. What that is? A letter from Hitler? Right." There was a pause before Archie spoke again.

"What about getting me that packet o' fags from that mantlepiece?"

The boy got the cigarettes, saying as he did. "You shouldn't really smoke. It's bad for you."

"Here," said the old man. "One minute you're askin' me to tell you a story, and the next minute you're getting' on at me for smokin'."

"Well, that's what the experts say."

Archie snorted. "See if you laid all the experts end to end ..... We'd maybe get a bit o' peace. But you're quite right. I shouldn't smoke." He took a long draw on the cigarette and coughed.

"Why do you do it then?", asked Andrew.

"Because I'm too auld tae know any better. Anyway, aboot the soldier who got the letter from Hitler. His name was Obadiah McElhose."

The boy laughed. "Was that his real name?"

"Aye. That was his real name. Whit's wrong with that?"

"It's just a funny name."

"I could think o' funnier. Whit aboot Panjandrum Horsetrough?"

Andrew laughed again. "Who was he?" he asked.

"He wasn't anybody. I just made it up."

There was a silence which Andrew eventually broke.

"Do you make up your stories, Grandad?", he asked.

"Whit d'ye mean, make them up?" asked Archie suspiciously.

"Well. Are they true stories?"

"What makes ye ask?"

"You know your war wound?"

"Aye. I know it fine. We've been going round thegither for a long time."

"Dad says it isn't a war wound. He says you fell down the stairs once when you were home on leave."

"How the devil would he know? He wasn't even born."

"I don't know," said the boy. "That's what he said."

"The trouble with your father," said Archie emphatically. "Is that he's middle aged. Ye get awful confused when ye're middle aged. It's all right if you're young like you or auld like me, but being middle aged is an awfy trial. Ye'll jist need to humour him till he grows oot of' it."

"I see," said the boy doubtfully.

"I bet you," the old man went on. "That he's aye on at you aboot how you don't work hard enough at school. And how he aye did his homework every night, and that you watch far too much television, and stuff like that."

Andrew said nothing, amazed at his Grandfather's insight.

"That's the signs, you see. You'll just need to humour him like I said, till it wears off. Do a wee bit extra homework now and again, jist to shut him up."

The boy made a face. "I hate homework", he said.

"Aye. Ah know. The thing is, the only time ye get to do it is when ye're young. The likes o' me is maybe sittin one night and thinkin' 'Here. Ah would like a bit o' homework.' But there isn't any."

Archie's grandson looked unconvinced. "Did you do your homework when you were a boy?" he asked.

"When I wis a boy," said Archie, neatly sidestepping the question. "We had slates and inkwells."

"Inkwells. What were inkwells?"

"Every desk had a wee round hole cut in it," explained Archie. "And in it was a wee wally pot. And in the pot wis ink. And we had pens with real nibs. You dipped the pen in the ink an' you wrote on the paper. An' if ye got fed up, ye could press down hard, an' the nib would spread oot an' ye would say: "Please Miss, mah nib's broke.' And when ye got a new yin, you had tae suck it for a minute or two, tae get it workin right, and by that time, if ye were lucky, the lesson was finished."

"We only have ball points," said the boy wistfully.

"There you are ye see. That's progress fur ye. There's no the same quality o' authors aboot since they did away wi' nibs. George Bernard Shaw an' H.G. Thingmy wrote wi' nibs."

Andrew considered this proposition in silence for a few seconds before he asked: "Were people cleverer in the old days when you were at school?"

"Less o' the old days. It's no' that long ago. It's only sixty years ago, no' a hundred and sixty."

The boy's imagination tried looking back through sixty years and saw the far end disappearing into mists of great antiquity.

"Were people different then, Grandad?"

"Different? D'ye mean did they hae long arms an' hairy feet?"

The boy smiled. "No. Not that. I mean were they ..... well ....." He searched for another word but couldn't find one. "Different," he concluded lamely.

His grandfather considered carefully.

"No' really," he said eventually. "Naw. Folk were much the same. It's jist things that have changed. Motor cars and footballer's shorts is different."

"There was no TV when you were a boy, was there?"

"Naw, nae TV. Funny though. We never missed it."

"Dad says people watch too much television."

"Ah know whit yer dad says," interrupted Archie. "Ah've jist finished tellin' ye whit yer Dad says. TV's all right as long as you ration it out with fresh air and homework."

Andrew felt it was time to change the subject. "There's sometimes good stories about the second world war on TV," he said unsubtly.

"War stories!" exclaimed the old man, as if in sudden recollection. "I was goin' to tell ye a story aboot the war."

"Yes. About the soldier who got a letter from Hitler," the boy prompted.

"Aye. Right. Where did I get to?"

"You hadn't really started. You just told me his name."

"Obadiah McElhose," Archie said. "Big Oaby we called him. Him an' I first met at Catterick, no' long efter we joint up. We were great pals, but to tell the truth, Oaby wisny very bright. In fact, no' to put too fine a point on it, he was thick. Thick as porridge. If he had sat an intelligence test, he wid a' been declared null and void. Maist people sweat when they're runnin'. Oaby sweated then he was thinkin'. It wis painful tae watch. But he wis the maist fearsome lookin' soldier ye've ever seen. He wis fifteen stone an' six foot five in his soaks, an' the expression oan his face wid a' knocked yer bunnet aff at twenty paces. Even when he wis smilin', his face looked as it if hud been left oot in the rain. But he widny have hurt a fly. In fact I used tae think he might a' been a conscientious objector if he hud a' known how tae spell it."

"What's a conch ..... What you said, Grandad."

"It's somebody who doesny believe in war."

"How could you not believe in war if there was one going on?"

"That's a good question. Ye can ask yer teacher."

Archie's eyes wandered to the clock on the mantlepiece. "Here!", he said. "Dye see the time? It's nearly six o'clock. Is that no ' yer teatime? War'll be declared shortly at your hoose if ye don't get a move on."

The boy moved towards the door.

"And, here. Tell yer Mum it's no fair you havin' tae buy me biscuits out o' your pocket money."

Andrew opened the door.

"And tell her I quite like Jaffa cakes."

"Okay, Grandad. Cheerio."

"Cheerio," Archie called, as the door closed. Silence fell on the room like a thick soft blanket. The old man got up and crossed to the window and watched his grandson running down the street. He watched until he was out of sight. "Swap ye mah war stories for that pair o' legs," he said aloud.

He became aware of the ticking of the clock on the mantlepiece. He crossed to the television set and switched it on.

"This is the six o'clock news from the BBC", said the television set.

"Good evening."

"'Good evening yerself'", said Archie McDougall. "Wid ye like a Garibaldi?"

IMMATERIAL WITNESS

Sammy stood undecided at the open door to the room. It was the faint glow from the gas fire that surprised him; caused him to hesitate. He could have sworn that the house was empty, having spent some hours watching it from a hidden vantage point across the road. Apart from the fire, everything was in darkness and completely silent. He stood perfectly still for several minutes before reckoning that the fire had been left on the keep the room warm while the owners were out. A bit unusual, but not outwith the bounds of possibility. It suggested, however, that they could return at any moment and he would therefore have to be quick. He began to move stealthily across the thick carpet to a writing bureau that he had just been able to make out in the glow of the fire. He had almost reached his goal when a voice said:

"Good evening."

Sammy froze, his heart leaping like a salmon trying to escape its natural environment. Then, as he was trying to collect his scattered wits, he turned and saw the indistinct outline of a man sitting in a high wing backed armchair which Sammy had passed in his totally focused approach to the bureau. The man was now positioned directly between himself and the doorway.

"Eh... hello," said Sammy "....Ah, just, em,... came in tae read the meter."

"Did you really," replied the man. "I would have thought the more usual procedure would be to ring the bell and wait until someone let you in."

As he spoke, Sammy was judging the chances of making it to the door. The man in the chair looked quite big. He decided against it.

"So you considered it within your rights to come in through the open window," said the man.

"Aye" said Sammy brightening. "Aye, that's it. Ah jist thought tae masel' they've probably said; 'We'll jist leave the windi' open in case the man comes to read the meter.'"

"People do that quite a lot, do they?"

"Oh, aye. Aye, Defin*ately*. Happens all the time." Sammy began to feel better. This person seemed to be exceptionally dim. "Here," he continued. "It's awfy dark in here, Will ah switch on the light?"

"No, thank you" said the man. "There's light enough."

"Ur ye hard up? Canny afford the electric. Is that it?"

Sammy saw the man's right arm make a sweeping gesture, indicating what seemed, in poor visibility, to be a richly furnished room. "Does it look as if I'm hard up?" he asked.

"Ye canny tell, nowadays," replied Sammy "It's maybe all on tick."

"I don't owe a penny on any of it," said the man. "I prefer the dark. What's your name?"

The suddenness of the question took Sammy by surprise. "Sammy," he said. "What's yours?"

"My name is immaterial," said the man. "You're not here to read the meter, are you?"

Sammy again contemplated the dash for the door and again decided against it.

"Well...eh... Aye. That's what ah'm here for right enough. We've got tae get in, ye know, Mr Immaterial. We canny have folk no' lettin' us in jist because they don't want to pay the bill, so we canny."

"So you just come in through a window?"

"See, the thing is," said Sammy "Mah boss is a hard man tae please. He gets awfy mad if ah don't read enough meters. He thinks ah've been skivin'. So if there's a windi open....." Sammy's voice trailed away and he spread his hands wide in an expressive gesture.

"You go through it to see what's worth stealing." said the man.

"Aw come on, Jimmy...Mr Immaterial. Ye don't think ah came in here tae pinch stuff, dae ye?"

"Yes, I do," said the man.

Sammy's mind, searching for a suitable response, ran up several blind alleys. After a short pause, he said: "All right. You got me. Whit're ye gonny do?"

"I haven't made up my mind yet."

Sammy began to feel slightly afraid of this man who wanted to carry on a conversation in the near dark.

"Look," he said. "Ah'm no' a violent person. Ah jist come in and see if there's anything worth takin'. Jist come in and go oot again. Peaceful like. Jist take a few things – no' too much. Ah'm no' greedy. Don't make a mess or nothin'."

"Why do you do it?" the man asked abruptly.

"Ah jist like it," said Sammy. The truthfulness of his answer startled him.

"You do it for the excitement?"

"Aye. Well.... No' exactly." Truth was not a well-stocked item in Sammy's larder. He had used a month's supply in a few unguarded minutes. "Ah've got a wife and weans. Canny get a job. Canny look after them proper. Worries me n' that. You got weans?"

"Alas, no," the man replied

"It's an awful responsibility, weans. Ye jist want tae do the best ye can." Sammy sighed. "But it's no' easy."

"Tell me," asked the man. "What would you do with a hundred pounds?"

Sammy's response as like an involuntary muscle twitch. "Have a good time," he said. Then, as his mind came into gear, added. "Gie the wife money for grub, buy something nice for the weans."

The man leaned over the side of the chair and reached into a dark shape on the floor. It looked like a holdall. He removed something and offered it to Sammy. "A hundred pound note," he said. "Take it."

Sammy swallowed, not believing what he had heard. But he took the money. He peered in the dim light. "A hundred pounds! Why are ye givin' me a hundred pounds?"

"Didn't anyone ever tell you never to look a gift horse in the mouth? Let's say I've just come into an unexpectedly large sum of money and I like your style. Incompetence with flair."

This last comment went straight over Sammy's head. "Ye don't have it in smaller notes?" he asked.

"No, I don't," said the man, brusquely. "Do you want it or not?"

"Oh, aye. Ah want it.... Except.."

"Except, what?"

"It's no' funny money, is it?"

"Counterfeit?" The man chuckled softly. "No it's perfectly genuine, I can assure you."

"Ok," said Sammy. "Thanks very much."

"Perhaps I'm getting soft" the man went on. "But if I give you another one, will you make me a promise?"

Sammy was so dazzled he would have promised anything. Not that he had any intention of keeping it. Making a promise was one thing. Keeping it was something else entirely.

"Yes," he said eagerly. "Ah've never not kept a promise. Ah'm really good at keeping promises."

"I want you to keep it for at least a month before you spend it."

"Aw, wait a minute, that's no' fair. It's no' easy to go aboot wi' that much money burnin' a hole in yer pocket. Whit aboot the wife and weans?"

"They'll be no worse off than they would have been had you never met me. And I can assure you that what I am asking has a real purpose."

"Whit's that, then?"

"It's an exercise in self-discipline, which I believe is something you lack. I pride myself in being good at reading a man's character. If you can keep this promise, your life will change for the better. Trust me."

Sammy took the second note. He wasn't really listening any more.

"I promise," he said automatically.

"But be warned," said the man. "If you don't do as I ask, the consequences will be disastrous."

"Aye, right, no bother. Ah'll no' tell the wife. Keep it for a surprise for her and the weans." Sammy replied. "Whit a nutter," he thought.

"Good" the man said "Now you can go. Just remember what I said."

Sammy tried to get a good look at the man before he left, but the light was too poor to see anything but a dark shape sitting unmoving in the big chair. He went gladly, but nervously, expecting a catch somewhere, but as he climbed out the window and across the garden to the street, he began to relax. He looked up and down the empty suburban roadway and seeing no signs of an avenging angel, began to walk quickly away, his step becoming increasingly lighter, in proportion to the distance between himself and the strange encounter.

He was as good as his word about not telling his wife for at least a month. This was not difficult, for he had no idea where she or his children were, nor had he any intention of finding them.

As for the rest of the promise, there remained enough resonance of the man's influence to cause Sammy to fidget about it for the whole of the following day. He had hidden one of the hundred-pound notes in a tea-pot in his one-roomed flat, but kept the other one close so that he could touch it periodically to confirm the whole thing hadn't been a dream. He walked the suburban streets as was his habit but couldn't settle enough to make the usual observations which enabled him to spot the Houses most pliant to his special skills. He had a few pounds in loose change that allowed him to purchase a pie and a pint in the middle of the day, and a couple of tins of beans he had in a cupboard at home got him into the evening with his promise still intact and a feeling of righteous self-denial just beginning to make him feel ill.

The following morning, the battle was over and self-denial, never a reliable ally, cowered in abject surrender.

Just over an hour after breaking his promise, as he sat in the pub with two acquaintances whom he had shocked by buying them a couple of rounds one after the other, he felt a heavy hand on his shoulder.

"Well, well," said a voice. "If it isn't Sammy. I want a word with you."

Sammy didn't need to turn around. He knew who it was.

Later, he faced two detectives across a desk in the interview room of the local nick.

"So. This man who gave you the hundred-pound note. Where did you meet him?"

“Jist bumped into him. Sort of accidental like.”

“Can you describe him?”

“Naw, it was dark.”

“You bumped into a perfect stranger in the dark and he handed you a hundred-pound note? The one you used to buy the drinks this afternoon. That’s the only one you have?”

“Aye.”

The detective, with a smug smile, produced another hundred-pound not and slid it across the table. “What about this one then?” he asked.

Sammy shrugged. “Dunno,“ he said.

“What if I were to tell you that we just found it in that tip you call home?”

Sammy remained silent.

The detective leaned forward. “And we’ve found something else,” he said. “We’ve found your fingerprints all over a house at No. 26 Heywood Place. Normally you don’t take enough for us to bother about getting the fingerprint boys out, but this is different, Sammy. We can’t let this one go, even if you are one of our best customers. So just tell us where we can find the rest of the money and we might make things a bit easier for you.”

Sammy, whose fingerprints were indeed high in the local police popularity chart, realised he was surrounded. He decided to tell the truth.

“That’s all ah’ve got“ he said. “Ah went in to see if there was anything lyin’ about, and this guy wis sittin’ in the dark in a chair in the front room.”

"And he gave you two hundred pounds, just like that."

"Aye."

"Well, I'm glad we've got that cleared up, aren't you?" said the first detective, turning to the other. "There you are, sitting quietly – in the dark – in your own front room, and in comes Sammy, looking for anything that isn't nailed down. 'Oh, hello Sammy,' you say, 'here's two hundred pounds.' That sort of thing happens all the time, doesn't it?"

"Definitely," said the second detective. "We've never had a case cleared up so quickly." Then, turning to Sammy, his tone changing: "Look, you've told us some wonderful and imaginative stories which we have all enjoyed immensely, but I have to admit that's the best one yet. There was nearly ten thousand pounds taken from that house, much of it in hundred-pound notes. We notify all the local banks, bookies and pubs, and lo and behold, two days later we hear that one of our best customers has come into money of the same denomination. I said to George here: "Well, who would have thought it? Sammy, of all people. As honest a man as ever swindled his grandmother. Come on Sammy, where did you hide the rest of it?"

"Ah haven'y got any more. Ah tell't ye. The man jist handed me the two notes."

"Ok. If you are telling the truth, this man will be able to clear you. A witness for the defence. All you need to do is give us his name, but I don't suppose your conversation ran to exchanging names?"

"Oh, but it did." Said Sammy triumphantly. "Ah tell't him mah name an' he gave me his."

“Which was?”

“He said his name wis Immaterial. Ah didn’y get his first name.”

And as much as Sammy repeated his story and protested his innocence, no one would believe him, not even the judge who sentenced him to five years. Worse still, the police said that even if he got out, they would never leave him alone until the recovered the rest of the money.

“Who would have thought it.” Said Sammy to himself. “That guy was nothing but a common thief!”

JOURNEY

I sat alone in the railway compartment, drowsily gazing at the wet, windswept, deserted platform. The wind blew the rain in flurries against the window, causing water droplets to chase each other diagonally across and down the surface of the glass until they dropped off and disappeared back into the night.

I could feel the power of the stationary diesel engine throbbing through the compartment floor; and the comfortable warmth, combined with a mild rocking of the carriage as it was buffeted by the wind, caused my eyelids to droop.

I closed my eyes and gave myself to sleep. Then, seemingly from a long way off, something was calling me, gently tugging at the coat sleeves of consciousness. Gradually, I responded, and in time became aware of a long-forgotten smell. A mixture of sulphur and warm oil, a hint of damp upholstery.... the smell of a steam train. I heard the low hissing sound of steam exhausting from a leaking valve, and above it a murmur of voices. I opened my eyes and realised that I was no longer in the same compartment. The rain and the wind and the empty platform were still there, but now the wind was snatching at a wisp of steam as it tried to drift up past the window.

I was sitting opposite a long bench seat covered in grey and black cut moquette, above which, spaced horizontally, were three photographs of holiday resorts. Above that again was a timber and net luggage rack supported on wrought iron brackets. The murmur of voices I had heard were coming from two of the four people who occupied the compartment, a young man and woman who were talking quietly, heads close together. They were dressed in what I took to be the style of the late nineteenth century; and opposite them on my side of the carriage was a man in his late fifties, similarly dressed. He was sallow faced, with sideburns and a luxuriant black moustache. The fourth occupant sat by himself in the far corner. He was less well dressed than the others, and held a small, half-empty bottle of whisky on his lap. He kept peering anxiously out into the night, every so often raising the bottle to his mouth and drinking, as if in an attempt to dispel whatever it was he saw beyond the window. None of the four seemed to be aware of me and I was in the grip of a strange feeling of contentment that constrained me from wishing it otherwise.

The sallow face man spoke to the young couple.

"Man", he said. "It's grand to be coming home for Ne'erday."

The young couple smiled but didn't speak.

"I've been travelling this two months past", the man went on. "All the way from India. But it's strange how the last part of a journey always seems the longest. Here I am but an hour from home, and it seems that I'm never going to get there."

The young man took a watch from his waistcoat pocket.

"Aye", he said, looking at the watch. "We're a wee bit late right enough." The older man snorted. "You'd think in this day and age, when we rule half the world we could get the trains to run on time. Four days to the New Year, and if this train doesn't get a move on, it'll be 1880 before it completes its journey. A man gets impatient to see his home and family after all these years away. Nearly five years it's been. The bairns'll be grown big. I'll have a job recognising them, and they'll need their mother to tell them who I am."

He suddenly smiled and continued: "But I doubt you two will be very interested in my story. It's my guess you're not long married."

The young woman looked down at her hands clasped in her lap. Again, the young man spoke for both of them.

"We're on our way back from honeymoon to set up home together."

"Isn't that great", said the older man, genuinely delighted. "Home for Ne'erday. To your own home for the first time."

As he spoke, there was an almost imperceptible movement and a creaking of axles. The deserted platform began to slide slowly into the night and there was a strangled shriek as the wind tore at the sound of the engine's whistle. The rhythm of the wheels as they passed over the rail joints gradually grew faster and the small railway station at which the train had been stopped finally disappeared into the rain-soaked night.

There was a sudden movement from the man in the corner. "We're away", he said to himself, getting to his feet and swaying slightly. "They'll no catch me now." The train jerked as it gathered speed and he collapsed back into the seat. "They'll no catch me now", he repeated softly, and took a long swig from the bottle.

The others, after an initial startled reaction, pretended not to have noticed. The young couple turned their attention back to each other, and the sallow faced man sat with a faint smile curving his lips, possibly searching the dusty corners of his mind for images of his wife and family. Then the internal scene became silent and frozen, tableau-like and I sat, not knowing whether or not I was part of the tableau.

I turned my attention away and saw watching the night streaming past the window and listening to the beat of the engine as it pulled its chain of coaches through the storm. Then without warning, there came a grinding sound and a jolting sideways lurch of the carriage as if the train had been switched at speed across a set of points to another line. Instinctively I turned towards my fellow passengers to see if they had been as startled as me, and instead, saw them fragmenting and dissolving, seemingly being absorbed into the fabric of the old compartment which, like the sounds of steam, gradually resolved and flowed and re-formed until I was back to my own reality; the sound of diesel and my empty compartment.

The pitch of the sound made by the wheels on the rails gradually rose, became sharper as we moved out over the water. The wind had driven a rent in the clouds and a pale moon shone on the dark turbulent waters of the Tay. As I looked down, I could see the moonlight reflecting wetly off the weathered pile caps, the only surviving elements of the old bridge.

ME AND ELECTRONICS

In computing terms, a scanner is a piece of electronic equipment that scans things and then delivers a copy of the item scanned to the computer. I thought it best to get the technical explanations out of the way right at the start.

Anyway, I have this scanner that scans things. Well, it did at first. Then it began to become a bit choosy. It continued to scan photographs but began to reject text. Whether it disliked my choice in literature, I'm not sure, but it would start on a page and then, half way down, it would just stop and could not be persuaded to go any further. To make matters worse, the computer would come out in sympathy and would freeze, staring at me, immobile from the monitor screen. I tried to outstare it, but that didn't work and as I eventually found, the only way to proceed was to switch off the computer and then switch it on again. This is known as re-booting – a very apt phrase.

At the end of the re-booting procedure, which takes a few minutes, I would get various messages from the computer, which I hope I will be forgiven for paraphrasing, allowing me to relay the meaning rather than the actual message:

'Fatal exception at co-ordinates, x,y,z' One would announce. 'If you want your incompetence to go unnoticed, please click here and I will do my best to get you out of the mess you've got yourself into.' (Had the sound been switched on, I couldn't have missed the long patronising sigh). No mention you'll notice, of incompetent scanners.

Or 'Windows was not shut down properly'. Well, I already knew that! 'Scan Check will now check for trails of muddy footprints on the hard disk. Please strike any key to continue'. At first I was rather wary of striking *any* key, in case of a retort saying 'Not that key, you twit!' But this never happened. On striking any key, the computer would go into a long routine of meticulous internal inspection before coming up with the immortal phrase: 'Scan Disk has detected 48,530 bytes of information hidden on disk. This may be absolutely vital or may just be gobbledegook taking up space for no reason at all. What do you want to do about it? If you want to find out what it is, click 'save' and Windows will put it into a virtually inaccessible file, which in the unlikely event of ever being found again will be unintelligible, for it will just be a succession of little squiggles and squares. If you don't want to save the 48,530 bytes, click 'ignore' and it will be thrown into outer darkness forever. Just don't come looking for it when you realise what a dreadful mistake you made'.

At first, this sort of information made me nervous, neurotic even, but now after dozens of similar episodes, I have become extremely blasé and cavalier in my dealings with bytes.

Anyway, coming back to the scanner. All the aforementioned trauma, although it allowed me to use my computer again, did nothing for the health of the scanner, which continued to be obdurate about reading.

It was at this point, prompted by advice obtained from a scanner helpline, that I made my bold pre-emptive strike. I decided to remove all trace of scanner from the computer's memory, and having done that, re-install the software that told the scanner what to do and how to behave, so that it and the computer could get along with each other without falling out.

I managed the first part with ease, so that the computer was now saying: 'Scanner? What scanner?' and refused to have anything to do with accepting the operating instructions. So now, instead of just not reading text, the scanner was also not recognising photographs. In fact, it wasn't doing anything at all. My expensive scanner was no longer pensive, it was just ex!

At this juncture, people made of weaker clay than I would have sat down and wept. Not I. I wept standing up. But then I had a brilliant idea. It was a Hewlett Packer scanner, so I would get onto Hewlett Packard's website, get further information, download all the latest operating software and live happily ever after.

Alas! The best laid plans of men and websites gang aft agley.

The 'agley' concerned my modem. A modem is a little electronic box through which a computer is connected via a telephone line to the internet. My modem was a venerable three-year old and the speed of its operation would have meant that I would have to be using the phone line for such a length of time that I would be cheaper buying a new computer and scanner which had been given proper counselling.

All right, so I'm exaggerating a bit, but I'm also getting on a bit and I wanted to be able to spend some time with my family before I go. Perhaps the best way of describing the relative speeds of my modem with its modern equivalent is the old comparison of the tortoise and the hare, except to imagine that the hare has been training for the Olympics and taking certain substances, whilst the tortoise has three legs and a bad case of gout.

So I went to PC World and bought a modem. Not the cheapest one, but not the dearest one either. I brought it home and following the instructions, inserted the CD that came with it, connected the modem to the computer and to the telephone line and switched the computer on.

'Windows will start up in safe mode' the computer said 'because you have done something incredibly silly.' (Again I paraphrase). 'Some of the operating systems may not work. If you *will* fiddle about with things you don't know anything about, what can you expect?'

I don't know if you've seen the new advert for PC World. It shows hundreds of PC World staff stamping their feet to lower prices and looking incredibly bright as they tell you about their wonderful technical staff who will solve all problems associated with their products without hardly batting an eyelid. My experience has always been somewhat different. I have never, and I mean never, had a problem solved by PC World staff. So I wasn't full of optimism when I went back to see if they could help.

"Nothing wrong with the Modem", said the technical expert, keen to improve customer relations. "You must have done something wrong."

I explained that I had followed instructions to the letter.

"Can't be anything wrong with the modem", said the T.E

"I'm not saying that there's anything wrong with the modem", I explained. "I was just wondering if this was a situation you had come across before. Maybe the installation disk has caused some sort of IRQ conflict."

"It won't be anything wrong with the modem", said the T.E. Then, brightening. "It's probably a virus."

"A virus that struck just at the point of connecting the modem?" I said pointedly.

He shrugged. “Can’t be the modem. All you do is plug it in.”

“So what you’re saying”, I said “Is that you can’t help me. You haven’t come across IRQ conflicts before?”

He didn’t reply. Just tightened his lips a bit and looked at me. He was probably thinking that daft old men shouldn’t be playing with computers. I turned and left, thinking that he probably didn’t know the difference between an IRQ and a broom handle. Neither did I, but it had been satisfying to call PC World’s bluff.

I phoned my daughter Amanda, who knows about such things.

“I bought a new modem”, I said.

“Good”, she replied. “The one you had came out of the Ark.”

“Not good”, I replied and told her that my computer was now acting like a wet lettuce.

“You didn’t load the CD that came with the modem?” she asked. She groaned when I replied in the affirmative. “That’s probably the problem.” She went on. “Leave it for the moment, and I’ll come over shortly.”

She said she didn’t like the modem I’d got. At this point I wasn’t very fond of it either.

“I’ll take it back and get a replacement”, she said.

“Can I come too?” I asked, “I want to punch the technical expert on the nose.”

She wouldn’t let me come, but to cut a long story short, she got a replacement which cost me another tenner, got onto the internet, downloaded the appropriate files and injected semblance of life back into the computer. She didn't have time to finish work on the scanner, so I did that myself. To my delight it scanned four pieces of text, which I was then able to process without much bother.

Next day, I fed another piece of writing to the scanner. Maybe it was too early in the morning, but it took one look, folded its arms and refused to read it. And of course, the computer folded its arms as well. With a sigh, I switched the computer off, then restarted it and had to wait while it went through the ritual about fatal errors and missing bytes. Then I typed the story directly into the computer. Later I told Amanda what had happened, and she said I should make sure the scanner was switched on before the computer. I thought this unlikely to make any difference, but I tried it just in case.

Lo and behold, it worked. Perhaps the computer just likes the comfort of knowing its old pal is there before doing any work. Anyway, it scanned the rest of the sheets and just to show there were no hard feelings it did not utter a single word of criticism.

Perhaps in the fullness of time, we may all become friends.

MINCE TOMORROW

As Andrew approached the bed, the old man's eyes opened suddenly. The boy's forward movement faltered.

"Grandad," he said. "You're awake."

Archie McDougall turned his head, his mind trying to focus. "It's you then, come tae see me?"

"Yes, it's me Grandad."

The boy sat down

"How are you feeling?" he asked

"Fine. Ah'm fine." Archie said slowly as his mind began to clear.

"How did you get in?"

"Mrs Thomson let me in"

"Did she come in hersel?"

"No. She just opened the door and went away again"

"That's good. The last time she let yer dad in, she came in hersel and started hoovering."

"What's wrong with that?"

Archie pushed himself up on the bed. "Fix that pillow for me son, would ye?"

The boy did as he was asked, so that his grandfather could lean back comfortably.

"That's better" said the old man. "How's school then?"

"Alright." Replied Andrew..... What's wrong with Mrs Thompson doing the hoovering?"

"Ye've a lot tae learn aboot wimmin," said Archie "Wan minit they're hooverin, then they're washing the dishes, an' the next thing ye know, they've got ye surrounded."

The boy looked puzzled but said nothing.

"There's nothin' mair frightening than a wumman intent oan good works," continued the old man. "They're like a steamroller under full sail," He lowered his voice and looked towards the door. "If ah encouraged her, she would be washin' mah semmit an' drawers afore ah knew what had hit me."

Andrew decided that the conversation had got beyond him, so he changed the subject.

"Will I make you a cup of tea Grandad?" he asked

"A cup of tea? Aye.... Naw! Ah tell ye what. If ye go into the cupboard in the kitchen, ye'll find a bottle o'lemonade. Would ye like lemonade?"

"Yes," said the boy.

"Good. You have a drink o'lemonade. An' beside the lemonade, ye'll find a bottle o'whisky. Jist pour me a wee drop an' fill the glass up wi' water."

When his grandson returned, Archie had re-arranged the pillows and was sitting up straighter than he had been previously.

"That's the stuff!" he said, accepting the drink.

"Now, then. It's nice to see ye! Cheers! How's the school?"

"Alright."

The old man lowered his glass, so that it was resting on the bedcover,

"Ye're an' awfy blether aboot that school o'yours," he said.

"Yes..... Grandad?"

"Aye, that's me."

"What actually happened?"

"Ye mean the ither night?"

"Yes"

"Ye know, " said Archie "Ah haven't had as many visitors fur years. First yer Dad wis up. Then yer Mum, Then the baith o' them the githe. An Mrs Thompson. And the doactor. And the polis. Even ye'r great aunt Jessie wis up, wi' that daft man o' hers. Ye know whit she said tae me?" he continued, warming to his theme. "She says, 'Whit huv ye been up tae noo, Archie? Ye're aye upsettin' everybuddy wae yer cairryin oan's' Whit a cheek! The last time ah seen her wis at Jimmy's funeral. Jessie wis aye like that." The old man shook his head. Some wimmin hus violent tongues," he said "If they hud mair muscles in their tongues the world wid be full o' battered husbands.... And then yer mum....She pit her airms aboot me an' hugged me. 'Are ye all right Grandad?' she sez. Archie made a face. "There's far too much huggin' goes on nooadays."

Andrew rose to his mother's defence

"I don't see anything wrong with that, Grandad," he said. She was just trying to make you feel better."

"Aye, well. Ah suppose she wis. But she should keep her haunds tae herself.' Ah'm all right. There's nae need for huggin' an' kissin."

The boy for some reason suddenly wanted to put his own arms round his Grandfather but resisted the impulse and asked again. "What happened Grandad?"

"Did yer Dad no' tell ye?"

"Well.... Not exactly. He just said you'd been hurt. But I heard him saying to Mum. 'If I get hold of them, I'll kill them"

"Did he say that? That wis nice of him. His heart's in the right place so it is. But ach, he's no really the killin' kind."

"He was pretty angry, Grandad. I've never seen him so angry."

Archie took a long slow drink of whisky.

"Ah wisny very pleased masel." He said

His grandson fidgeted in his chair.

"Ah wis sittin hain mah tea', Archie went on. "Potted meat an' potatoes it wis.. oor butcher does a good potted meat, when there wis a ring at the door. When ah opens it, there wis this fella an' a lassie. 'We're frae the cooncil' she says, wi' her blonde hair doon tae her shoulders. 'We're checking up on old age pensioners." The old man's eyes met his grandson's then looked down at the glass in his hand. Ah wis jist goin tae ask to see their credentials, when the pair 'o them jist walked in an' shut the door behind them. 'Where's yer money Grandad?' The fella says, nasty like.

"Grandad?' ah says. Less o' the grandad! Ah'm fussy aboot who calls me grandad!" And the next thing ah know ah'm oan the floor."

The boys hands were clenched so that his knuckles showed white.

"Did he punch you Grandad?"

"Ah'm not sure, " said Archie. "But ah tell ye, he widny have done it if ah'd been five years younger. Ah used tae be real fast oan ma' feet."

"If you'd had a gun you could have shot them," said Andrew.

"It's maybe jist as well ah hadny," said the old man with disdain. "Shootin' people isny a very good idea, even toerags like yon."

"I wish I had been there Grandad. I would have stopped them."

Archie smiled

"Aye, so ye wid son. They widny have tried onythin' if you hud been there. Naebuddy wid try onythin' oan wae the pair o' us. We're just like yon two that used to be on telly – d'ye mind? Scratchy an' Hutch."

"What did they do then?" asked the boy

"He wis staundin' ower me, an' she wis rakin' aboot the place. 'It'll likely be in a drawer,' he says

'Try the tea caddy,' ah says.

She empties the tea caddy upside doon in the sink. There wis nothin' in it but tea.

'Don't get smart, old man,' the guy says. "He wisny ca'in' me Grandad any more. That wis aye somethin"

"Where is it?' he asks, lookin' doon at me, an' proddin' me wae his toe.... Jist as well he was wearin' sannies.

"Sannies?" Andrew asked. "What's sannies?"

"Sannies? Sandshoes! They've got some daft name fur them nowadays. Whit d'ye ca' them again?.... Strainers?"

"Trainers, Grandad"

"Aye, well, Strainers or Trainers, that's whit he had oan his feet. Ah wid recognise them again anywhere." He smiled. "Imagine the polis askin' me tae go in an identification parade o' sannies!"

"How can you joke about it Grandad?" asked the boy angrily.

"If ye didny laugh, ye wid greet."

'Come on old man' he asks, 'Tell us where it is an' ye'll no' get hurt.'

'If ah tell ye, will ye go?' ah asks.

'Aye, we'll go. That's all we want. The money.'

'Well, ah ses, it's somewhere ye widny think o' lookin'. It's in mah wallet in mah jacket pocket, ower the back o' that chair.' The lassie dives ower, an' takes oot mah wallet. 'Twenty quid,' she says.

The fella looks doon at me again. Ah mind o' thinkin' it wis funny that he hud a real honest face. 'Is that all ye've got?' he asks.

'Aye, whit did ye expect?' ah says, 'Ah'm no exactly Aristotle Thingmy.'

'It's hardly worth the bother,' He says to the lassie, as if ah wisny there. She looks round and sees a fancy vase oan the dresser. She picks it up. "This'll maybe be worth somethin' she says. 'Leave that alone,' Ah shouts. 'That belonged tae mah wife!' That seemed tae please her, fur a smile comes ower her face, an' then she drops it oan the flair, bursting it tae smithereens. 'You stupid bitch.' Says the fella, movin' over and slappin' her across the jaw. 'Somebody'll hear that.' Then he kicks me in the ribs again.

'Stay there' he says. 'If ye move, ah'll come back an really hurt ye'. An wi that, the pair o' them were away."

The old man sighed and took a long drink from the glass. "Were you not scared, Grandad?" asked the boy.

"Scared? Naw. No at the time. It all happened that fast, ah didny have time tae be scared. Ah mind o' thinkin' that if the pair o' them wis tryin' tae get intae the human race, they wis goin' the wrong way aboot it. The thing wis, ah must o' had the flu' hangin' over me, for when they went away, ah started fur tae shiver so much that ah could hardly get up.

But ah managed it, an ah phoned yer Dad. An he comes roon, an' he phones the polis an the factor. Ye know whit the doactor sez? He says.. 'Ye've had a shock tae yer system Mr McDougall.! Ah could have telt him that an' saved him the bother o' comin'. At least he didny ask me whit wis up wi' me. When ye send fur a doactor they usually ask ye whit's up wi' ye. Then he says ah've tae stay in mah bed fur a day or two an' he'll write oot a prescription for pills tae help me tae sleep. 'Never mind the pills,' ah says. 'Jist write oot a line fur a boattle o' whisky'

He laughs and ' pits his pen away

'Aye, maybe your right Mr McDougall,' he says. 'A drop of whisky in moderation'll probably be jist as good.'

But he didny gie me a prescription for it, an when he's goin' oot the door, ah shouts 'Ah'll send ye mah fee in due course.'

He laughs again, 'Ah think you'll recover,' he says

Then ah hears him mumblin' away tae yer Dad in the kitchen, gie'in him aw the medical patter. Doactors!" said Archie scathingly, taking another leisurely sip from his glass.

"What happened when the police came?" asked the boy.

"They took my fingerprints." Archie replied

"Your fingerprints?"

"Aye." They wanted tae separate them from the ither yins on the tea caddy."

"Maybe my fingerprints were on the tea caddy," said Andrew.

"Mebbe they were. But they'll no' arrest you, even if ye do call me Grandad. The sannies rule you out. Then they took fingerprints aw ower the place. Even off the broken vase."

"It's a shame about Grannie's vase." The boy said.

"Yer grannie hated the sight o' it," replied Archie. "Ah won it fur shootin' at a sideshow."

"Then why did you say?..."

"It kept the lassie frae thinkin' aboot ither things. Soor minds tend tae curdle quick."

"Grandad?" The boy hesitated.

"Aye?"

"I'm glad you're alright."

"Ah'm fine son. Don't you worry. It takes mair nor Bonnie an' Clyde tae upset me. An' it's fair made me intae a celebrity. Like I won the world cup of somethin'. Everyboddy's been up tae see me. An' Mrs Thomson'll be in, in a wee while, wae mah tea oan a tray. Trouble is, ah bet it's biled fish.' She's a nice wumman, but ah bet it's biled fish!"

"Don't you like biled... boiled fish?"

"Canny stand the stuff. But ah widny like tae hurt her feelins."

"Maybe it'll be mince, Grandad," said Andrew

"Naw I don't think so. Ah'm no at that stage yet. Ye've goat tae take things in the right order when ye're no' weel. First, it's the beef tea, then when ye're a bit better it's scrambled egg, and then next, maybe a bit biled fish in a white sauce. Ye don't get mince till ye'r mair or less back oan ye're feet. That's the way ye're granny used tae work, anyway."

"Are you going to be back on your feet soon, Grandad?"

"Oh aye, likely. Tae tell ye the truth ah'm no very sure there's anythin' wrong wi' me now. The flu' went aboot as quick as it came."

"You should be careful," said Andrew, "Dad says you're not as young as you used to be."

He's a smart man, yer dad!" Archie replied sharply. "Did he work that out himsel' or did he get help? He's no as young as he used tae be either. Neither are you!"

"Yes I know Grandad. He just meant....."

"Ah know fine whit he meant."

There was a momentary spark of mutual irritation.

The boy stood up. "I'll need to go now. Is there anything I can get you?"

"Is it that time already?" Archie looked at his watch.

"Yes," said Andrew. "But I'll be back tomorrow, and Dad will be up later tonight."

"Off ye go then." Archie responded. "Ah'm fine. Ah'm no needin' anythin'. Jist be careful on yer way home. Oh and by the way", he continued in an offhand manner. "No' that ah'm aw that worried, but make sure ye shut the door tight."

"Okay Grandad."

After the boy was gone the old man lay still for a long time. Then, suddenly, there came, quite unbidden, deep dry silent sobs that wracked his whole body. He suffered this for some minutes, until, losing patience with himself, he swore aloud and swung his feet to the floor.

Half an hour later, when Mrs Thompson came in with his tea, he was up and dressed, and had the table set.

“Mr McDougall!” she said, startled. “You’re up!”

“Aye” he replied, “an feelin’ a lot better.”

“That’s good.” She laid the tray on the table. “I thought you might like a wee bit haddock in white sauce.” “Fish!” he replied, “Whit a nice surprise!”

Mrs Thomson smiled her pleasure. “I hope it’s warm enough.”

“It’ll be fine,” said Archie. “It’s been really good of ye tae bring me in mah meals like this. But it’s aboot time ah wis getting’ a grip oan masel.

Ah’ll need to get oot in the fresh air.”

“Oh, do you think that’s wise?”

“Best thing for me. Ah can’t have the boy seein’ me in bed like that again.”

He squared his thin shoulders.

“So ah think ah’ll have a wee toddle round tae the butchers in the mornin’. He gestured towards the fish.

“Mince tomorrow”, he said emphatically.

MISTRAL AND THE GREAT WHITE BIRD

This is the definitive Teenage Romance
It has all the correct ingredients:
Girl Friends
Boy Friends
Body Matters
Fashion
Cosmetics
Pop Music
Parent Problems
Environmental Issues
Adventure
World Travel
Relationships
Rik
Disco Dancing
Kissing
Strong Arms
And many other Important Factors

Mistral stopped squeezing her blackheads and turned to look at Lasagne who was sprawled on the bed.

"Why aren't you wearing knickers?" she asked

Lasagne lowered her long black eyelashes and drew her blue taffeta dress down to her knees.

"My mum confiscated every pair I have", she explained with a trace of anger in her voice.

Mistral stared at her in disbelief. "What a thing to do!" she said. "Mothers can be the pits sometimes, can't they?"

Lasagne gazed at the ceiling and pouted.

"She burst into my bedroom, without knocking, collected everything off the floor and positively hurled them into the washing machine! Anyway, I've got tights on." She raised an elegant leg a little way off the bed and turned it so that the calf showed. "Don't you think that hole looks a bit like a butterfly?" she asked.

"Yes it does a bit", Mistral agreed turning her attention back to the blackheads. There was silence for some minutes before Lasagne spoke again.

"You were going to tell me about your new boyfriend", she said.

"So I was", agreed Mistral. "He's really fantastic. I think we were meant for each other. He's got long legs and broad shoulders, and the pimples give his face a mysterious look." A shiver ran deliciously down her back. "And the way he looks at me with his left eye makes me go all funny... That's the blue one", she explained.

"He sounds positively fab", Lasagne giggled. "I bet his name is Rik."

"Cuthbert", corrected Mistral.

"Cuthbert!" Lasagne echoed. "Why isn't he called Rik?"

"Well, to tell you the truth, he comes from a rather poor family. His father works for the co-operative."

"Ooo. Quelle hard fromage!" squeaked Lasagne. "I want someone beautiful and rich. So that he can give me my heart's desire."

"What's that then? Your heart's desire?" Mistral enquired.

"Love and togetherness. My head resting on his shoulder. His strong arms protecting me."

"You don't need money for that. That's what it's like with Cuthbert and me. And it's exciting, for he's going places and I'm going with him."

Lasagne put an index finger into the hole in her tights, attempting to make it look more like a butterfly.

"Has he left school, then?" she asked.

"Oh yes. Ages ago. He's got a steady job with the council... He cleans sewers."

Lasagne surveyed her elegantly manicured nails and spoke softly, almost, but not quite, to herself:

"That's nice. He won't notice your B.O."

Mistral drew her breath and turned her head away so that her friend wouldn't notice the hot tears that had welled up in her eyes.

"What a horrible thing to say", she quavered.

Lasagne was suddenly full of contrition.

"Oh, Misty", she said. "I'm sorry! I didn't mean it. You haven't really got B.O. I don't even notice it when we're out in the fresh air."

Even as she spoke she knew she was only making things worse. Sobs were choking Mistral's throat so that she couldn't speak. Lasagne leapt from the bed and wrapped her arms around her, holding her friend and her breath at the same time.

Gradually the sobs subsided. Lasagne released Mistral and retreated to sit on the end of the divan bed. She began breathing again.

"You are the best friend I have in all the world", she gasped painfully, "And I love you very very very much."

"Do you really?" asked Mistral, turning her tear-stained face towards her.

"Yes. I really really do."

Mistral struggled to bring a smile back to her lips.

"I know you do. Only a truly loving friend could have found the courage to tell me.."

She pulled a length of tissue from the recycled toilet roll on her dressing table and began blotting the tears from her face. Her naturally bright personality began to bubble up and take charge again.

"Tell you what I shall do", she announced. "Starting next week, I'm going to have a bath every Friday, whether I need it or not! And in the meantime, I'm going to use Mum's deodorant oil all over. She gets it from the Body Shop. It's completely natural. Absolutely no animal products in it at all." She smiled contentedly, thinking of all the baby seals frolicking safely in the North Atlantic blissfully unaware that it was only because of her and thousands like her that they would be able to grow up into big ugly seals. The thought restored her to complete happiness.

"Would you like to hear my new record?" she asked.

"Yes please", Lasagne replied. "What's it called?"

"I Ain't Got Time To Kiss You Today Cos I Gotta Save The World." Mistral put the disc on the turntable.

When the stylus dropped into the groove, the room erupted with raucous purple sound. A strip of wallpaper detached itself at the ceiling and drooped downward like a wilting flower.

"Isn't it brilliant!" Mistral screamed above the noise. "Look what it does to the duvet cover."

She picked the duvet off the floor and laid it across the bed. A faint pattern of mauve stripes was appearing on its surface.

"Isn't it brilliant!" she screamed again.

"Brilliant!" shrieked Lasagne. "What group is it?"

"The Cherubums!" roared Mistral at the top of her voice. "Rik Grunge and the Cherubums."

"Rik!!" squealed Lasagne transported with joy. "Fab!!" She rolled about on the bed until the hole in her tights began to look really really like a butterfly.

After a few minutes the music stopped as abruptly as it had begun. The only sound remaining, apart from the ringing in their ears, was the creaking of floorboards as they eased back into position.

"How did they come to be called the Cherubums?" asked Lasagne.

"Rik was a boy soprano in a Cathedral choir", Mistral explained. "So I suppose that's where he got the idea. But he had to leave when his voice broke and he – you know – became a man." They both giggled then Lasagne sighed and said:

"It's all right for you. You've got a boyfriend."

"I know", breathed Mistral happily. "The most wonderful man in the world. But I've been keeping a secret from you. Cuthbert's bringing a friend to the disco tonight."

"Is he called Rik?" asked Lasagne hopefully.

"No. Mustapha."

"Mustapha? Are you quite sure?"

"Well, no. Not absolutely sure. It might be George or something like that."

The hole in Lasagne's tights was becoming a bit big for a butterfly.

"Is he nice looking?" she asked. "Has he got broad shoulders and narrow hips?"

"I don't know. I've never met him", Mistral replied. "But if he's a friend of Cuthbert's he's sure to be dreamy."

She surveyed the jars of creams and lotions borrowed from her mother's bedroom. She selected one called 'Wild Garlic' and began to prepare for the evening ahead.

Lasagne stood up and tried to smooth out the wrinkles in her dress. It wasn't easy. She looked wistfully at her friend.

"Oh dear", she said. "I wish I was small and had a nice wobbly bottom like yours."

Mistral stopped rubbing Wild Garlic into her skin and turned towards her friend.

"Goodness Lasagne", she protested. "It's me who should be envious of you. You're so slim and elegant."

Lasagne was suddenly afraid she was going to be embraced, so she spoke quickly.

"But I've got no really round and squishy bits", she said. "Not like you."

"You don't need them", said Mistral. "Not really. You can wear anything and still look beautiful. Not like me."

"Even in this old thing?" Lasagne enquired, still smoothing out wrinkles.

"Even in that old thing. Goodness. You don't know how fortunate you are. Just wait. I bet Cuthbert's friend will fall madly in love with you at first sight."

When they arrived at the disco, the boys were already there, waiting just outside the entrance. Cuthbert immediately embraced Mistral, pressing her tight against the metal chains and buckles on his jacket. Then before her face began to come up in lumps, he released her and made the introductions.

"This is Mustapha", he said. "Mustapha, this is Mistral and this is her friend Lasagne."

Mustapha was short and swarthy and had a moustache that made him look older than he probably was. He greeted Mistral courteously and then turned towards Lasagne. She had just time to notice dark mysterious brown eyes before she felt his moustache tickling the back of her hand

“Pliss to meet you, lovely Lasagne”, he said.

Mistral nudged Lasagne in the ribs.

“What did I tell you”, she hissed. “L.A.F.S.”

“Now pliss”, said Mustapha, taking Lasagne’s hand and leading her towards the entrance to the disco. “We go out to this wild place and jiggle.”

He produced a huge roll of paper money and peeled off a note which he handed to the girl at the cash desk.

“Hello pliss”, he said. “Four out.”

Behind him Lasagne smiled and held up four fingers.

The girl gave Mustapha her best customer liaison glare.

“Far out yourself, sunshine”, she retorted and began to look for large amounts of change. But Mustapha had gone, taking Lasagne with him. Cuthbert waited for the money.

“He’s absolutely loaded”, he whispered to Mistral. “I’ll give him this later.”

Once inside they found a table at the far end of the dance floor. Mustapha was obviously attracted to Lasagne and kept looking deep into her eyes.

“My Father Sheik”, he said suddenly.

“Oh dear, I am sorry”, Lasagne replied. “What’s the matter with him?”

“Sheik!” Cuthbert hissed. “You know. Like in the desert.”

"Seventeen Wivies", Mustapha continued, holding up six fingers.

"How perfectly awful", Lasagne commented. "Do you have to keep your bedroom tidy and call them all Mother?"

"Ninety-five camels", Mustapha went on, not holding up any fingers.

Lasagne looked into his limpid brown eyes and wished she could speak fluent Arabic. She couldn't, but thought she knew a couple of words.

"Qattar Papyrus", she said brightly.

Mustapha looked puzzled for a moment, then smiled, revealing a row of white even teeth.

"Qattar Papyrus to you too, lovely Lasagne", he replied.

Suddenly and unexpectedly, Lasagne found herself dreaming of lying on a silk-covered sofa in a tent in a desert, eating Turkish Delight.

Then Mustapha took her by the hand and led her to the dance floor.

He turned out to be a terrific dancer, his body writhing and twisting in perfect time with the beat of the music. After a while Lasagne stopped to brush the dandruff off her shoulders.

"Oh dear", she said. "I'm really sweating."

"Qattar Papyrus", said Mustapha, grasping her and pulling her tight to his short swarthy body. "I am fallen out loaf with you. I am besooted. My loaf has no jumps."

Somehow, almost mystically, Lasagne knew exactly what he was saying in his heart.

“Oh, Mustapha”, she breathed. “I feel the same way.”

“Qattar Papyrus”, cried Mustapha with passion, sweeping her back into the rhythm of the dance. “This is our song.”

Mistral and Cuthbert were still seated.

“Don’t they make a lovely couple?” Mistral commented, gazing affectionately at them in their tight embrace, Mustapha’s nose pressed into Lasagne’s chest.

“Yes”, said Cuthbert absentmindedly. Then more urgently:

“Come close beside me Mistral. There’s something I must tell you.”

Mistral snuggled up to his leather jacket, her ear hard against a length of rightly polished chrome steel chain.

The aphrodisiacal smell of body lotion combined with sewer gas made her senses reel.

“What is it Cuthbert?” she asked.

“On Thursday”, he began. “On Thursday… Oh Mistral, you’ll never believe it… It’s something I’ve strived for, dreamed about, but never thought would come to be..”

Mistral was astonished to see tears well up in his eyes.

“What is it, Cuthbert?” she repeated anxiously.

He reached out and cupped her face in his strong bony hands. His blue eyes burned into both of hers. The brown one looked past her left ear. He took a deep breath and blurted out:

"On Thursday I'm piloting Concorde to New York!"

Mistral hadn't thought it possible that her senses would reel any more than they had been doing, but they did.

"I don't understand," she heard herself saying.

"It's through the Youth Opportunity Scheme", said Cuthbert proudly. "I was chosen from forty thousand applicants"

Stupidly, all Mistral could think of was that Thursday was the day before Friday, when she was going to have her bath.

"Oh, Cuthbert", she breathed, steam beginning to rise from her body. "Oh Cuthbert."

It was then that he kissed her. A soft, triumphant, caring kiss. The gentle, magic moment when two souls unite in single, eternal bliss. A moment when she knew she would be his forever, waiting patiently while he flew off into the wide blue yonder of all their tomorrows. She was so proud of this man, who had climbed doggedly out of the sewers to fly the greatest aircraft in the world. But the best part of all was that he loved her. She would have fallen to the ground had he not held her safely in his strong bony arms. But he didn't so she didn't. Her eyes were beginning to glaze over when they were interrupted by the return of their friends.

Mistral could see Lasagne was excited by the way she was breathing.

"Quelle news, Mistral!" cried Lasagne. "Mustapha wants to give Dad twelve camels...", she held up three fingers. "So that I can go to Arabia with him. Isn't it exciting! And they have toilets in their tents and everything."

Mistral wondered if her friend wasn't being just a touch impetuous, but she was not going to be negative.

"Oh Lasagne, how absolutely wonderful! I'm so pleased for you..... Cuthbert's going to fly Concorde to New York!"

"That's nice", Lasagne replied absently. "I expect Dad can keep them in the back garden as long as the neighbours don't object."

Mistral was a bit put out by the offhand manner in which her best friend had received her fantastic news, but, well, she was her best friend and because of that she could forgive her.

"I'll write to you", she said, wondering if tents had post codes.

"Thanks", replied Lasagne, hoping not to be embraced.

The following Thursday, they all travelled together to Heathrow in one of Mustapha's father's Rolls Royce's. Mustapha went off to arrange delivery of a down-payment of two camels which Lasagne's father had accepted in a moment of near catatonic insobriety as a gesture of pre-engagement good faith. Cuthbert went off to get into his pilot's uniform.

"Oh, Mistral", said Lasagne tearfully.

"Oh, Lasagne", said Mistral tearfully.

They embraced, and Lasagne held her breath until she thought her lungs would burst. Then she fled towards Mustapha and her future, thinking of the friend she was leaving behind and of Turkish Delight in a tent in the desert. Tears ran down her cheeks and her breath came in great rasping sobs.

Mistral watched her until she had disappeared among the throng in the terminal and wished she could write poetry.

Then she forgot Lasagne, for Cuthbert was striding towards her, like a Greek god in a pilot's uniform. Her mind reeled, and she would have fallen to the ground, had he not caught her in his strong bony arms. He was becoming quite an expert at it.

"Oh Cuthbert", she breathed.

"Oh Lasagne", he said in his strong bony voice. 'I'd never have made it had it not been for you."

It seemed as if her heart would burst and the terminal building was full of birdsong.

"I'm so proud of you", she said simply.

She knew that his strong bony mind was already at sixty thousand feet over the Atlantic and was ready when he said:

"I must go now, my darling. But I'll be back on Saturday. Will you be here for me?"

"How need he ask?" she thought and said: "Of course my dear. How could it be otherwise?"

He stooped and kissed her eager parted lips. "You are my Alpha and my Omega", he whispered. "I couldn't get from A to B without you."

And with that he was gone, striding off with his broad shoulders and narrow hips under the fluorescent lights. She realised with a sudden realisation that only now did she know what a Greek god in a pilot's uniform looked like from the back. She wept silently, wishing that Saturday was already with her.

She joined a crowd of people waiting to see Concorde take off. They courteously made space for her, standing aside so that she might have a better view.

She waited for what seemed like an eternity before the slender droop-nosed aircraft appeared and taxied to the end of the runway. She was in a frenzy of excitement and anxiety and would have swooned if Cuthbert's strong arms had been there to support her. But they weren't, so she didn't.

Then, with a roar like a thousand demons, the great white bird sped down the runway and soared gracefully into the night sky. Mistral called out Cuthbert's name though she knew he wouldn't hear.

The crowd around her held their breaths. Who could blame them. It was still only Thursday.

MYSTERY TOUR

The touring coach rocked slightly as Jean MacFarlane, looking slightly dishevelled, mounted the steps.

"Oh dear", she gasped. "Sorry driver, I didn't realise it was so late until I heard the time on the radio. Oh dear. I'm all out of breath."

She took the nearest available seat, beside a grey-haired man, who smiled at her as she sat down.

The coach driver closed the door, the engine burst into life and the bus moved slowly into the stream of traffic.

After a few minutes of fidgeting in her seat, Jean, already warm from her exertion and becoming warmer in the heat of the coach, stood up to remove her coat. Politely, the man rose also, took her coat to place in the rack and offered her the window seat, which she accepted. Jean introduced herself. He said his name was Andrew Davidson. There was a short pause before he spoke again.

"It took some time before I plucked up the courage to come on one of these trips." He hesitated. "No. Not courage. That's the wrong word. No. It was more a question of facing facts. Vanity, perhaps." His expression changed. "My apologies", he went on "That was a rather clumsy thing to say."

Jean smiled. "I know exactly how you feel", she said. "I sometimes find myself thinking, 'What am I doing here among all these old people?' Silly, really."

"Not silly at all", Andrew replied. "On the few occasions I look in the mirror nowadays, I find some old man staring me straight in the eye daring me to recognise him." He shrugged. "One day I will. But not yet."

"Good for you", said Jean. "My sentiments exactly."

"Not you surely", said Andrew, trying to recover from his earlier gaffe.

"When I saw you get on the bus, I wondered why you would want to come on an over-sixties trip when you so obviously didn't qualify."

Jean gave him a half smile, half grimace, but felt pleased. It had been a long time since she had been given even a backhanded compliment.

As the bus travelled towards the Clyde coast, and both the city and the initial small embarrassment became more distant, they found themselves talking comfortably, finding much in common and, subconsciously, the feeling that each had known the other much longer than was actually the case. Then the early morning clouds dispersed, and the sun came out.

"It looks as if we're going to get a lovely day", Jean said.

"Looks like it", Andrew agreed. "It may even be warm enough for us to sit on the open deck."

Jean noted the 'us' and wondered if he was thinking of a busload 'us' or a smaller number. Aloud she said: "I'm getting quite excited. It's so long since I took a sail down the Clyde."

When they arrived at Wemyss Bay and had got off the coach, Andrew asked her if she would consider spending the rest of the day in his company. She hesitated only briefly.

"If you like... Yes... Thank you. It's pleasant to have company... Someone to talk to."

As they walked out along the pier, Jean caught the sharp smell of the seashore. She looked down between the tarred boards and saw the oily water moving great fronds of seaweed against the barnacled timbers and felt again the lifting of her heart she used to experience as a child at the start of each fortnight's holiday with her parents.

"Takes you back, doesn't it?" said Andrew.

She nodded in agreement, enjoying both the nostalgia and the empathy.

As they walked up the steeply sloping gangway on to the car ferry, he said "They're not the same, these things. Not like the old steamers. Not the same life about them. Impersonal."

Like the rest of the bus party, they decided it wasn't warm enough to sit on deck, so they made their way to the forward cabin where they could see across the water.

"Isn't this nice", said Jean. "I'm quite excited... Oh." She broke off in embarrassment. "I said that already, didn't I?"

"Yes, you did", said Andrew smiling. "What was it Stevenson said? It is better to travel hopefully than to arrive."

"That may sometimes be true", Jean replied, "But not today. It'll all be good. Travelling and arriving. Look, they're casting off."

The background noise of the diesel engines became more intrusive, the ship's bow began to angle sway from the pier and the ferry began to move slowly out into the Firth of Clyde.

Andrew stood up. "I'll go and get us a cup of tea."

When he came back he said: "Paper cups, I'm afraid. There's progress for you."

"Never mind", said Jean, taking one of the cups. "It's still tea." She sipped and made a face. "Well I think it's tea."

So they sat together and drank what they believed to be tea together and looked at the sea and the far shores, the pleasure heightened for each of them by the company of the other.

Presently, at Jean's suggesting, they left the shelter of the cabin and ventured out on to the open deck. It wasn't warm, but it wasn't exactly cold either. A slight breeze was ruffling the surface of the water so that slivers of light sparkled all around. The gazed across the Firth to the familiar silhouette of the Arran hills.

"Isn't the Sleeping Warrior clear", remarked Jean.

"Yes it is", Andrew replied, and as Jean turned she found his eyes looking into her.

"Yes", she repeated hurriedly and looked away again.

They must have been leaning against the rail for some time before they noticed a dense bank of fog directly ahead.

"That's odd", Andrew commented with a frown. "I could swear that wasn't there a moment ago..."

As he spoke, the car ferry slid into the mist and the sun was blotted out. Instantaneously, the air temperature dropped, and almost immediately they began to experience a strange feeling of detachment. One by one, it seemed, their senses were being drawn away into the mist. First touch, then smell and taste and sound, and finally sight. It seemed they were becoming part of the sea, of the ship; and then they were wholly of the mist, which was swirling, not around them, but through them. They were unaware, drifting with the mist; absorbed.

How long they existed – or didn't exist – there was no way of knowing. But there came, in time, or in no time, a faint sensation of warmth on their skins. A tiny stimulus that caused them to try to move towards the source, like primitive organisms seeking light. Imperceptibly, the warmth grew, and with it, they grew, and formed, and began again to breathe and to hear and see, and finally, to feel the reality of the ship's rail through their fingertips.

A breeze caressed their faces and the sun danced on the wavetops. They were Jean and Andrew, sentient beings.

For a long time, neither of them moved or spoke. Then:

"Jean, are you all right?"

"Yes..." Hesitatingly. "Yes, I'm all right"

Her reply brought him fully to life.

"Can you hear?" he asked rhetorically. "The engines." The fast tenor of the diesels had been replaced by a slow baritone throb. He looked around. The ship's deck was different. Wider. Cleaner. Different.

"Look", he exclaimed, and pointed.

A huge paddle wheel was thrashing the water into white foam.

"My God, look!", he said again. "I know this ship. We're on the Jeannie Deans."

The deck, previously almost deserted, was crowded with passengers.

"Those people", said Jean "See how they're dressed! Like when I was a child. I had a little frock just like that when I... when I..." Her voice faltered and faded.

Andrew took a long deep breath and sucked in the sea tang. There was something else. He became aware of his heart beat, slow and powerful, like the rhythm of the ship's engine.

"Don't you feel different? Don't you feel it?" he asked Jean.

"Yes. I feel it", she replied, and as she spoke, two teenagers passed, arm in arm. "I feel... like that" she said.

And now that the initial shock had passed the strangest thing in the whole strange affair was that neither of them was afraid. They wanted to be there. They felt energy coursing through their veins. They wanted to laugh in sheer delight. And they did. Each took the hand of the other and they went down into the heart of the ship.

If confirmation was needed, it was provided by the engine room. They looked through the steel half door, smelling the sweet mixture of hot engine oil and steam and watched the shining reciprocating piston rods translating the thrust of the cylinders into the circular movement of the great paddle wheel shaft.

"It is real", said Andrew. "It really is the Jeannie Deans." I knew – know – this engine room so well.

They stood and watched for some time, then made their way back to the upper deck. As they reached the top of the last steep flight of steps, Jean stopped.

“Do you realise what we just did?” she asked rhetorically. “We ran all the way up. Ran up! And I’m not the least out of breath.”

“Neither am I”, said Andrew. “Come on. Let’s keep moving.”

They made their way along the crowded deck to the stern, where two musicians, one with a piano accordion and the other with a fiddle, were entertaining the passengers. They leaned against the rail, watching the creamy wake trailing into the distance and listening to the music as it rose and drifted where the seagulls wheeled.

“Magic”, Jean whispered. “Pure magic. I see it, but I can’t quite believe it.”

“I believe it”, said Andrew. “It’s there. And it’s wonderful. In the full meaning of the word.”

She looked at him and saw every line in his sixty-something face. Only the light in his eyes was different.

She was startled when he said, “You have the most beautiful eyes, Jean.”

One of the musicians was coming round with a velvet collecting bag. Andrew reached into his pocket and put in a coin. The man smiled and moved on.

“He didn’t notice”, said Andrew.

“Notice what?”

"The ten pence piece. I gave him a ten pence piece."

Jean giggled. "He probably thought it was two shillings. He'll think you're rich." There was a pause before she spoke again. "You'd think they would notice our clothes. We must seem very odd, dressed as we are."

But no-one gave them more than a passing glance.

"Do they see us as we are, or as we were? Are we in this now, or as we will be? As we appear to each other, or as we feel inside?"

Andrew gripped her hand tight. "Forget the introspection", he said. "Just be."

The deck was alive with passengers. People talking, people laughing. People singing to the music. People of their past that was now.

By this time the ship was abeam of Ascog, steaming into Rothesay Bay, and they watched the shore slipping by until the 'Jeannie Deans' swung round towards the pier. There was a soft judder as she nudged the heavy timbers and shortly after there was the rattle of the gangways going out.

"What shall we do first?" Andrew asked as they walked down the pier.

"You decide", said Jean.

He bought her a large ice cream cone from a man with a barrow and with their free hands linked, they walked along the sea front.

"They're all so old-fashioned", Jean commented.

"Not like us", said Andrew, smiling.

Jean looked at him. "Why are we not afraid?" she asked. "We leave Wemyss Bay in the 1990's on a car ferry and arrive in Rothesay on a paddle steamer in, I don't know... late forties, early fifties? By rights we should be scared out of our wits." She stopped walking.

"Look, Jean", said Andrew. "I don't know how or why it happened. But it has happened. We're not on drugs. We haven't had anything stronger than tea. We have apparently travelled back somewhere between forty and fifty years, yet we don't look any different, at least to each other. But I feel different. Younger and stronger. Full of life. I just want to enjoy the experience. Don't you?"

"Yes", replied Jean. "Yes I do. I feel so alive. I feel..."

"Go on", he encouraged.

She looked away momentarily, then returned his steady gaze.

"I feel very happy."

Andrew laughed joyfully. "There you are then", he said. "Race you to that lamppost."

To her utter amazement, she found herself running after him, ice cream in hand, until they both collapsed, laughing, on a bench.

"What about that then", said Andrew triumphantly. "Not only do you feel like a teenager, you're acting like one."

"So are you", she said, making a face. "Acting like one, talking like one. Anyway", she went on "I can't imagine why a teenager like me should be falling for an old man like you... Oh!" As she realised what she had said, she blushed to the roots of her hair.

Andrew just smiled and said simply, "It's mutual."

They took a tramcar to Ettrick Bay, sitting on hard sparred seats. As it clanked along to Port Bannatyne, the conductor came to collect the fares. Andrew gave him a pound note, wondering if it would be rejected as counterfeit, but "Is this the smallest you've got?" was all the man said. Andrew nodded and got two cardboard tickets, plus a ten-shilling note, three half crowns, a shilling and sixpence in change.

"It's like one of these theme parks", he said to Jean. "Except it's real."

They joined the throng of holidaymakers on the beach, they paddled in the sea and Andrew bought two double nougats. "Sixpence each", he said. "No expense spared."

An hour later they took the tram back into Rothesay where they bought two fish suppers, eating them from the paper as they walked slowly up the steep streets behind the town.

They came eventually to a lane between two fields of barley where they stood at a five-barred gate. The sun was low in the sky and a capricious breeze was chasing lively shadows across the surface of the ripening grain.

And then, quite naturally, Andrew took Jean in his arms and they clung together, each feeling a turbulent, adolescent passion, furiously, gloriously alive. It was the timeless antithesis of the mist. It was all they had and all they needed.

But like the mist, they were called back, this time not from the depths but from the mountain top, and time began to tick again.

It didn't for a moment occur to either of them that they wouldn't go back, that their place in time might be altered, that now could be other than now.

They went hand in hand down into the town out along the pier and on to the deck of the 'Jeannie Deans' which was wisping smoke from her funnels and preparing to leave.

They sailed out into the gloaming Firth, into the night and into the mist.

And they were absorbed by the mist and went back to the ending.

They awoke as the coach was nearing the end of its journey, pulling to a halt in the street, now lamplit, from where it had left in the morning.

They were last off. A fine drizzle was falling and Jean pulled her coat collar up round her neck.

"Did you notice", she asked. "When the others were getting off? We got four knowing looks and a wink."

"Just because we spent the day together?" said Andrew. "What a scandal! Come on, I'll see you home."

She had a flat on the second floor of a Victorian tenement and they were both slightly out of breath as they stood on the stone flagged landing in front of her door. Andrew was the more affected of the two.

"Quite a climb", he said and shrugged. "There was a time..."

"Oh, you get used to it. Helps to keep me fit, I suppose."

There was a slightly awkward silence, like their meeting on the coach.

Then Jean plucked up the courage to say something that had been on her mind for the last couple of hours.

"We met before, didn't we? When we were young. On the boat it began to come back to me. And on the bus – I had the feeling that you remembered too."

"I remember", said Andrew. "It was like today – a day trip to Rothesay. A long time ago. I met this girl. She had her hair curled in round her neck – what was the style called?"

"A pageboy bob", said Jean.

"...She was beautiful...full of life. I recall a day filled with sunshine and laughter. For the life of me, I don't know why we didn't arrange to meet again."

"Nor do I", Jean said. "That part has gone from my memory. Perhaps we became separated in the crowds going home."

"Perhaps", agreed Andrew. "I don't remember the journey home. Only that glorious day. But if you would agree to have dinner with me some evening, we may remember more."

"We may indeed", said Jean.

NOBODY'S PERFECT

Dr Marihuano put down the telephone and hurried through to the reception area.

"Charles", he said. "I have to go out on urgent business. I have to go now." He looked at his watch. "I have only one more patient due this afternoon. Mrs Home, at three-thirty."

"Home at three-thirty? That's a rather odd name."

Dr Marihuano's response to this was immediate irritation.

"There is nothing to be facetious about, Charles. Listen carefully. Tell Mrs Home... tell her... Apologise on my behalf. Apologise profusely.. but don't.... overdo it. Don't be obsequious. That may make her suspicious. There is nothing for her to be suspicious about. This is a genuine emergency. Be apologetic, be polite, be brief – but not too brief. Look up the book, make another appointment. That's it."

"Is the emergency really serious?" Charles asked.

"No, no. Urgent. Not serious. Troublesome perhaps. Worrying perhaps. Not serious, no, no. No, I hope not. I sincerely hope not." The doctor took off his white coat and put it over the back of a chair. "Polly won't be back from her dental appointment until after four."

Polly was the regular receptionist.

"That's OK", said Charles. "I'll be OK."

Charles was twenty-eight, but because of greying hair, looked older. He kept the place clean, made a capable if slow job of typing letters and very occasionally, like this afternoon, acted as receptionist. He was intelligent, articulate and mildly schizophrenic. The doctor had employed him as a favour to Charles' father, an old friend, but in truth, given the pittance he was paid, he had turned out to be an asset to the practice.

"Did you take your pills at lunchtime?"

"Yes. Yes, I did", Charles answered untruthfully, not wishing to add to the doctor's present worries. Shortly after the door had closed on Dr Marihuano, Charles picked up the discarded white coat and put it on. He looked at himself in the mirror, turning one shoulder forward and then the other. He frowned and shook his head. Then he produced a pair of spectacles from an inside pocket and put them on. This time his mirror image pleased him.

He smiled sweetly at it and then went through to the consulting room. He opened a drawer of a filing cabinet, which the doctor in his haste had omitted to lock and fingered his way through the files until he came to the one he wanted. He sat behind the large glass topped desk and began to read Mrs Home's case history, sometimes frowning, sometimes smiling, sometimes shaking his head. Then he returned the file to the cabinet and went back through to the reception area.

Mrs Home arrived five minutes early. She was a woman in her late thirties with auburn hair and deep set blue eyes.

Charles rose from his chair and extended his hand in greeting. "Mrs Home. How nice to meet you. But I am afraid I have regrettable news. Dr. Marihuano has been called away on urgent business – an emergency. It arose too late to contact you, so he has asked me to convey his most sincere apologies and to arrange another appointment as soon as mutually convenient." He opened the appointment book, then paused as if in thought. "Unless – unless – only if you wish it of course – you might wish to talk to me."

Mrs Home looked at him and saw a rather good-looking man in his early forties who carried with him an air of quiet assurance.

"Would you?" she asked. "I was really most anxious to speak to the therapist today... A lot on my mind, as always... Haven't I seen you somewhere before?"

"You may have seen me here. The good doctor and I have many discussions – arguments even. Not specific cases you understand – generalities." Charles beamed a smile of outrageous sincerity.

"Don't you have to know something about me? Surely you have to know my... erm... circumstances?"

"It's interesting that you make that point," Charles said. "A recent study commissioned by the Institute of Psychiatry on the effect on the patient of a sudden change of therapist showed that in fifty seven percent of cases there was an immediate improvement. The effect of a new mind on an old problem perhaps. Not", he added hurriedly, "That I see you as a patient. It may be that in truth, I am the patient and you the doctor. Each meeting of minds should benefit both participants. We can never tell in advance who may benefit more."

The pupils of Mrs Home's eyes widened so that deep blue darkened to indigo. "What an interesting notion", she said. "All right. Let's do it."

Charles opened the door to the consulting room and with a gallant sweep of an arm shepherded the lady through.

When she was seated, he produced her file from the cabinet and asked, "Do you want me to read this?"

She nodded.

He placed the file on the desk and riffled quickly through the pages, much in the manner of a conjuror with a pack of cards. The whole process took under ten seconds.

"Well now", he said. "Shall we proceed?"

Mrs Home radiated disbelief. "You couldn't possibly have read my file in that time", she said.

"I took a course of speed reading at Keele University", he said. "I came first."

The lady seemed unconvinced.

Charles clasped his hands together and placed them on top of the file.

"Tell me about the horse", he asked.

She gasped, and colour flooded into her face. "How could you possibly.... Oh dear. I'm so ashamed."

"Nothing to be ashamed of", said Charles. "The horse is a noble, not to say elegant animal. In any case, I believe the charge of kleptomania was ill-advised. Hippomania would, in my view, be a more appropriate term."

"Yes, but just riding off with it – on an impulse – when the jockey's back was turned..."

"Do you know", said Charles, leaning forward and speaking in a confidential manner, "I was once at Edinburgh Zoo and had this sudden rush of affection for a penguin. It was waddling towards me rather like a drunken toastmaster. I wanted to hide it under my coat and take it home with me – just to get it away from the awful fish they were feeding it. I didn't of course, but the impulse was very strong."

"Goodness", said Mrs Home. "How very strange."

"Not at all", said Charles. "Love – affection – in its widest sense – is the very glue of civilisation. Without it we'd be in anarchy." He paused, then asked: "Have you ever been in Anarchy, Mrs Home?"

The lady's eyebrows rose quizzically.

"I often sing that little song to myself", Charles went on.

"Which little song?"

"Roses are blooming in Anarchy", he sang softly and tunelessly.

"I think..." said Mrs Home, beginning to rise from her chair.

Charles raised a hand.

"Please. I'm sorry. I apologise. Just a little joke. I hoped to make you smile. I expect you have a wonderful smile."

Mrs Home smiled.

"There you are, you see", said Charles, smiling himself. "Quite wonderful! Thank you for that. I shall remember that smile tonight as I drift into sleep."

"You know, I think I'm feeling better already", said Mrs Home. "You really are a most unusual therapist."

"I accept your compliment gratefully", Charles said. "But I must insist that we speak as equals. Woman to man, patient to patient, philosopher to philosopher. Now, shall we begin with your problems or with mine?"

Mrs Home assumed the question to be rhetorical and gave a reprise of her smile.

"Elinor", she said.

"Elinor then... Excellent.." Charles tapped himself lightly on the chest. "Charles.. Now, let me see... You say your husband is often very distant?"

"Yes."

"And on what sort of frequency does this occur?"

"I'm not exactly sure. It varies. Probably about seven or eight times a year."

"Not all the time, then?"

"No."

"And the times when he is close... and presumably caring... that makes you happy?"

"Close and caring don't always go together. I can have problems with that."

Might it be that you prefer him to be distant?

"No, I can't say that I particularly like that either."

"These periods when he is distant. Do they last very long?"

"Sometimes only a week, sometimes much longer."

"And do you have any idea what causes this?"

"Oh, the usual with men. His work."

Charles fiddled with the folder on the desk. "You are quite sure about that?" he asked.

"Oh yes. Quite sure."

"Hmmm. And how exactly does your husband create this feeling of distance?"

"By air"

"By air?"

"Yes. That's the quickest way to Hong Kong. His company has an office there."

There was a long silence, broken eventually by Charles.

"Dr Marihuano appears to have taken a less literal interpretation of 'distant'", he said. "Didn't his line of questioning alert you to this?"

Elinor Home shook her head. "I don't recall his asking much else about it", she said. "He just made a note on his pad and changed the subject."

"What we would call leaping to a confusion", said Charles, lifting he folder from the desk. "I think we should dispense with this meantime." As he resumed his seat he said: "Let's talk about ships and shoes and sealing wax."

Elinor leaned forward in her chair. "Alice", she said in delight. "How I loved that book when I was a child."

"I still do", said Charles. "...and then, if we are in expansive mood, we can move into the area of cabbages and kings... Will you begin?"

"We? Oh dear... I can't think of anything offhand."

"Try nibbling on the little cake labelled 'eat me'" Charles suggested.

Elinor grinned, then said: "I've always had this dream of making the desert bloom..."

"Excellent", said Charles. "And have you thought of how this could be achieved?"

"Yes, I would lay two huge pipes between the Arctic and the Sahara. One would carry hot air northwards to blow on the ice, and then as the ice melted, the other would carry water southward to irrigate the desert."

Charles slapped his right hand on the desk. "What an absolutely wonderful idea", he exclaimed. "Have you mentioned this to anyone else?"

"Once to my George ... my husband."

"And what did he think about the idea?"

"He said it was quite idiotic." said Elinor

"Oh dear, how sad. I am sorry."

"He said it in such a dismissive tone. I was quite crushed."

"You misunderstand", said Charles. "My sorrow is for your husband. It must be devastating to live enclosed in walls of pragmatism. There aren't any windows. You can't see the view."

"He says I'm woolly headed and impractical."

"How blind he must be. Don't you see. The Arctic is at the top of the world. Hot air rises, so it will rise up one of your pipelines and the water will flow down the other." He said this with such authority that he almost believed it himself. "Have you ever thought much about the letter 'J?" he continued.

"The letter J?"

"Yes. If you look at the dictionary, you will find that there are about one hundred and forty pages devoted to the letter S. There are only fourteen pages of words beginning with J. I want to start a society for the promotion of words beginning with the letter J."

"I see", said Elinor doubtfully.

"Oh, I know what you're thinking. Why don't I start with words beginning with X? Alas, X is a lost cause. Only just over two pages of words, and of them, only xylophone has any chance of survival. There is for instance Xystus, a word for a covered portico said to be used by athletes for their exercises. Ask any of today's athletes if they've used their xystus recently and they'll think you're accusing them of taking drugs. Then there's xema, a genus of fork-tailed gulls. A word, according to my dictionary, arbitrarily invented in 1819. I have no doubt that it was invented by someone trying to save X words from extinction. Sad, but there it is. I shall have to leave X to its fate. But there's still a chance for J". Charles leaned back in his chair, "Joy, Juniper, Jodphurs", he recited. "Jejeune, Jubilant, Jurisprudence.. Aren't they wonderful words?"

"Jingle, Jangle, Jungle", Elinor offered. "Justice and Jubilee"

"You understand!" Charles cried. "So what we must do is attempt to introduce – invent – more J words. Lewis Carroll did it."

"Jabberwocky!" Elinor said triumphantly.

Charles clapped his hands. "Exactly", he said. "How would you get along with jonquilophile?"

"One who loves daffodils ... like me! I would be happy with that."

"Jasperology!"

"You've got me there", Elinor admitted.

"The study of opaque quartz containing clay", said Charles.

"Hmmm ... a bit abstruse, perhaps."

"You may be correct", Charles agreed. "But abstruse words are much loved by jabberers and judges who expound them in joyous juxtaposition."

"Ah now, Charles", said Elinor. "Now you are just showing off."

They went on in this vein for some time, each becoming more animated until Charles, glancing at his watch said: "I'm afraid we shall have to stop now. Time has overtaken us."

"Oh dear", said Elinor. "I was really enjoying myself."

"As I was. But to coin a cliché, all good things must come to an end. However," Charles continued, "Before we finish, I must say that I have seldom come across a more normal, well balanced individual than you. You have no need of further sessions."

"And I must say that it is a long time since I felt so happy with myself. But Dr Marihuano..."

"Dr Marihuano will have to get along without you. I suspect that he gets more out of your appointments than you do. Not that I condemn him for that. We are all motivated by self-interest."

"You mean he likes the colour of my money."

"Perhaps there is a little of that", said Charles, "but no, I think he likes the colour of your mind... and perhaps, how you smile."

Elinor blushed deeply. "Surely you don't mean....?"

"That he is attracted to you. Yes indeed. But please don't think there is anything sinister in it. He just enjoys your company... As I do."

"Aren't you being a bit unprofessional?" asked Elinor

"Goodness, no. Just completely honest. Give me your hands."

Elinor stretched her hands across the desk and Charles took them in his. "Repeat after me", said Charles. "I hereby empower myself."

"I hereby empower myself"

"To live my life as I wish it"

"To live my life as I wish it"

"To recognise the strengths in me"

"To recognise the strengths in me"

"And to forgive myself the weaknesses as I forgive the weaknesses in others"

"And to forgive myself the weaknesses as I forgive the weaknesses in others"

Charles released her hands. "That", he said. "Is psychiatry in a nutshell."

Elinor laughed.

"And just remember", he added. "I was the nut you heard it from."

"You really are a most extraordinary man", said Elinor. "And I can hardly believe the change in me over such a short period. But I've taken in all that you've said, and if you will give me a sheet of paper, an envelope and a pen, I shall leave a note for Dr Marihuano. I've decided to take your advice and be positive. Take charge of my own destiny."

"Excellent", said Charles. "But only on one condition. Do not mention me in any way. Attribute your wish to discontinue treatment to his skill and dedication. Lay it on a bit thick." He leaned across the desk and lowered his voice. "He has a rather fragile personality. A little flattery will cheer him up no end."

After she had written the note and sealed the envelope, Elinor rose and extended her hand. "How can I ever thank you", she said. "This has been a momentous day for me. I hope we shall meet again some time. Socially, of course."

"I can assure you, Mrs Home... Elinor. We shall certainly never meet in a professional situation. That is a complete certainty. I won't wish you luck. You won't need it."

They shook hands warmly and Mrs Home left, humming softly to herself. After she had gone, Charles removed the white coat and draped it carefully over the chair where Dr Marihuano had left it.

When Polly returned from her dental appointment, he was removing medical books from a shelf, dusting and replacing them in alphabetical order.

"Do you think he has ever read any of these?" Charles asked.

"Old Acid Head?" Polly replies. "No chance. He's only ever had two books of his own and he hasn't finished colouring the first one yet. Sorry", she apologised. "Very old joke... I take it he isn't in, then?"

"Had an emergency call. Shot off like a startled rabbit – a well-adjusted startled rabbit, of course."

"Of course," Polly echoed.

A few minutes later, Dr Marihuano returned. He went straight through the reception area and into his office without speaking. Charles followed after a short interval. He was sitting behind his desk looking somewhat ill at ease.

"Hmmm", he said as Charles handed him the envelope. "Resignation. Letter of. Can't stand the heat get out of the kitchen. Eh?"

Charles sighed inwardly. He almost always said this when Charles handed him an envelope. "From Mrs Home", he said.

Dr Marihuano opened it and began to read.

"Well, well", he said, obviously speaking to himself. "Dear, dear. Interesting. Interesting. Pity in a way. Excellent... Flattering. Yes, I must say. Excellent, excellent. Well, there you are then", he concluded, putting the letter down. "No use crying over spilt milk." He looked up at Charles.

"Mrs Home has decided to discontinue treatment. Considers herself fully recovered. Not too surprising. She was showing a continuing improvement. I suppose if I have a fault it is that I'm too successful for my own good, eh? How did she seem to you?"

"Very cheerful", said Charles. "She was humming a tune as she left."

"Oh?"

"I think it was from that old operetta, em, The White Horse Inn. You know.... 'Farewell, farewell, I bid you all a fond farewell'... or is it 'goodbye'?"

"I really don't know Charles, nor do I care. Now, please leave. I have to go out again almost immediately and I have some papers to gather together before I go."

Charles turned towards the door, then stopped and asked. "Your emergency case work out all right?"

Dr Marihuano looked up, seemingly startled. "What? Yes. Yes of course. As always. Difficult. But reasonable outcome. Quite reasonable under the circumstances. Yes, fairly reasonable, I did my job. Yes, I think so. Definitely. Very probably. Please go, Charles."

Charles went.

Shortly after, Dr Marihuano came bustling through to reception. "Off again", he said. "Lock up at the usual time Polly. Set alarm, etcetera, etcetera. Usual routine. Same time tomorrow. Work, work, work." The door closed behind him.

Polly raised her eyebrows. "Seems a bit uptight, even for him", she commented.

"That's what I was thinking", replied Charles. "Something to do with his emergency, perhaps."

"Perhaps. But no use wondering. We'll never know. We're just the hired help."

About fifteen minutes later, a nondescript, middle-aged man with thinning, sandy coloured hair stuck his head round the outside door.

"Dr Marihuano in?" he asked.

"He has just gone", said Polly. "Won't be back until tomorrow. Do you want to make an appointment?"

"Perhaps you can help me."

"Sorry, I'm not a doctor."

"No, no. I'm looking for information about the incident. I'm from the Evening Courier."

"What incident?" asked Polly and Charles simultaneously.

“He was trying to talk a woman down off a roof. I got a call from my office to come here and interview him. Get the background. I don't know much else, except that he failed. The woman jumped. Not badly hurt I understand. A broken bone or two. Then he disappeared. They sent me here to find him. Get the story.”

“He was called out to an emergency earlier this afternoon”, said Charles. “He came back briefly a short time ago. He seemed a bit agitated. That's all we know. He never divulges anything about his work. Not allowed to.”

The man took a notebook from his pocket. “Perhaps you can tell me a bit about him. What he's like. Background stuff.”

“Absolutely not”, said Polly. “You'll have to speak to him. I know what the papers are like. We say something, and you print something quite different.”

“Not me”, said the man. “Absolute honesty. Straight down the middle. That's me.”

“Well that's where you'd better go. Straight down the middle of the corridor outside”, said Charles. “We're saying nothing.”

The man persisted for a little longer, but eventually gave up and left.

Polly and Charles were preparing to go home when the phone rang.

Polly answered it.

“What!?” Charles heard her say. “Goodness me! No, I didn't know. No, I can't help you. I'm sorry I can't help you. No.

I've told you already." She went on in this vein for a short time until she banged the phone down in exasperation.

"What was that all about?" Charles asked.

"That was the newspaper", said Polly. "They were having another go at digging the dirt on Dr Marihuano. It seems the woman he was trying to talk down was on the roof of his own house. But that isn't the worst of it. You'll never guess who it was."

"Someone we know?"

"I'll say", said Polly. "It was his wife! I can't say I'm all that surprised. I've often wondered how she puts up with him. He's always so uptight. How his patients survive beats me. I've often thought that I could do a better job than he does." She looked at Charles. "Or you, even."

Charles laughed. "Me?" he said. "Chance would be a fine thing."

ONE TWO THREE

Robbie came down from the warmth of the coach on to the cold wet forecourt of the depot. He could see the fine drizzle falling through the pale light from the lamps. There was a thrum and smell of diesel engines. Several people walked off into the night, heads down as if defeated in some way. Robbie didn't do that. He lifted his head so that he could feel the fineness of the rain on his face. This was his rain, back home rain. Out on to the high street, walking past grey building and corners of dark shadows and puddles of pale white light. He was good at walking – and running – and throwing himself flat on the ground and firing his gun.

"You're the best, Bobby", the sergeant always said.

One, two, three. One, rifle to shoulder. Two, take aim. Three, pull the trigger. You're the best, the sergeant always said. He always shut his eyes as he pulled the trigger, but nobody knew. His boots were always shining and his buttons bright.

Walking was easy. He could walk forever.

See Jennie first. Then home to Mum and Dad. Should go home first, but never mind. They didn't think he'd be home until tomorrow. They'd be surprised to see him tonight.

Jennie was the only one who wrote him letters. Except his Mum of course. He'd known lots of girls, but they weren't interested. They'd always gone off laughing before he thought of anything to say.

Jennie wrote about all that was happening at home and he wrote back. Well, he told David what to say and David wrote it. Good letters they were. David knew what to put down and what to leave out.

As Robbie moved away from the town centre it became darker, for remnants of the blackout still lingered in the suburban streets. It didn't bother him for he was going to see Jennie and tell her he would like to marry her.

One, take off his forage cap; two, take her hand; three, tell her he loved her. One, two, three. He had practiced it often. He walked down her street, hesitated by the gate, hesitated before he rang the doorbell. Jennie's mother opened the door. She seemed surprised.

"Oh, it's you, Robbie."

"I'm back. I'm not going away again. Is Jennie in?"

"No." Her voice was flat, like the look on her face.

"I want to talk to her."

"Well you can't. She's not in. You'll have to come back later." The door began to close. He wanted to say something, but he couldn't think what.

"Good night", he said as the door shut tight.

He went towards the beach and walked along the damp deserted promenade. No light except the far-off twinkle from a few windows across the bay. A light breeze was blowing, sending small waves slapping against the sea wall.

He began speaking to himself. "One", he said. "Jennie's not home. Two, I don't know where she is. Three, keep walking."

He kept on walking right to the end of the promenade. Then he turned and started walking back. He wished he could think of what to do next. He enjoyed walking, but it wasn't helping him to think.

A patch of light caught his eye and he altered course without conscious thought and began walking towards it, attracted as a moth by a candle. As he drew near, he saw a long Nissen hut with big double doors at the front thrown open. There was the sound of music and of voices and laughter.

Robbie was approaching from the side and he could see a man leaning against the back of the opened door smoking a cigarette. As Robbie approached, the man looked up.

"Hello lad", he said. "You look a bit lost."

"No," replied Robbie. "I know where I am."

"Going inside, then?" the man asked.

"I don't know", Robbie replied. "What is it, inside?"

"I thought you said you knew where you were."

"I do know. That thing shouldn't be there. It's right in front of the town hall."

"Smart lad", said the man. "Been away for a long time?"

Robbie looked at his watch. "Nearly two years", he said slowly. He shook his hand and wrist and held the watch to his ear. At that moment, the town hall clock began to chime. Robbie stood, his head nodding to each stroke of the bell. The man watched him, blowing cigarette smoke and saying nothing.

The clock stopped chiming. “Ten o’clock”, said Robbie and adjusted the hand of his watch. “It doesn’t work very well”, he said.

“It’s a homecoming dance for you lads”, said the man. “You’ll get a couple of free pints, and sandwiches and sausage rolls.”

Robbie became aware that he was hungry. “I’ll go in”, he said.

“Free”, said the man. “No charge.”

Robbie went round the door and into the light and waves of heat and the smell of beer and perfume and sweat and damp wood. He screwed his eyes against the glare. Up one step and onto a wooden floor. At the far end, beyond the shuffling and bobbing, a band was playing. A piano, a fiddle and an accordion. Black suits and white shirts. Proper musicians. There were seats all around the walls, with hardly anyone sitting. On the left were trestle tables set with food and drink. Robbie walked carefully along between the people dancing and the edges of the seats.

“Could I have something to eat, please?” he asked.

A middle-aged woman in a green uniform smiled at him.

“Help yourself, dearie”, she said.

Robbie took a bottle of beer and loaded four egg sandwiches and two sausage rolls carefully onto a paper plate.

“Hungry?” commented the woman, still smiling.

“Yes”, said Robbie.

He made his way carefully to one of the seats, sat down and began to eat. He was really hungry, and the food was good.

Soon it was finished but he was still hungry. He placed the bottle of beer carefully on the floor and went back to the tables. He stood, shifting from one foot to the other until the same woman said: "Don't wait to be asked, dearie. Just take what you want."

Robbie took another three sausage rolls and went back to his seat. He ate two of the sausage rolls and then the music stopped, there was clapping, and people began to sit down beside him.

He was happy and wanted to talk to someone, but before he could think what to say the music started again and he was left sitting on his own. He finished his beer and went back for another.

"All right dear?" asked the woman in the green uniform.

"Yes thanks", said Robbie and went back to his seat. He watched them all dancing and thought of him and Jennie dancing, except he couldn't dance. He didn't know how. It looked good fun. Everyone was smiling as they danced. He smiled at their smiles and sipped his beer.

The band was playing Twelfth Street Rag. He had heard it before and he remembered the name. Twelfth Street Rag. He began to rum te tum to the music and tap his feet. It was hard not to tap your feet. Rum te tum te tum tum. They were all swishing about fast, holding each other close. He drank his beer and thought what a happy place this was. He sat back in his hard chair and closed his eyes, listening to the music. He raised the beer bottle to his lips and took another long swig. He could do that. Lift the bottle to his lips with his eyes closed. It would be nice to dance with Jennie if she was here and if he knew how. The thought had just left his mind when there she was, running across the dance floor towards him.

"Robbie! You're home!" She wrapped her arms around him and gave him a hug and Robbie was just thinking about hugging her back, when she stepped back, looking at him. "It's so nice to see you again."

Robbie smiled, feeling really happy to have found her. She was so pretty. Her eyes were alive and dancing as if the music was still playing.

"Robbie, this is George."

There was a tall man beside her in Air Force uniform.

"He's a pilot", he said.

The man offered his hand and Robbie took it, pumping vigorously up and down. Then he let go and there was a silence.

"He's a special friend", said Jennie.

"Like me", said Robbie.

"Yes. Sort of."

Sort of wasn't as good as. Robbie smiled at Jennie and then at George.

"I've had six sausage rolls", he said.

They both laughed as if it was some sort of joke.

The music started again, and Jennie gave a quick glance at George, then turned to Robbie and asked "Would you like to dance with me?"

Of course he would. Of course.

"I don't know how", he said.

"It's easy", said Jennie. "Come on, I'll show you."

George didn't seem bothered.

"Arm across my shoulder. That's it. Now. One two three, one two three. You'll get the hang of it."

Robbie's head was going one two three, but his feet weren't listening. He didn't care. Here was Jennie close to him and smiling like in his dreams. They stumbled. One two three.

"I've got all your letters", Robbie said.

"And I've got all of yours. They were really nice letters."

One two three. One two three.

"What kind of dance is this?"

"A modern waltz."

One two three, one two three. Jennie gave a little cry and hopped on one foot.

"You'll get the hang of it", she said.

"I went to your house and you weren't in. Your mother was in."

"When did you get back?"

"About seven o'clock."

"Tonight?"

"Yes. I went round to your house."

"Slide your feet Robbie. You don't have to pick them up as if you were walking. Listen to the beat. One two three. One two three. That's it. You nearly got it then."

Robbie swallowed and tried hard to concentrate.

"I love you Jennie", he said.

A look of surprise came into her eyes.

"Oh, Robbie." That was all she said.

One two three, one two three. They bumped into another couple. "Sorry." One two three. Robbie's head was hurting.

"Do you want to stop?"

"Yes please, Jennie, it's too hard."

They wound their way back to the seats through the dancing and the music.

George was standing waiting.

"That didn't take long", he said.

"No", said Jennie.

"My head's hurting", said Robbie.

George said, "I'll get you a beer."

"So what are you going to do now you're back?" asked Jennie.

"Don't know. Stay with Mum and Dad first."

Smiling, Jennie took his hand. "You'll be all right", she said.

When George came back with the beer, Jennie stood up.

"We'll have to be going now, Robbie'.

George looked surprised.

'Will we?' he asked.

Jennie bent down and kissed Robbie on the cheek.

"Look after yourself Robbie", she said quietly. Then she took George by the hand and they went off through the dancers.

Robbie shut his eyes tight, lifted the beer to his lips and listened to the music and the shuffling feet.

When you listened carefully, it was quite sad music. One two three, one two three.

PENALTY

Jimmy clattered noisily up the stair, listening intently as he went to the echo of his footsteps, trying to merge the sound of each step with the echo of the preceding one. As he passed the first landing, he danced a little jig on the worn stone flags, then with a sudden burst of energy took the next flight two at a time. He arrived at his own door, lifted the letter box and shouted:

"Mum, it's me! Is the dinner ready?"

His mother heard his call and came from the kitchen smiling to herself. The smile vanished as she opened the door.

"How often have I told you not to shout through the letter box? Come in before I clout you."

Jimmy, who could judge her mood with accuracy knew she wasn't really angry, but he lowered his eyelids and said. "Sorry Mum. Is the dinner ready?"

"If you are so anxious to get to the match you should have been in earlier!"

'It's funny,' thought Jimmy, 'how grown-ups never answer a question straight out. They always have to say something about your hair being untidy or your nails being dirty or something.' But he knew that his dinner was ready. His mother's voice would have had a keener edge if it hadn't been.

He threw his jacket over a chair, went over to the sink and started washing his hands.

"And your wrists," called his mother from the cooker. He rubbed the fronts of his wrists on his wet hands and then on to the towel.

"Sandy Gray's back at the outside right," he said. "Thank goodness. That reserve they had was hopeless."

"Watch you don't burn your mouth," said his mother, putting a plate of steaming soup on the table.

He took his meal almost without tasting it, his mind already in the stadium, imagining the goals his team would score. They had to win this one he thought. Rovers were sixth from the top of the league and today's opposition were near the bottom and besides, hadn't won any of their last six away games. If Rovers won and the top five teams all lost, they'd be third top and within striking distance of the league leaders.

It was all terrifically exciting, for in all the years Jimmy had supported them they had never been higher than the middle of the league. He knew that the team they had now were the best they'd ever had and that the best player in the team was Dave Thomson, the outside left. Dave was Jimmy's hero. An almost God-like figure who could turn on a defence and cut it to ribbons with a couple of body swerves and a perfect pass.

A dozen or so pictures of him in action were pinned on the bedroom wall, and in a scrapbook was a dossier complete even to the size of his boots. Indeed, Jimmy knew enough about him to be able to persuade many of his school mates that he and Dave were in regular contact – friends almost.

He lifted the five pound note that his mother had laid on the table, and draped his scarf around his neck.

"Ok. Mum, I'm away then."

His mother's "Be careful" was cut in half by the banging of the front door. At the end of the street he joined a trickle of men and boys walking towards the football ground; a trickle that became a stream and finally a broad river, dammed up in front of the turnstiles.

He pushed his way towards the boy's gate and listened impatiently as each click let someone into the ground.

At last after waiting for hours it seemed, he thrust his warm five pound note through the hole in the wire grille and got a few cold, impersonal coins in exchange, the pressure he was exerting on the turnstiles at last yielded movement, and he was in.

He ran up the steep slope and stood for a moment at the top of the terracing, taking in the familiar scene. The green oblong of turf, neatly lined off, the white goalposts with their nets and the semi-circle of bare earth bearing witness to goalmouth frenzy, the fluttering corner flags; all seemed to be waiting expectantly like him, for the kick-off.

There was added delight today, for he saw that the television cameras were set up, the main one high on a scaffolding, just behind where he normally stood. This was great, because of course it meant that he could watch the Rovers' victory again in the evening. The broad steps that went down between the sections of terracing had to be taken in a loping run, for if Jimmy walked he found that one stride wasn't big enough and two were too much; so that the only comfortable way was to run with long strides.

He was soon in his favourite place, right down beside the low wall dividing the terracing from the running track that went all round the ground. He positioned himself near the end of the left touchline so that he would have a good view of the goalmouth and of course, Dave Thomson, who made the left wing the most exciting area of the pitch.

He put his hand in his pocket and took out one of his sweets. He waited more patiently now for the kick off, for it was enough for the moment to be inside the ground and to feel the excitement grow with the crowd. Gradually the wall beside him was occupied by other boys of his own age, most of whom he knew from school. Some, like himself, just stood leaning with their elbows on the wall. Others jostled and occasionally wrestled with one another for a better place. Some, to the delight of all, would shout a rude remark at the back of one of the half dozen policemen who were slowly patrolling the track. Not that any of the policemen paid any attention, but it was all part of the game. From where Jimmy stood he couldn't see the tunnel where the players emerged, but he watched and waited patiently for the signs. First of all there was a faint murmuring from the crowd in the enclosure opposite the stand. Then the ball boys appeared and after a short interval, the visiting team ran out to thin cheers from their supporters and some cat calls from the local boys.

Another short delay preceded roars of approval from the enclosure and heralded the arrival of the scarlet and white Rovers.

The game was scarcely fifteen minutes under way when Jimmy realised that it wasn't going to be an easy victory after all. The play surged from end to end, as first the Rovers and then United came near to scoring. Half time came and went with neither side getting the upper hand, but now that the teams had changed ends, Dave Thomson was close at hand and things seemed brighter.

"Davey, Dav-ey," chanted Jimmy as his hero beat the right half and sent an inch perfect pass to the centre forward.

"Easy, eas-y!" chanted the crowd as the centre forward's thundering shot singed the top of the cross bar.

But it wasn't easy. Time and time again Rovers crowded United's goalmouth, but the goal would not come.

Then, about ten minutes from time, Dave Thomson collected a pass from his centre back, gathered it on the run, moved past a midfield player as if he wasn't there, beat the back with a contemptuous body swerve and was in the clear, heading towards the goalmouth.

Another United player, spotting the danger, ran in from the far side of the field, but it seemed he could be too late to catch Dave, who was now inside the penalty area and gathering himself for a shot. But the defender, coming from behind, threw in a final desperate tackle, missing the ball, but catching Dave Thomson's ankle.

Jimmy, who had the cry of 'goal' welling up inside him, became almost apoplectic.

"Penalty!" he screamed in unison with a thousand voices as his hero crashed painfully to the ground.

The confusion reigned, for Dave Thomson picked himself up almost immediately and swung an angry punch at the face of the man who had brought him down.

Jimmy couldn't see what happened for a time after that, for the combatants were surrounded by their team mates dragging them apart.

When finally, order was restored, Jimmy discovered to his horror that Dave Thomson was being ordered off. The player's protestations were being ignored by the referee, who stood imperiously, one hand holding aloft a red card, the other pointing to the dressing room.

"No, Ref. No!" shrieked Jimmy, sick with frustration.

But he had to go off. Everyone, even Jimmy, knew it. It just seemed so unfair. The man who had started the trouble was getting off with a yellow card and Dave was having to take the long walk back to the tunnel.

Then Jimmy, who was sharing every minute of his hero's torment, did something he had never done before.

As the dejected red and white clad figure approached the near touchline Jimmy jumped the wall, dodged the sudden grasping hands of a policeman and ran towards Dave Thomson. He didn't even think of what he was going to say or do, he just desperately wanted to convey something of his depth of feeling. As he ran, he heard the policeman running after him, but he didn't care. If he could only get there first!

The player looked round just as the boy was almost upon him.

"Dave..."

Dave Thomson's hand came up flat and fended the boy off.

"Get lost, son!" he said angrily and walked on.

Jimmy screwed his eyes tight shut to stem the sudden humiliating tears.

"Come on lad," said the policeman as he led him back to the terracing.

"Get back to where you belong. Look! McKay's taking the penalty."

But Jimmy didn't look. Nor did he hear the roar when the ball hit the back of the net. He made his way up the terracing and out of the ground, all the while trying to understand what had happened. It hadn't occurred to him that Dave would not want to know how he felt. Suddenly he hated Dave Thomson. He would never go to see him or the Rovers again. He thought of how he would pull all of Dave Thomson's pictures off the wall one by one and burn them along with his once treasured scrapbook. As he climbed the stairs towards his front door his feelings finally found expression.

"Big fairy!" he shouted to the walls. The echo, blurred and distorted shouted the words back as he rang his doorbell.

"Jimmy!" said his mother as she opened the door. "What on earth's the matter?"

He sensed that she was about to put her arm about him.

"Nothing!" he shouted. Pushing her away, he ran to his room and slammed the door behind him. His mother sighed, shook her head and went back towards the kitchen.

"That boy," she said to her husband. "Sometimes I don't know what to make of him."

Inside his bedroom, Jimmy stood glowering at the gallery of pictures on the wall. But he didn't, as he intended, tear them up. Angry as he was, he couldn't bring himself to do it.

It was only when his father switched on the sports programme later in the evening that he remembered about the presence of the TV cameras at the match. The excerpts shown were, of course, the most exciting ones, and despite his mood he became absorbed again in the events of the afternoon. Then the action leading up to the penalty was on the screen.... The foul, the punch, the ordering off. And then to Jimmy's absolute horror, the camera began following Dave Thomson as he made his lonely way back to the touchline. The possibility that his humiliation would be shown to all the world had never occurred to him. If his parents, his pals, saw what had happened, he would never be able to hold up his head again.

"Surely, they won't..." But they did. As Dave approached the touchline, into camera range came Jimmy, running hard, scarf flying behind him.

Jimmy shot out of his chair, as if jabbed by a pin. His first impulse was to run to his bedroom, but instead he stood transfixed, watching his figure on the screen.

"You little Devil!" he heard his father gasp.

Into view, in long shot, came the policeman, about five strides back. Jimmy's arm was seen coming up as if to embrace the player, then just as Dave Thomson turned towards the boy, the policeman's bulk blocked out the view, a heartbeat before the hurtful push. Miraculously, the image left in the mind was of mutual commiseration between player and admirer. Jimmy's spirits soared. He had been on the telly. Everyone would have seen him with Dave Thomson. He gave a quick glance towards his father who was looking at him with the kind of expression that asks silently for an explanation.

"Did you see me and Dave Thomson, Dad," he said, excitedly. "I bet you don't know what he said to me?"

And before he met his pals tomorrow, he would have an even better story.

PENSIONERS CLOSE

The wee tenement, also known as Pensioners' Close, was stuck on the end of the long grey sandstone block like the full stop on the end of a sentence. No-one knew how it had come to be, for it was quite unique. Some said that the Victorian builder had run out of stone or money, some that he had had material left over. Whatever the reason, a single storey tenement allowed the tenants many of the advantages of tenement life, with few of the disadvantages. Obviously, there were no stairs to climb, and because there were no stairs to climb, there were no noisy parties overhead; there was no chance of someone else's burst pipe bringing down your ceiling; and above all there was no regiment of muddy feet tramping through the close to reach the upper flats. It was this last that mattered most to three of the tenants and it was this also that was the root cause of the brief unpleasantness.

There were four eponymous occupants; three widows and a widower. For the most part they got on well together, the character of each adding to the sum of collective harmony.

Front right was Lizzie McIvor. Lizzie was a large, sturdily built woman who liked 'to keep her eye on things'. It was she who spearheaded petitions and complaints to the factor regarding potential improvements and maintenance of the property. It was she also who took upon herself the duties of chasing away noisy children and of preventing them from chalking the walls.

The flat behind Lizzie was occupied by Hughie Sim. Having been a joiner to trade and remaining a handyman by nature, he attended to all the minor jobs outwith the responsibility of the factor. As Lizzie was once heard to remark: 'It's better than havin' to get a man in.' He also had a plot, or allotment, which provided the close with fresh vegetables through a large part of the year. Hughie kept more to himself than did the ladies, preferring television to conversation, scorning 'standin' all day bletherin 'aboot nothin', and refusing the majority of invitations to 'come in for a wee cup of tea'. In truth, he was addicted to the 'box', it and his allotment being the boundaries of his life, except for a once-weekly and normally brief outing to the 'Station Bar' on pension day.

Opposite Hughie, on the left of the close, and like him overlooking the back court, lived Meg Simpson. In temperament and in appearance, Meg was the South Pole to Lizzie's north; small and softly rounded; a diplomat who often had to work hard at reconciling opposing views, particularly between Hughie and Lizzie. Meg had a soft spot for Hughie. Had they been forty years younger, she might have been prepared to think that she fancied him, but now the only thought she would allow was that, being a man, he needed looking after.

The last tenant, who lived front left opposite Lizzie, was Ina Blair. She was small, like Meg, but thin, with big short-sighted eyes that seemed even bigger behind her strong spectacles. Ina was the gatherer of local news. She had a nose for it and it was often said that she knew what was happening before it actually happened. There was nothing malicious about her. It was just that she had an insatiable desire to know what was going on and a compulsion to tell others about it.

One thing that the three ladies had in common was a fierce pride in the appearance of the close. It was by far the cleanest close in the neighbourhood. As was common practice, each took a week in turn; but whilst other closes were cleaned only once a week, Lizzie, Ina or Meg, whichever was responsible, made sure that her close was up to the mark at all time, giving it a 'wee touch up' whenever necessary.

Hughie, however, was more bohemian by nature, as a quick glimpse at his flat would have confirmed. Although he was wise enough never to say it, the constant attention given to the close irritated him and he would have been content to have it swabbed down with a bucket of water once a month if it was really required. Long ago, the women had mutually agreed that it wasn't worth letting appearances deteriorate under Hughie's administration and had decided to exclude him from the rota on the basis that it would cause them less work.

This suited Hughie and he was sensible enough to respect their attitude. When he returned from working at his allotment, he would take himself and his muddy boots via a gap in the back-court fence and come in by the rear entrance to the close, which was only a few steps from his door. And so even Hughie contributed his part, if only in a negative way, and life went on unruffled until the day that Ina Blair left to visit her daughter in Canada for three months.

Lizzie and Meg had been out at the close mouth seeing Ina into the taxi and had been joined at the last minute by Hughie who was self-conscious about conspicuously waving people away to Canada, or anywhere.

After the taxi had moved away and they had turned to go back indoors, Hughie made the light hearted but insensitive remark that triggered off the conflict.

"Well," he said, smiling, "That's wan set o' feet less tae dirty yer close. Of course, its wan set o' hands less tae wash it. The pair o' ye will need to watch the place doesny get a bad name the week it isny done."

So saying, he made his way to his flat, quite unaware of the effect his witticism had made on Lizzie.

"Did ye hear that!" she exploded to Meg. "Oor close! Oor close indeed! Ah'll gie him oor close! It's no thanks to him the place doesn't get a bad name!"

"Lizzie, Lizzie," Meg said soothingly, opening the door to her flat. "It was only a bit of a joke. You know what he's like. Come on in and have a cup of tea."

"Ah know fine what he's like," replied Lizzie, still fizzing. "He's never cleaned the close all the years he's lived here, and he hasn't got the decency to offer to take Ina's turn. Ah'm no'one to make a fuss, but he's damn well no' goin tae get away with it."

Meg, who was by now filling the kettle, tried to calm her down.

"We all agreed it wouldn't be worth the bother getting Hughie to take his turn," she said. "Anyway, I quite like cleaning the close. It gives me a lot of pleasure when it's done. Surely we'll manage it together for the wee while Ina's away."

"It's the principle o' the thing, "Lizzie retorted stubbornly. "He lives in the close. He should take his turn."

"I would be ashamed to have a man cleaning the close," said Meg.

"Ashamed!?" Lizzie's voice rose. "Ashamed!? Why should a man no' wash the close? Tell me that. This isny oor mothers' days. What aboot wimmen's lib?"

"Ach, Lizzie. Wimmen's lib is just for young lassies without much sense. And anyway, he would just make an awful mess. Come on, we'll have a cup of tea and some buttered scones and think about it."

"There's nae point butterin scones. Nor me neither! They young lassies aren't so daft. No. My mind's made up! Hughie Sim will huv tae take his turn or ah'll sort him out, good and proper! Ah'm away to tell him right now!"

"Lizzie," pleaded Meg. "Wait and have your cup of tea. There's no good having a row on an empty stomach."

"No, Meg. Mah mind's made up!" Lizzie raised a finger in admonition. "And Ah'll tell you something else! If I catch you doin' it for him, you'll hae my turn tae do and all!" So saying, off she went, slamming Meg's door behind her.

Hughie was watching a boxing match when the doorbell rang. He gave a sigh of resignation and reluctantly pushed himself out of his armchair.

He walked slowly towards the door, his eyes still on the TV.

"Ah wid like a word wi' ye Hughie," said Lizzie, when he opened the door.

"Aye, aye," Hughie replied absently, starting back towards his armchair.

Lizzie followed him into the room, her purpose momentarily deflected as she took in the newspapers scattered on the floor and the pile of unwashed dishes in the sink in front of the window.

"Sit doon. Sit doon," said Hughie, making a vague gesture towards a chair which was draped in what looked like last week's underwear.

"No thanks," said Lizzie sharply. "Whit ah've got tae say'll no' take long."

"Aye, aye. Good, good," said Hughie, his attention still with the boxing. Lizzie crossed her arms and glared at him.

"Meg and I would like ye tae take Ina's turn at the close," she said with only partial trust and with, for her, great restraint.

"Is that so?" Hughie responded absentmindedly, his eyes on the television set.

Lizzie's temper, never strong, broke.

"Are ye listenin' Hughie Sim," she roared. "Ah'm saying' that-you've-got-tae-take-Ina's-turn-at-the-close!"

The message that she had something important to say finally got home to Hughie, somewhere between a short jab and a left hook. Startled, he stood up and faced Lizzie.

"Goad almighty!" he retorted. "Ye're aye shoutin' at somebody, aren't ye. Ye get mair like mah auld sergeant-major every day!"

"Well,!! Are ye or aren't ye?!"

"Ah'm ah or ahm'nt ah whit?"

The veins were standing out on Lizzie's neck by this time and her face was an unpleasant shade of puce. She took a deep breath.

"Are – ye – goin - tae – take – Ina's – turn – at – the – close?!"

Hughie's eyes widened and, demonstrating a courage few would have thought he possessed, pushed his head forward so that he was staring her right in the eyes.

"Naw!" he said.

Lizzie blinked. "Naw?!"

"Naw!" Hughie repeated. "Ah've never washed a close in mah life, and ah'm no' startin' now!"

Lizzie didn't shrink from the eyeball to eyeball confrontation. "Ye've never washed a dish or a semmit either, by the looks o' things," she retorted. "But ah'm tellin' you this! Either ye take your turn o' the close, or ah'm goin' tae the factor!"

"What's he got tae dae wi'it? He'll no' wash the close for ye."

Lizzie took a step back and waved a finger under Hughie's nose. "Don't you worry. He'll soon pit yer gas at a peep! It's in the lease that anyone wae a door tae the close has got tae take a turn at cleanin' it."

Hughie forced his face into a grin. "He canny get me for that," he said, "Ah clean mah door regular."

That was enough for Lizzie. She retreated, or at least, made a fighting withdrawal. She opened the door, and turning, shouted. "Ah'm tellin ye, Hughie Sim! If ye use the close, ye help tae clean it. Either that or ah'll see ya get pit oot on yer ear!" So saying, she slammed her second door that day, completing the treble a few moments later when she went into her own flat.

Meg, who was having her cup of tea and buttered scone, flinched and sighed when she heard the doors bang, but determined not to become involved, at least not for the moment.

It was about half past ten the following morning when the sounds of hammering began. Meg and Lizzie opened their doors almost simultaneously and looked at each other questioningly.

Meg nodded towards Hughie's flat. "It's coming from there," she said.

Lizzie, never slow on decision, marched forward and rang the bell.

The hammering stopped and there was silence for some seconds.

"Whit is it?" Hughie's voice was muffled behind the door.

"That's whit we would like to know," Lizzie shouted.

"It's nane o' your business," came the reply.

Meg moved forward. "All that noise gave me a fright, Hughie. Can you not tell us what you're doing?"

"Ask Lizzie McIvor," came the reply. "She started it."

Meg and Lizzie exchanged glances. Lizzie shrugged. "Ah don't know what he's talkin about," she complained.

Meg crouched down and pushed open the letter box. "Open the door, Hughie, so we can talk properly."

"Ah canny open the door." Ah'm nailin' it up."

Lizzie snorted. "The auld fool's taken leave of his senses."

"No he hasny," came Hughie's voice. "You tell't me that if ah used the close, ah had tae wash it. Well, ah'm nailing up the door so a canny use the close. And if ah canny use the close, naebody can make me wash it."

Meg was still crouched by the letter box. "But Hughie," she asked. "How are you going to get in and out?"

"Through the window of course," replied Hughie, and the sound of hammering resumed.

Almost for the first time in her life, Lizzie was rendered speechless, and the two women retired to her flat to discuss this bizarre development.

Once inside, Lizzie said: "Ah think he should be locked up. He's gone too far this time."

Meg's main desire was to prevent the situation escalating any further.

"He may be right, you know Lizzie," she said.

"Rubbish," was the retort. "There's bound to be something in the lease about nailin' up doors."

"I doubt it," said Meg. "It's hardly a thing anyone would think of."

"Well, ah think we should report him to the polis. Let them sort it oot."

"I don't think the police could do anything. He's not committing a breach of the peace inside his own house. And even if they could, do you really want the police round? The story would be everywhere. We'd never live it down."

Lizzie considered this in silence, then eventually said "Maybe you're right Meg. But we canny leave things the way they are."

"Why not?" Meg countered. "It's not causing us any inconvenience. It's not us that'll have to climb in and out our window."

"The neighbours'll find out whit's goin' on and we'll be a laughing stock," said Lizzie.

"Hughie won't say anything and neither will we. I think we should let it be for a while. He'll soon get fed up of the idea."

"Ay, well. Maybe you're right," said Lizzie reluctantly. "But he's no goin' tae get away with it. Ah'll sort him oot eventually."

Privately, Meg didn't really think that letting the situation drag on was a very good idea, but she couldn't think of a way to resolve it quickly. So the two women agreed that in the meantime, they would pretend that nothing had happened.

Inside his flat, Hughie opened a can of beer and switched on his television set. There was an open university programme on. It was entitled 'Sociology: Living with your neighbours.' He wondered if there would be anything mentioned about washing closes.

And so a nervous stalemate obtained in Pensioners' Close. It lasted just under a week; until the following Thursday, the day that Hughie made his weekly foray to collect his pension and visit the Station Bar.

He returned to his flat in the faint afterglow of two pints of best, happy with his lot and with the comforting recollection that had been his constant companion since the event, of having bested Lizzie. He eased up the window and crawled in, successfully avoiding the dishes in the sink.

'Time for the last race,' he thought, and went to switch on the television.

For a moment he thought he was in the wrong house. There was no television set. He looked wildly round the room; even, in desperation, peering under the table. There was no television set. He collapsed into his armchair. "Oh, my goad," he said aloud. "Somebody's pinched it." He looked round the room again, to see if anything else was missing. Not that there was anything else worth taking except for the clock he had been presented with when he retired. The clock was still in its accustomed place on the mantlepiece.

'Serves me right for havin' tae leave the windae open,' he thought ruefully. 'Lizzie McIvor's going tae laugh her heid aff when she hears aboot this.' He thought of going to the police, but quickly decided against it on the grounds that it might raise other problems.

About two hours later, just as darkness was falling, Meg heard a knock on her window. Startled, she turned and could just make out Hughie's face in the fading light.

"It's me. Hughie," he called. "Can ah hae a word?"

"Come round to the door, then."

"Whit aboot Lizzie? Ah'm no' wantin' her to catch me in the close."

Meg suppressed a smile. He was like an unruly schoolboy trying to avoid retribution.

"Lizzie won't see you. She'll be at her tea. On you go. I'll open the door."

Meg opened the door and he sidled in. Then as she made the inevitable cup of tea, Hughie told her of the disaster that had befallen him.

"Oh, my goodness, Hughie," said Meg. "And you so fond of your television."

"Ay. And it's comin' intae winter. It's no sae bad when ah've got the plot tae work at, but ah don't know whit ah'll dae wi masel' in the winter. Ach! Ah suppose ah asked for it, haein' tae leave the windie open. But it'll be a terrible miss. Ah huvny even got a wireless."

"I don't suppose you can afford another one. Or hire one?"

"No' really. Ah've only got a few pounds comin in from mah company pension on top of the old age pension. Ah'm no' poor enough fur the social and no' rich enough tae buy wan. Ah wis never wan fur savin' money. Ah'll need tae go and think aboot whit ah could cut oot so a could pay wan up." Hughie sighed and peered into space, imagining a televisionless future.

Meg poured two cups of tea and sat down across the table from him. There was a long silence, eventually broken by Meg.

"Hughie," she said thoughtfully. "I would like to suggest something. I just don't want you to be annoyed."

"Suggest away," replied Hughie, hope appearing on his face.

"The thing is," said Meg. "I hardly ever watch television. What if I gave you mine ..."

"Oh, naw. Naw Meg. Ah'm no' havin' that. It's real decent of ye tae offer, but ah couldny take yer TV." As he spoke, he was finding it difficult to believe that anyone with a television set would hardly ever watch it.

"I listen to the wireless most of the time," Meg continued. "There are very few programmes on TV I would want to watch. There's far too much violence and sport and stuff I'm not interested in. I prefer my wireless. Anyway," and here she reached out and touched the back of Hughie's hand. "If there was something on that I really keen to see, you would maybe let me come in and watch it with you."

Hughie looked at the kindly brown eyes looking softly into his. 'She's really an' awfy nice wee buddy,' he thought. Aloud he said "Naw, naw, Meg. Ah couldny ....."

With consummate timing, Meg withdrew her hand and looked hurt.

"Meg. Meg!" said Hughie, jumping into the trap. "Ah don't mean ah wouldny want ye in tae watch the telly with me. Ah meant ah couldny take it. It wouldny be right."

Meg pressed home her advantage. "I wouldn't have offered if I hadn't thought it over," she said. "It would really please me if I thought it was being properly used. I often think it's an awful waste it sitting there doing nothing most of the time."

Hughie was weakening. "Ah couldny take it for nothing," he said. "Ah would have to give ye something for it."

"Well, if that would please you," said Meg. "I'm sure we could come to some sort of arrangement."

"Jist you say what ye want. Ye would maybe huv tae get it in Installments, but ...."

"I don't want money, Hughie. But there is something you could do for me."

Hughie's mind immediately leapt to the wrong conclusion. He looked round the room thinking painting and papering. "Anything ye want. Jist name it."

There was a brief silence before Meg said: "It would make me very happy if you would take Ina's turn at the close. It's only for a month or two. You would only have to do it four or five times. And then you can open your door and sneck your window."

The trap was closed with Hughie in it. Fortunately, his character was in one respect similar to Meg's – anything for a quiet life. And he did have a sense of humour. After a short pause, his face wrinkled into a smile and he said: "Ye're an awfy woman, Meg Simpson. But aw right. It's a deal."

The delight on Meg's face pleased him more than he had expected.

"Meg," he began, then hesitated.

"Yes, Hughie?"

"How are we going to get your set intae mah flat? It's quite a big one."

"We'll just need to take it through the windows," said Meg. "It's dark now, and if we're careful, Lizzie won't know anything about it."

Hughie was relieved. That had been the real point of the question.

"Right then," he said. "Are ye quite sure aboot givin' it tae me?"

Meg nodded, and between them they managed to manoeuvre the set through Meg's window. Then, having slipped quietly out of her door and into the back court she balanced the set on Hughie's windowsill while he climbed in. You'll have to move your dishes," she hissed.

Hughie nodded and did as she suggested, then pulled the set through the window. She waited a few moments before Hughie reappeared to give her a conspiratorial thumbs up. She smiled in return and made her way stealthily back to her flat.

The next morning, to the accompaniment of the sound of nails being drawn from wood, Meg went to Lizzie's to tell her the news.

"Ye see, Meg," said Lizzie. "All ye've got tae do is tell them what's what and stand firm. Huh! Men!" The contempt in her voice was tinged with triumph.

"Please, Lizzie," Meg pleaded. "Don't be crowing over him or making funny remarks. You'll just start him all over again."

"Crowin'? Me? Ye know ah'm no like that. And tae tell ye the truth, ah'm no that keen on him washin' the close anyway. Ah can jist see the sort o'mess he'll make of it. It wis jist the principle o' the thing. Ah'll maybe tell him no' tae bother."

"You'll do no such thing"" snapped Meg. Lizzie was taken aback by the unexpected sharpness in her voice. "It was you that forced him into it in the first place."

Lizzie sighed. "Aye, all right Meg. Ah'll leave it be."

As Meg turned to go, Lizzie enquired: "Are ye all right. Ye're awful stiff looking."

"I've just hurt my back a little. I must have strained it lifting something."

"Ah hope," said Lizzie with a smile on her face. "That ye're not goin' to need Hughie to do your turn o' the close and a'."

Meg returned the smile. “No, I don’t think it’s as bad as that.”

That evening after Meg had finished her tea and washed the dishes, she made her way to an object covered with old curtain material in the corner of the room. She removed the cloth, switched on Hughie’s television set and settled down to watch Coronation Street in a mood composed in equal parts of contentment and guilt.

SPACE

Albert Armstrong, works foreman of Cameron Engineering had just locked the main workshop doors and put off the lights. As he entered the office block, John Cameron, who owned the company was coming along the corridor.

"Everything in order then, Albert?" Cameron asked.

"Yes Mr Cameron," Albert replied. "Except... have you seen young Davie?"

"Davie?" inquired Cameron

"Aye, young Davie the apprentice. I haven't seen him since I sent him in here to shut off the central heating boiler."

"No. I haven't seen anyone."

"That's funny," said Albert.

"He may have shut off the boiler and gone home." Suggested his employer.

"No, I don't think so. I told him to report back." Albert walked along the corridor and disappeared through a door at the far end. When he returned a few moments later he was shaking his head.

"The bloody boiler was still on," he said. "Bloody kids!"

“Ah well, no harm done,” said Cameron. “Let’s go home.”

“Little sod!” breathed Albert fiercely. “I’ll sort him out tomorrow morning.

Then he hesitated. “Just a minute, Mr Cameron.” He went back out through the office door.

“Davie!” he shouted. His voice echoed around the vast building. He was just about to turn back when a voice came out of the darkness.

“Ah’m up here!”

Cameron appeared behind Albert.

“What was that?” he asked

“God knows!” replied Albert, shouting again. “Davie?!”

“Ah heard ye the first time.”

“Davie? Is that you?”

“Naw, its somebody else. He’s a ventriloquist.”

“Don’t get smart. Where are you?”

“Ah’m up here!” repeated the voice.

“Up where?”

“Pit the lights oan, an ye’ll find oot.”

“I’ve just put them off!”

“Ah know that” said the voice. “That’s why ye canny see me.”

Albert made his way to the lighting board and pushed up the isolator, illuminating row upon row of idle metal working machines.

"Where the hell are you?" he shouted

"Up here," repeated the voice. "Up in the roof."

Albert peered up beyond the level of the suspended lamps and just managed to make out a figure at the far end of the building, twenty feet up. Davie was standing on a roof truss, holding onto one of the diagonal struts.

"God Almighty!" breathed Albert, then raising his voice. "What the hell are you doing up there?"

"Staunin oan a roof truss."

"I can see that...but why?"

"Because if ah didny, ah wid fa'," came the reply.

Cameron appeared at Albert's shoulder

"That's not him up there, is it?" he asked incredulously.

Albert was confused and exasperated.

"Well, it's not you an' it's not me, so I suppose it must be him," he retorted sharply.

"What is he doing?" asked Cameron

"Making me very angry!"

Cameron decided to be assertive. "You up there!" he called firmly.

"That's right," David interrupted. "Me up here. You down there."

"Don't be so cheeky!" retorted Albert. "That's Mr Cameron you're talkin' to."

"Pleased to meet you, Mr Cameron. Ah'm called Jist."

"Jist?"

"Aye, Jist the apprentice."

"I really think you should come down, young man. I know what your name is."

"Why don't you use it, then?"

Cameron turned to his foreman. "He's not doing his employment prospects much good," he said. "I suggest you get him down before I sack him."

"Davie!" called Albert. "You'd better get yourself down here before you get yourself into trouble."

"Trouble! That's a laugh." Davie retorted vehemently. "Whit dae you know about trouble?"

"A lot more than you do."

"Tell us why ah'm up here then."

"That's easy. Because you're thick."

"That's right. Because I'm thick. That's your answer tae everything."

"What's *your* answer?" asked Albert.

There was a long pause before Davie answered. Eventually he said "Ah jist need a bit o' space."

Albert shot a puzzled look at his employer, then looked back up at the figure on the roof.

"Space?" he shouted. "Whit d'ye mean, space?" There's plenty of that down here."

"No' that kind of space," countered Davie. "Space, space."

"Whit did he say?" asked Cameron.

"Space space!" Albert answered.

"Space, space?" Cameron repeated. "the boy's demented. What's he talking about?"

"What're ye talking aboot?" shouted Albert.

"Ah need to think, Ah jist want space and time tae think."

"Think!" Albert retorted contemptuously. "You?" Then changing the tone of his voice. "Get yer arse down here! Now!"

"Aw right!" Davie called. "Ah'll be doon in a minute. But yis better staun clear. Ah'm gonny jump."

"Jump?!" Albert echoed. "Jump? You'd better not do that. You'll hurt yourself."

"That's the general idea," said Davie

John Cameron was slightly deaf. "What is he saying now?" he asked.

"He says he's going to jump. He wants to kill himself."

Cameron drew his hand cross his forehead. "Oh no." he said nervously. "He can't do that I'm trying to run a business here."

"You can't do that," shouted Albert. "It's against the rules."

"Gross misconduct," prompted Cameron.

"That's gross misconduct," Albert called up. "You'll get fired."

"Aye right!" Davie retorted. "In the crematorium."

"Don't get smart wi' me son! Ah'm the foreman here! Don't you forget it!"

"Albert," hissed John Cameron. "Try and humour him. We don't want him to do anything stupid."

"It's hard to change the habits of a lifetime," snorted Albert. "Ah'll humour his backside with mah boot." Then, shouting again: "See you Davie. You're a useless little arsehole!"

"So everybody keeps tellin' me" Davie agreed. "That's wan o' the reasons ah'm gonny jump."

Cameron grasped Albert by the arm. "Do you think he really means it?" he asked anxiously.

"Ah'm not sure." Albert replied. "But if he's as good at jumping as he is at sweeping the floor he'll only make it halfway."

Cameron continued to hold Albert's arm. "Do you think he really means it?" he asked again.

Albert, irritated, pulled his arm away. "I don't know. I can't read his mind. He hasn't got one."

"We must get him down." Said Cameron. "Remember we've got that group of customers coming tomorrow. I don't want anything going wrong. I could lose a lot of business."

"Whit're ye whisperin' aboot?" Davie shouted.

"We were just saying," Albert shouted back. "That if you're going to jump, you'd better do it now, so that we can get the blood wiped up before the morning."

"Albert." Hissed Cameron vehemently. "You're doing it all wrong."

Then raising his voice called: "David. Have you heard of John Donne?"

"Naw. Dis he work in the office?"

"He was a preacher and a mystic. He once said: 'No man is an island. Ask not for whom the bell tolls. It tolls for thee.'"

There followed a long silence, during which Albert considered his employers state of mind and found it wanting.

Eventually Cameron broke the silence.

"Do you know what that means, David?"

"Aye," retorted Davie. "It means you want tae be up here an' all. Ah'll let you jump first."

Cameron groaned, feeling that the situation was getting beyond him, but he persevered.

"Why don't you come down, David. I'm getting a stiff neck talking up to you like this."

"That'll be a change frae talkin' down tae folk."

Cameron sighed and turned to Albert. "We don't seem to be making much progress," he said.

"You're right," Albert replied. "I'll away and 'phone the Police, or the Fire Brigade. They'll soon get him down."

"No, no no, not that. We'd have reporters swarming all over the place. And we'd be here all night. These people have different priorities. I want this sorted out quietly."

"What are we going to do then?" asked Albert.

"You're the foreman. You're used to him. Do something useful!"

Albert looked up and snarled. "You! Get your arse down here! Now!"

"That's no good Albert," said Cameron. "Try to make him feel good about himself."

"Good about himself!" Albert retorted. "How do you make something like that feel good about himself. There's nothing to work on."

"Of course there is. But if this is the way you always speak to him, he'll find it difficult."

Albert snorted with rage. Cameron called up to Davie:

"You've had your bit of fun. Made us look silly. So why not come down and we can all laugh about it.

“Naw!”

“All right, then. Tell me why you went up there in the first place.”

“Ah don’t know,” Davie said. “And it wisny the first place, it wis the second place.”

“But why?”

“Because the first place wasny good enough.”

“He’s trying to make a monkey out of you, Mr Cameron,” said Albert, loud enough for Davie to hear.

“Just be quiet a minute, Albert,” Cameron retorted. “Look, David,” he continued. “You’re a sensible lad. I’ve often said that to Albert...”

“Balls” interrupted Davie. “You’ve never even noticed me. You’ve never even spoken tae me. Ah wis never important enough. But ye’re speakin’ tae me now. I’m important now, ahmn’t ah no’.”

Albert felt that he’d been silent long enough. “No, ye’re no!” he shouted. “You jump. We put you in a box. Somebody sings hymns, and next week we get another apprentice. That’s it: Finito!”

“For God’s sake, Albert,” said Cameron. “That’s psychologically unsound. You’re encouraging him to jump.”

“You’re a rotten bastard!” shouted Davie.

“Aye! Ah’m a rotten bastard. An’ you’re a useless bastard. The difference is, I’ve learned to live wi’ it!”

"David" called Cameron. "Don't listen to Albert. He's just a bit over-wrought. Tell me what's worrying you. I'm sure we can work something out."

"It's just everything." Replied Davie after a moment. "A whole lot o'things. Life an' stuff like that!"

"Could you perhaps be a little more specific?" asked Cameron. "What sort of things?"

There was a long pause before Davie answered.

"The thing is…." he began slowly.

"Speak up!" shouted Cameron. "I can't hear you."

"The thing is," said Davie raising his voice. "Ah think ah'm good at things, but then it turns out ah'm not. Like at school ah wis good at maths but ah never passed any exams. An'ah thought ah wis good at fitba' but ah never got picked fur the team. An' he." Davie pointed at Albert. "Is aye tellin' me ah'm useless at everything."

Cameron glared at Albert then turned to look at Davie again.

"I'm sure Albert was only wanting to encourage you," he said.

Albert was stung by the black looks from his employer.

"Ah never told you you were useless, you half-baked little moron," he shouted.

"See whit ah mean?" retorted Davie. "But that's no' everything…That's no' the worst of it."

"Go on then," coaxed Cameron, and in a lower voice to Albert. "Keep quiet! You're making things worse."

Albert grunted but said nothing.

"Go on then!" Cameron repeated.

"It's mah girlfriend" said Davie. "That's the real problem... She's pregnant."

Albert laughed.

"Ah thought ye said you weren't good at anything," he shouted gleefully. "You must have had all the gear organised properly for that job. More than you can manage in here."

"It's no funny!" shouted Davie with just the trace of a sob in his voice. "Ah didny want anythin' like that tae happen. Noo she's sick wae worry, an ah' canny help. Ah couldny support her an' a wean. It's just a helluva mess, so it is!"

"Look son," called Albert in a more conciliatory tone. "That sort o' thing happens all the time. Some lassies do it deliberately jist to get hold on ye."

"She's no' like that," Davie interrupted furiously. "She widny do that. It jist happened! It jis came over us sudden."

"I believe you, David" called Cameron soothingly. "But you're certainly not going to help her by....by..."

"By jumpin off the roof!" Albert shouted. "Never mind. We'll get her in to scrape ye off the floor."

Davie's body swayed, as if to fall, but he retained his hold on the cross bracing and found his equilibrium again.

"God almighty!" shouted Cameron. "Then lowering his voice, "Albert! Will. You. Keep. Your. Mouth. Shut! I've told you.

There are important clients coming tomorrow and I don't want the place crawling with police. If he jumps, you're fired." He looked up at Davie who was still poised, white faced, on the roof truss.

"David!" he called. "Don't you see that this is the worst thing you could do for the girl? She'll need you!"

"Aye, well, maybe," Davie replied with some doubt in his voice. "But ah don't know whit ah kin dae fur her."

"Do her parents know?" Cameron asked.

"Naw. She's feart tae tell them. She thinks they'll throw her oot. They don't even know she's goin' wae a fella."

"What about your own parents? Would they help?"

"Ye must be jokin" Davie said. "Mah auld wumman's been trying' tae get shot o' me fur years, so mah sisters kin hae a bed each."

"What about a place of your own?"

"Whit, Oan the money you pay me! That's a laugh!" "He's got a point there," said Albert to Cameron. "Listen. Let me speak to him. Ah'll see that he doesn't jump."

John Cameron agreed wearily. He felt that the situation was getting beyond the point where his managerial skills were effective. "But just remember," he said. "If he jumps, you're fired."

"Davie," called Albert. "Girls aye blame the boys. But they've got a choice as well."

Davie appeared to consider this.

"D'ye think so, Mr Armstrong?"

"Definitely." Replied Albert. "And I bet her parents wouldn't throw her out. I'm a father myself and so is Mr Cameron. We would understand, wouldn't we, Mr Cameron?"

"What? Yes. Yes indeed," Cameron replied absentmindedly, his thoughts on what he could do tomorrow if things went wrong.

"So I think you should have a word with the girl's father. Get it all straightened out."

"Ah don't think that would be a good idea, Mr Armstrong," said Davie.

"He'd go absolutely mental."

"You know him, then?"

"Aye, and he knows me. But he doesny know ah'm goin' out wi' his daughter, never mind getting' her pregnant."

"But you know him. That's a start."

"The trouble is," retorted David. "He disny like me, an' ah don't like him."

Davie," said Albert soothingly. "You young folk think everybody's against you. He's probably quite reasonable."

"Naw, he's no." Davie replied. "He's like Attila the Hun. Thinks he's a hard man."

"Look," said Albert patiently. "You tell him everything. He'll be alright. You'll see."

"Ah'll think aboot it," said Davie from his lofty perch; then he called: "Mr Cameron?"

"Yes?"

"Whit would you say if it wis your daughter?"

"My daughter? Elspeth? Don't be silly David. Elspeth's several years older than you."

"Age disny come in tae it when ye love somebody." Davie replied.

"Elspeth?" repeated Cameron in a dazed voice. "Elspeth wouldn't..."

He had been about to say, 'Elspeth wouldn't take up with the liked of you,' but stopped himself in time.

"Elspeth's engaged," he went on nervously. "You're not.... serious are you?"

"Whit would you say if ah was?"

"Well I would say ..." Cameron took out an handkerchief and wiped his brow.

"I would say....em...em.."

"Cut it out Davie!" Albert shouted suddenly. "Mr Cameron's got enough worries without you tellin' lies about his daughter. It is lies, isn't it?"

"Naw, no really lies... it was jist fur instance like. Ah just wanted tae hear whit he wid say."

Cameron heaved a clearly audible sigh.

"Well! There you are then," called Albert. "He didn't go mental, did he?"

"It wisnae his daughter," said Davie

"Yes, but he thought for a minute it might be."

"No, I didn't," Cameron whispered hoarsely. "The very idea of Elspeth being interested in that young lout is quite preposterous!"

"Aye, you're right," replied Albert softly, looking up. "What lassie in her right mind would fall in love with that?"

Davie thought the remark had been addressed to him.

"What did you say, Mr Armstrong?" he asked.

"I was just saying to Mr Cameron that your girl's lucky to have someone like you to worry about her."

"You're jist sayin' that tae get me tae come doon," said Davie suspiciously.

"No. No, really," Albert tried to press home his advantage.

"A girl could do worse. You're young and healthy. You're nearly good looking. And"...Here he swallowed very hard before continuing. "I don't really think you're useless. It's just my way of doing things. You'll make an engineer yet, don't you worry."

"D'ye really think so, Mr Armstrong?"

"Certainly," Albert replied. "And if you have a word with your lassie's father everything will turn out all right, believe me."

"D'ye really think so?" Davie repeated.

"Definitely." Said Albert.

Cameron thought that Albert was now handling the situation well. The silence was eventually broken by Davie.

"Ok" he called. "Ah'll come down if ye promise ye'll no give me mah books."

"I promise," Cameron and Albert shouted simultaneously.

"Right then," said Davie "But there's something ah huv tae say furst."

"Go on then son," Albert called encouragingly. "Anything ye want."

He and Cameron were all smiles.

"Well," said Davie to Albert. "Ah hope ye take it like Mr Cameron…but – its Jeannie. It's your Jeannie, Mr Armstrong."

The smile dropped suddenly from Albert's face.

"Is this another joke?" he shouted.

"Naw, naw, its nae joke. Ye don't see me laughin' dae ye? It's Jeannie right enough. Like ah said. Ah didny want tae get her intae trouble. Nor me either," he added as an afterthought.

Albert's face turned first white, then brick red.

"Jump, you little bastard! Jump!" He roared

And before Cameron could restrain him, he was climbing the ladder towards to cab of the overhead crane. From the cab he clambered onto the roof truss where Davie was standing.

"Albert!" Cameron shouted, terrified. "Come back down! The boy'll jump."

"He'll no jump," replied Albert. "He never meant to jump. He was wanting to break the news from a safe distance. An' ah'll tell you something else. He'll not jump another lassie either; not once I've got his balls on a jar on the mantlepiece."

"Oh God! Oh God!" Cameron moaned, picturing bodies falling, police and reporters advancing and important clients heading for the horizon. He sat down on the bed of a lathe and buried his face in his hands. He remained in this position for some minutes, not wanting to look, but listening in dread for the sound of falling bodies.

Albert was breathing heavily and holding on tightly to one of the steel diagonals supporting the roof truss.

"Right then, Davie," he said. "What's it to be. Suicide or murder?"

Davie was at the opposite side of the truss. Between them stretched a single piece of angle iron, about three inches wide and fifteen feet long.

"Right then," said Davie. "Ah'll come out where there's nothin' to hold on tae. If ye want tae knock me down, ye can meet me in the middle."

At this point Cameron looked up and saw the boy walk forward, arms outstretched like a tightrope walker.

"David," he called "What are you doing?! Oh my God! Albert! Get back down here!"

"Mr Cameron's talkin' tae ye," said Davie to Albert.

"Don't worry about Mr Cameron," retorted Albert. It's me you have to deal with. You comin' to get me then?" There was a silence, during which Albert continued to cling white knuckled to the roof truss.

"Cat got your tongue?" Davie asked.

"I'm thinking," replied Albert.

"Thinking?" said Davie. "Ye canny think when yer knuckles are aw white like that.... Ah'll jist go back so's I can haud on tae this diagonal. Then if ah start pushin' with mah legs, like this...., the hale roof truss begins tae wobble...." Albert wrapped his arms tightly around the strut at his end and closed his eyes.

"Stop it, David." Shouted Cameron. "For God's sake stop it!"

"It's all right, Mr Cameron," Davie shouted back. "Ah'm teachin' him tae haud on the way he teaches me mah trade. It's ca'ed the fear o'God method, or pit the shits up them... In't it Mr Armstrong?"

"Cut it out, Davie," Armstrong growled, his eyes still tight shut.

"In't it, Mr Amrstrong?" Davie repeated.

"Aye, Right. Whatever ye say. Jist stop doing that!"

"Ye promise ye'll no throw Jeannie out?"

"Yes, Yes! I promise. I don't know where you got that idea from anyway!"

"From Jeannie."

"Well she was wrong."

"Dae ye promise?" Davie repeated.

"Yes, yes. I promise!" said Albert.

Davie stopped shaking the roof truss, and after a short pause, Albert said: "Right, I'm going back down. I'll have to let go. You'll not start shaking the steelwork again?"

"Naw."

"You promise?"

"Promise."

"You coming down?"

"Nae reprisals?"

"No reprisals. You coming?"

Davie followed Albert as he made his way shakily down the ladder.

When they both had reached the floor, Albert grabbed Davie by the back of the collar and hissed: "Right, you little bastard!"

"Albert!" Cameron shouted. "What are you doing?"

"I'm just taking him up the back of the workshop for a wee talk." Albert replied.

"No you're not," barked Cameron with uncharacteristic firmness. "We'll go up to my office and deal with this in civilised fashion." Then as Albert seemed about to argue. "Now! Let's go!"

They walked off in procession, Cameron leading, Davie in the middle and Albert bringing up the rear, stiff armed, with his hand still holding Davie firmly by the collar. He released his grip only when they were in Cameron's office.

John Cameron crossed the room and sat down behind his desk, indicating to the others to sit in the two chairs on the other side. He felt much more confident now that he was in his familiar position of power.

"David," he said firmly. "You have just put me through one of the worst hours of my life. Further, although you may not be aware of it, your actions have contravened clause twelve of your contract of employment, leaving me no alternative but to consider the contract void."

Davie half rose to his fee. "Dis that mean ah'm fired?" he asked.

"In a word, yes," Cameron replied.

Davie collapsed back into his chair. But you promised ye widny....if ah came doon!" he promised feebly.

"An offer made under duress is invalid in law," retorted Cameron.

Davie looked confused.

"Whit dis that mean?" he asked.

"It means being in a position where you have no real choice."

"Aye," said Davie. "That's how it was wi' Jeannie and me. It jist came ower us sudden."

Cameron sighed. "Look David," he said patiently. "I really cannot have employees threatening to jump from the roof. It could ruin the business."

"Ah didny mean tae ruin your business, Mr Cameron." Davie replied.

"Ah didny even mean tae go on tae the roof. It jist seems tae come over me sudden."

Albert looked at him fiercely. "An awful lot of things seem to come over you sudden," he growled.

Davie sank deeper into his chair. "Aye, well," he replied defensively. "It's jist human nature so it is."

"What's human nature to some, isn't human nature to others," Albert retorted. "Once you get a bit older you'll learn to control your emotions. Isn't that right, Mr Cameron?"

"What?" Cameron suddenly realised that self-analysis was not one of Albert's strong points. "Yes! Yes indeed! Quite. Emotional instability is something I would prefer to do without. I'll have to let you go, David."

"That's no' fair. Ah huvny done any harm."

"Tell that to my nervous system! You'll have to go, David."

"Are you not being a bit hard on him, Mr Cameron," said Albert, surprising everyone.

"For God's sake, don't you start, Albert." Said Cameron. "Ten minutes ago you were going to castrate him."

"I was just a bit irritated. I was just letting off steam."

"I'm not a charity. I need reliable staff, not acrobats."

"Would you keep him on if I promised he'd cause no more trouble?"

"No!! And you'd better watch your step. You're not indispensable either."

"Mr Cameron." Davie tried to interrupt.

"Shut up Davie." Said Albert.

"Listening to you out there," Cameron continued, "I thought you would have paid me to get rid of him."

"I'm thinking about Jeannie," said Albert. "If she's daft enough to want to marry him, he's going to have responsibilities. That'll maybe bring him to his senses."

"Mr Cameron...."

"Will you shut up, Davie," said Albert.

"I don't know," Cameron replied doubtfully. "I wouldn't want family feuds upsetting the workshop."

"No feuds," said Albert firmly. "Would there, Davie?"

"Ah don't know. Ah suppose so....Mr Cameron..."

"What is it Davie," Cameron said irritably.

Davie cleared his throat and said: "Ah want tae hand in my notice."

"Well, there you are," said Cameron with a sigh of relief. "That's the end of the matter."

"Wait a minute," Albert said. "Wait a minute... where would you get another job?"

"Mah Auntie Maggie said she could gie me a job."

"What sort of job?"

"Sort o' caretaker and handyman. Keepin an eye on things an' stuff like that."

"Where does your Aunty Maggie work?" Albert asked.

"She's a sort of manager at a place called the Juno Massage and Sauna."

"I've heard about that place," said Albert. "I'm surprised at your Aunty. That's no place for a young lad like you."

"Naw it sounds quite good. She says there's a lot o' big shots go there. She knows them all. Says ah could make contacts. Maybe impress one o' them. It's real high class."

Albert exploded. "High class, my arse. From what I hear, it's full of weirdos and perverts. Isn't it Mr Cameron?"

Cameron who had started looking at Davie with a glazed expression on his face shook himself to life. "What? Yes! No! I don't know! I have no knowledge of these places...My wife..."

"Yes?" prompted Albert?

"What?"

"You were saying about Mrs Cameron"

"Was I?" said Cameron. "Yes. Quite... Yes.... My wife chairs a committee that's trying to get these sort of places closed down. Your aunt knows all the clients?"

"So she says."

"Well now," said Cameron. "Well now. There you are then. Dear dear. Quite."

"We can't allow the boy to work in a place like that, can we Mr Cameron?" asked Albert.

"Albert's got a point there, David," said Cameron. "You don't want to go rushing into a job with no future. I do care about my employees, you know."

"So he can keep his job?"

"I didn't say that. But if he wants to leave I would like to think he could do better than that."

"I'm sure you would," said Albert.

Cameron glared at Albert. "What does that mean?"

"Like you said," replied Albert. "You care about your employees."

"Yes, well. You can't create a successful company if you don't care about people.....David... Do you really want to leave... Throw away your apprenticeship?"

"Well..." Davie began.

“I can see you are hesitating,” said Cameron. “If we can agree that nothing will be said about what happened here tonight – and that goes for you too, Albert – if that is fully understood, you can keep your job.”

“Thanks, Mr Cameron. Thanks very much. Ah didny really want tae leave. It wis jist wi’ everything....everything...the way things wis going’ on...Ah didny know whit tae do... an’ mah aunty said...”

“David,” interrupted Cameron. “Just go. Just get out. Please.”

Albert stood up, and grasping Davie by the arm, pulled him out of his chair and towards the door, where Davie turned and said “Goodnight, Mr Cameron, Thanks.”

Once outside, Albert asked: “Your aunt doesn’t really work at the Juno, does she?”

Davie looked puzzled. “Aye,” he replied.

“You mean you didn’t know what you were doing, as usual?”

“Ah just wanted him to know ah could get another job if ah wanted. Anyway, thanks for stickin’ up for me,” said Davie, then gasped as Albert pushed him hard against the corridor wall.

“Look,” said Albert. “If you were a prize in a raffle I wouldn’t buy tickets. As a prospective son-in-law, I rate you somewhere between Mickey Mouse and Little Bo-Peep. So if I belt you one, it’s just come over me sudden. Right?”

“Ah might belt ye back.”

Albert grinned ferociously. “I’ll take the chance,” he said. “Now you’re coming home with me and we’re goin’ to sit down and talk things over with Jeannie and her mother - except you'll keep your mouth shut and do what you're told."

"That's no fair," protested Davie.

"That's as fair as it's goin' to get," said Albert. "But first, we're goin' for a pint. I think we both need one. No, we'll have two pints. One to pretend that we're goin' to get on with each other, and one to pretend it matters."

"What, d'ye mean by that?" Davie asked.

Albert grinned again. "You think I'm a hard man. Wait till ye meet her mother. You can maybe dance along roof beams, but you can't walk on water. You were wanting space. Forget it. You've had all the space you're going to get!"

THE BODY IN THE CUPBOARD

I hadn't intended to be early. It just happened that way. I was never any good at organising time. So I was half an hour early for the Creative Writing evening class. When I arrived, there was just me and the Janitor. He was sitting in his office by the entrance, watching television. I raised an arm and called 'Hi' in the passing and went on into the gloomy recesses of the Victorian building, through its long curving corridors. The high ceiling accentuated the silence and the shadows.

I opened the door to room nine, switched on the lights and went in. I put my notebook on a desk near the back, so that I would be as far away from the Tutor as possible.

Maybe that was why I was early. A sort of Freudian time slip. The Tutor was usually enveloped in a cloud of garlic fumes; a minor satellite for the hole in the ozone layer. He wasn't French nor Italian. Perhaps he was afraid of vampires. Or perhaps he just liked garlic or was trying to extend his body space. If the last, he had certainly succeeded with me. Three rows of desks minimum.

I looked at my watch. Still twenty minutes early. I fidgeted about for a bit, then decided to go back into the corridor for a smoke. They don't allow smoking in the classrooms. It has something to do with the atmosphere of study; a suggestion of decadence that wouldn't square with the sum of the squares on the other two sides. I preferred it to the smile of pine disinfectant or sweaty little feet, to say nothing of garlic.

I flicked my lighter and the small flamed caused the corridor lights to dim briefly in embarrassment. I drew the cigarette smoke deeply into my lungs and coughed satisfyingly for about fifteen seconds.

When my eyes cleared I was looking directly at a door. It must have been there for all of ninety-five years, yet I had never before noticed it. Idle curiosity got the better of me. I turned the handle and pushed, fully expecting it to be locked, so I wasn't surprised that it didn't budge. Then, just to make sure, I put my shoulder to it and heaved a little harder, still without success. Finally, in a great leap of intellectual competence, I tried pulling. The door opened. Its opening revealed a large walk in cupboard which was empty except for a woman. I didn't say 'Hello' because she was lying on the floor with her eyes closed. She was wearing a brown jacket and skirt with matching shoes, and I remember thinking even through the initial shock, that the outfit did nothing for her. But the main thing, the thing that really leapt at me and caught me by the throat, was the notion that she was dead. I had met strange people in strange places before this, but they all had, to a person, been more of less vertical and more or less capable of holding up one end of a conversation. This one wasn't either. Besides, there were three ugly gashes across her neck and a knife sticking out of her chest.

Most people faced with this situation would have panicked... I'm fairly average, so I panicked. I found myself in the Janitor's office being told firmly to pull myself together. This wasn't as easy as the Janitor thought. I was fairly far apart. But my babbling and gesturing must have got some message through, because he started off down the corridor like a speeding Janitor. I followed closely like a wheezing smoker. He stopped abruptly at the open door.

"What body?" he was asking as I cannoned into him. Then we both sort of said "Whoof." As he sank to his knees, I put my hand on his head to steady myself. Then I looked and felt a sudden close affinity with Old Mother Hubbard. Bare cupboards as far as the eye could see. Feeling bewildered, I wiped the hair cream from the palm of my hand. The Janitor was dusting off his trousers and pulling himself up to his full five foot three. He towered under me.

"What body?" he repeated

There didn't seem to be much of an answer to that, but I tried. "But there was," I protested. "Definitely. Ghastly brown suit...Knife..."

He gave me a look full of unspoken obscenities, turned on a contemptuous rubber heel and left. I felt hurt and humiliated, not to say puzzled. It's not often that the corpse flees the scene of the crime. I decided to flee it myself. All the way across the corridor and into the classroom. This turned out to be my second worst move of the evening. There, two desks from the back and three from the left, was the corpse, neatly laid out on her back so that the weapon operandi or vivendi or whatever you call it could be clearly seen sticking out of her front. Bodies in cupboards were one thing. Bodies as classmates were quite another. I decided to leave, I still didn't like the suit.

The Janitor didn't seem particularly pleased to see me again so soon. "Deary me," he said, or words to that effect. My mouth was opening and closing without issue for some time before I managed: "It's back!"

He took some persuading, but he must have been one of those rare birds; a Janitor with human blood flowing in his veins. He heaved himself to his feet, sighed deeply and followed me back to the classroom. This time he believed me. He tried my codfish impression and said: "It's Mrs Henderson. She's a teacher here. I saw her just today, at lunchtime, she was eating a pie in the dining hall."

I didn't think she had died of food poisoning. The clues pointed elsewhere.

"How was she moved from the cupboard?" I asked and at that instant each of us realised that if the movee was here, the mover could not be far behind, perhaps considering the elimination of witnesses.

"We'd better call the Police," the Janitor said.

"Oh, my God. No," said the corpse, sitting up suddenly. "You'd better not do that."

The Janitor fainted. I'd never seen a Janitor faint before. It was quite interesting. Not that he fainted any differently from anyone else, but I'd always imagined them to be made of sterner stuff.

I suppose it was a bit callous, but I turned my thoughts to the corpse. I had been trying to calculate the odds against resurrection.

"A real work of art, don't you think?" she said, speaking through her waxen death pallor. She was fingering the slashes on her throat as if they were a cherished string of pearls. She removed the knife from her chest just as the Tutor walked in. He evaluated the whole scene in an instant and spoke with a certainty denied us lesser mortals.

"The Janitor's lying on the floor behind that desk there," he said. "What happened?"

"He fainted," I explained... I wasn't feeling too well myself.

"Why aren't you in the cupboard?" he asked the corpse

"I was," she replied. "I thought I'd get into the cupboard well before anyone arrived for the class. Then I heard someone trying to get in. She pointed at me. "Then he opened the door. He was certainly impressed."

I didn't argue the point.

The Tutor curled his fat top lip.

"You've ruined the whole thing," he said brusquely as he could with his fat top lip curled.

"Ye..es" I replied, unencumbered with curled lips. "What about the Janitor?"

"Nothing to do with the Janitor."

"No. I mean. Shouldn't we be doing something?"

The Tutor looked down.

"Yes," he said decisively. "We'd better bring him round."

"Would you please fetch a glass of water?" I asked the corpse.

"Priscilla," she replied. "Certainly."

"No need for that," the Tutor interrupted. "Just slap him gently about the face a bit."

I've never slapped anyone about the face, let alone a Janitor.

"No," I said.

"No?" he repeated as if he couldn't believe his ears. "No? Oh, for goodness sake… I'll do it myself." He knelt down thus enveloping the unfortunate man in his garlic poisoned outer atmosphere.

'Who'd be a Janitor?' I thought

There was a short burst of slapping which brought no immediate result. I hoped the Tutor wasn't going to administer the kiss of life. Fortunately, he stood up as soon as he'd done slapping and the Janitor's eyes began to open. I waited for him to say, 'Where am I?' but he didn't.

"There you are, you see," said the Tutor. "No need for water."

It is unsettling when deeply held articles of faith are flattened in the steel vice of reality. It makes you think your intellectual house is built on sand.

The Janitor spoke.

"Water," he croaked

Here was a Janitor among Janitors.

At that moment, two of my fellow students arrived.

"Take the Janitor to a glass of water," commanded the tutor, in a brief but brilliant display of lateral thinking.

The sound of rubber heels scraping squeakily along the corridor faded into silence and more refugees from an evening in the bosom of their respective families arrived, notebooks in hand, to take their seats. The corpse sat at the front, removing make up. Eventually the Janitor's watering party returned flushed with success and the class had its full complement, plus one.

An excited buzz was going around the room. I decided to swat it.

"I would like a full explanation of this charade," I said loudly.

The other students looked both interested and puzzled. The Tutor looked at me, I knew he wouldn't take implied criticism sitting down. He stood up.

"Harrumph, "he said, pregnant with lucid sentences.

"An idea for a short story," he aborted. "Class to see the body. Experience the initial shock. Write about it. Invent plot, etcetera, etcetera. Mrs Henderson agreed to help."

"Pricilla," said the corpse.

"What about Mrs McGovern," I protested. "She's got a weak heart."

Mrs McGovern was a florid faced lady two from the right, second front row.

"Quite," said the Tutor, as if that was just part of the great tapestry of life. It was then that I saw him for what he really was. A man who concealed counterfeit corpses in cupboards without considering the consequences, human or alliterative.

"It's all right, George," said Mrs McGovern. "I'm on new pills."

'Et, tu, Mrs McGovern,' I thought

The tutor glanced a 'there you are then, smart arse' at me and began to explain to the group how I had ruined the wonderful scheme he had so carefully worked out; and to which Mrs Henderson. - Priscilla. - had given so much of her time; inferring that I had, without doubt, caused much great literature to be stillborn.

He was just saying ‘and therefore’ when I pulled out the little silver-plated revolver that I had concealed about my person and shot him right in the middle of his therefore. A small, perfectly circular black hole appeared midway between his eyes and a look of surprise came across his face as I saw him fall forward across the nearest desk, smashing it to firewood.

“And therefore,” he said. “We shall have to fall back on a more mundane agenda, since the element of surprise has been lost.”

‘Not on me’ I thought slipping my metaphorical revolver back into my actual pocket. I sighed. So much for my belief in janitors, tutors, bodies in cupboards and now, psychokinesis.

I didn’t go back to the class. It wasn’t the tutor or the garlic, or that we could only smoke in the corridor. The muse, the urge to write had gone. Besides, the Janitor maintained a stubborn belief that the whole thing was somehow my fault.

He refused to let me in.

THE FLAT

The flat occupied the top floor of a building high on a hilltop and the lounge windows looked out across the rooftops of Marchmont to Arthur's Seat and the Firth of Forth beyond.

Years of neglect had left the interior gloomy and dilapidated, and the first time George walked through the door, he was overcome by a sudden mood of loneliness, a feeling which turned immediately and illogically to an empathy and a desire to make the place his; the desire turning to determination when he saw the magnificent view.

When he later discovered the flat had belonged to an old lady who had lived there since birth, first with her parents, and then alone, he had the fanciful notion that the brief feeling of loneliness he had experienced to be the last whisper of her being, lingering in the emptiness that had once been the centre of her life.

Once bought, he spent a great deal of money on its renovation, and when it was finished, the flat had an elegance he wouldn't have believed possible. The eyes of the lounge seemed to look over the city with a confidence that had been missing for a very long time.

As they began living together, George and his flat, he gradually became conscious of an almost palpable feeling of welcome whenever he crossed the threshold. It was more than just the pleasure he felt in the classical proportion of the rooms and the style of the furnishings, it was almost as if the flat found as much pleasure in him as he in it.

Then, one evening in late October, when nightfall had preceded him to his front door, in the time that elapsed between putting the key in the lock and switching on the hall light, that feeling of loneliness, of emptiness, he had felt the first time, returned. In the way of many people who live alone, he spoke aloud.

"It's the darkness", he said to the hall.

But it wasn't just the darkness. Although the feeling went as quickly as it had come, in its place came the realisation that being on his own was no longer the perfect state of existence it once had seemed.

As he prepared his evening meal, he wondered if it was the solitary life his imagination had given the flat's previous owner that had triggered the mood. Then unexpectedly there came to his mind a recollection of a programme he had watched about the male Bower bird, which spent a huge amount of time preparing an avian palace, thereafter waiting expectantly for a mate to come and share it with him. He smiled to himself. Perhaps that was it. Instinctive behaviour driven by the biological clock. In this notion, even if he didn't really believe it deep down, George found an explanation, a connection, between his flat and the longing in him; and found himself thinking of the dark-haired girl who smiled a lot and worked in the front office....

It was the next night that he came home and found the hall light burning. Although initially irritated at his carelessness in leaving it on, he found it comforting, for there was no moment of loneliness. He thought it just possible that it was the result of a subconscious act. He even considered making a habit of it but dismissed the idea as conspiring with self-delusion.

The following evening, the light was on again, so before leaving for work in the morning he made a particular note of switching it off. When he got home, to his disbelief, it was lit. Then an explanation occurred to him. Somehow the hall light had got wired through the circuit for the central heating and as he had recently set the heating to come on an hour before he came home, so the light was coming on with it. The idea satisfied his practical mind and on subsequent nights he indulged himself in the feeling of welcome.

Meanwhile, at his place of work, he found himself paying increasing attention, at a distance, to the girl with the dark hair and ready smile. She had an intelligent face and the way she moved pleased him. With some feelings of guilt, he used his senior position to examine her personal file. Her name was Gabrielle Smith and he discovered that she was twenty-four and unmarried. He realised that this told him practically nothing, except that she was twelve years his junior. In all probability she would be sharing a flat with a male who was more than just a friend. He sighed and put away the file.

When he arrived home that same evening, he laid his coat and his briefcase on the telephone table in the hall and went to the kitchen to switch on the electric kettle. It was his habit, before he left for work, to fill the kettle and plug it in, so that when he returned all he had to do was flick the switch.

He was stopped in his tracks not because the kitchen light was on, but because there was a wisp of steam rising from the spout of the kettle. He felt a cold finger on his spine and made an immediate search of his flat for an intruder, but there was no one there, nor any sign of disturbance. The hall light was one thing, this was quite another. He telephoned a friend, an electrical contractor, who came round later in the evening and spent over an hour checking the electrical circuits.

"All in order", he said eventually. "There's no earth leakage, no feed-back on neutral, no crossed wires."

"So what's the explanation then?" he asked.

"Absentmindedness? Momentary blackouts?" suggested his friend.

"You're saying that I'm switching things on without realising it", said George. "Early onset of senility, losing my marbles?"

His friend smiled. "Don't put words in my mouth", he said.

That night George dreamed he was making love to a woman with tightly bobbed hair who kept calling his name. He awoke to darkness and the sound of her voice still whispering in the bedroom. Then the hall light came on.

George had thought a lot about how he could introduce himself to Gabrielle without making it too obvious. In the event, it was arranged for him. One afternoon she came into his office carrying a thick file.

"Excuse me Mr Gibson", she said, handing him the papers. "Mrs Anderson asked me to let you examine this contract before it goes out. It has some implications for your department. You may want some alterations or additions."

He smiled. "Miss Smith, isn't it?"

"Yes", she replied, continuing: "There's a bit of a rush on, I'm afraid. It has to go out in tomorrow's midday post."

"Mrs Anderson hasn't left me much time then, has she?" he asked rhetorically. He looked at his watch. "It's almost four-thirty; I'll have to do it now. Will you tell Mrs Anderson that whoever worked on the contract will have to stay on with me."

"I drew it up", Gabrielle said. "And I don't mind staying late."

It was almost nine o'clock before they completed their task, and as they were preparing to leave, George said: "I don't know about you, but I'm starving. There's a fairly decent restaurant about ten minutes from here. I think the company owes us a meal, don't you?"

Gabrielle hesitated briefly, then to George's delight, accepted with a smile.

As they ate, they talked and found that they had many common interests, not least of which appeared to be a growing interest in each other. As they drank their coffee, George, with only a brief flutter of apprehension, asked her if she would consider accompanying him to the theatre later in the week.

Gabrielle smiled and said: "Yes, I'd like that."

After he had taken her home, he drove back across the city, his mind in pleasant turmoil.

It was one of those nights in early December when a bitter wind from the north sought to eliminate the spark of life wherever it lay exposed. George, in his preoccupation, hadn't noticed it, but after he parked his car, he caught the full mind-numbing blast. He was therefore more grateful than usual for the light and the warmth with which he was greeted. What he wasn't prepared for was the additional wave of heat coming from the gas fire in the lounge which, judging by the white incandescence of the radiant bars, had been on for some time. However, his mood was such that he wasn't disturbed by this new phenomenon. He poured a large whisky, raised the glass and said: "Here's to us, my beautiful flat."

During the months that followed, as the New Year came, and January rolled into February and February into March, George became so used to the flat's caring ways that he took it for granted. He accepted, without a thought, the lit hall, the boiling kettle, and on particularly cold evenings, the warmth of the gas fire. In any case he was too besotted with Gabrielle to think of much else. Except that when he slept, some nights he dreamed of Gabrielle and some nights he dreamed of the woman with the tightly bobbed hair; and on the nights he dreamed of Gabrielle he awoke to an icy cold bedroom. On the nights he dreamed of the other, he wakened to warmth and the whispered sound of his name following him from sleep.

It was strange that as George and Gabrielle were now so much in each other's company, he never took her to his flat. Gabrielle wondered if it was old fashioned propriety, for he was like that in some ways, but she made no comment. It was even stranger that the thought hadn't entered George's head.

Then one evening, after they had enjoyed an excellent meal in a quiet hotel, he asked: "Will you come shopping with me tomorrow?"

"Shopping?" she repeated.

"For an engagement ring."

Her reply was to lean forward and kiss him.

He bought her a ridiculously expensive diamond mounted in twenty-two carat gold, then they decided that they were hungry and they went like teenagers to a fast food restaurant.

"A Burger King and a diamond ring", said Gabrielle. "You are a prince among men."

"What took you so long to find out?" George asked.

"I've always been suspicious of the motives of older men", she countered "Although you have consistently confounded them."

"In what way?"

"You've never asked me back to this wonderful flat of yours – to listen to your CD's or to see your etchings."

"Don't get too pushy", he said. But he took her there that night.

The flat was in darkness. George switched on the hall light and threw his coat on the telephone table.

"Would you like a coffee?" he asked.

"Let me", said Gabrielle. But as she picked up the kettle she gave a scream and the kettle fell, spilling water across the floor.

"I got an electric shock", she gasped.

George led her to the lounge and sat her on the settee.

"Let's forget the coffee", he said. "We'll have a whisky instead."

Gabrielle shivered, and George lit the gas fire. Then he poured two large measures of whisky.

"Feeling better?" he asked coming to sit beside her.

Gabrielle moved close to him.

“It’s a lovely flat”, she said. “I thought you were exaggerating, but I was wrong.”

There was a romantic film on television and they watched it, sitting together, enjoying the closeness. Later, George lifted the hair from the side of her face and kissed her neck. At that instant the television screen went blank. George swore and got up and began fiddling with the controls.

“Never mind, George”, said Gabrielle. “Who needs it? Come back here.” She patted the seat by her side. He gave the TV a final futile thump, then went back to her. This time he kissed her full on the lips. Some minutes later he disengaged himself gently and said: “Look Gabrielle, I think it might be a good idea for me to take you home.”

Gabrielle had known for some time that she had found one of that endangered species, the gentleman.

‘You disappoint me George’, she mocked. ‘I was beginning to hope that lust was gaining the upper hand’. She reached down and removed a silk garment from her handbag. She spread a brief nightdress across the arm of the settee and said: “I came prepared to encourage your baser instincts. I had hoped that if I put this on you would carry me through to the bedroom.”

George swiftly decided that the first duty of a gentleman was to please his lady. “Put that on and I’ll carry you anywhere”, he said.

Gabrielle got up and went towards the lounge door.

“Give me a couple of minutes and I’ll be back wearing this and my most seductive smile. Nothing else, I promise.”

The moment she left the room, the television came back on again. George watched it for a time, then got up and switched it off. It was only then that he heard the sounds coming from the direction of the hall. It was Gabrielle, pounding on the bathroom door.

“It’s jammed tight”, she called when she realised George had arrived. “I’ve been shouting for ages.”

“Sorry”, he called back. “I couldn’t hear anything above the television.”

“I thought it had broken down.”

“It came on again, just after you left.”

“Can you get me out of here?”

George had been attempting this while they spoke.

“I can’t force it”, he said. “I’ll have to cut through the lock”

“Hurry up then George, will you? I can’t think of anything more designed to dampen my ardour than standing half naked in an ice-cold bathroom.”

“Get close to the radiator”, George called.

“The radiator’s cold”, came the reply. “I can’t get it to work. The valve’s fully open.”

George cursed under his breath and went to get tools. On his way back, he put his hand on the hall radiator. It was warm.

He attacked the door with a violence born of anger, and when he was finished, he was appalled at the damage. The beautiful pitch pine facings lay splintered on the floor; great strips of wallpaper had come off the wall, taking lumps of plaster with them, revealing uneven brickwork and ugly sections of dirty, unmachined wood. He had disfigured his flat, and he felt a shudder of guilt.

"A couple more minutes", he called. "I can get at the lock now." He cut through the stem and pushed the door open. Gabrielle was sitting fully clothed on the toilet seat, her nightgown across her lap. "Perhaps I should go home, George", she said. "It doesn't seem to be our night."

In reply, George picked her up and carried her towards the bedroom.

Halfway across the hall, the light went out. As they entered the bedroom, Gabrielle's head struck the doorpost, and George was forced to admit to himself that their romantic evening was descending into farce. Before they reached the bed, he felt Gabrielle's body begin to shake convulsively and as he laid her down, he tried to find soothing words. Then he realised she was rocking in silent laughter.

"Oh George" she spluttered. "We're brilliant, aren't we? Romeo and Juliet, Daphnis and Chloe, George and Gabrielle."

George lay on his back beside her.

"Laurel and Hardy", he added.

Later, their mood changed and they made love for a first and perfect time.

In the lounge, the gas fire went out. The incandescent bars cooled slowly through orange to cherry red, then faded into the darkness of the room.

George and Gabrielle lay in each other's arms and slowly drifted into sleep.

It must have been about three in the morning when George awoke and was renewed in his delight of the woman who lay beside him. He began to touch her skin with his lips and with his fingertips until she awoke to the pleasure of it. And as they loved again, there issued from the fire in the lounge, the disapproving hiss of cold, grey gas.

An hour passed and George was still awake, listening to the sound of Gabrielle's slow regular breathing, intrigued by the thought that he loved her too much to waken her again. He smiled into the darkness, then turned on his side and closed his eyes.

At that instant, in the lounge, a tiny spark jumped across the poles of the fire's igniter. From the spark there grew a small orange ball and from the ball, a genie of yellow flame that roared and threw itself against the walls and against the eyes that looked out across Edinburgh. The lenses blew out violently, arcing down through the darkness, bursting into a thousand pieces on the ground below, leaving the sockets burning in a blood red, sightless glow.

The force of the explosion threw George and Gabrielle to the bedroom floor. Gabrielle, still imprisoned in sleep, gave a high animal-like wail. George, with the benefit of terrified consciousness, pulled a cover from the bed and wrapped it around her. He opened the door and found the hall full of smoke. Tongues of flame were licking along the ceiling.

"Stay put!" he shouted. He pulled the bedroom door shut and ran toward the far end of the hall. The door to the landing wouldn't open. He could feel the heat from the lounge fierce on his naked back and it was becoming difficult to breathe.

He put a foot on the wall by the door and heaved on the handle with all the strength he could muster, but it wouldn't yield. He pounded despairingly on the panels of the door.

"Christ!" he screamed, pulling again on the handle. "Do you want me dead?"

The door swung open. The draught of cold night air filled his lungs, cooled his body – and caused the flames to reach along the hall ceiling with renewed vigour.

As George ran back towards the bedroom, he was aware of the wail of sirens.

The bedroom door was immovable. "Gabrielle!" he yelled. "Gabrielle." He felt smoke reaching into his lungs as he threw his weight repeatedly at the door. Then, as oblivion reached out, he felt something being wrapped around him and hands pulling him away.

When he awoke in hospital, his first thought was of Gabrielle and to his enormous relief; he was told that she was safe. She had been rescued by a fireman who broke through the bedroom window from a turntable ladder and who found her lying, apparently unhurt, on the floor where George had last seen her.

It wasn't until she was in the ambulance that they had noticed the deep disfiguring gash that ran down the left side of her face from forehead to chin. Although the fireman denied it vehemently, it was assumed that it had been caused by a jagged piece of glass as she was being carried to safety through the broken window,

George had suffered minor burns and severe bruising to his upper body, which was painful but not disabling. When eventually he got permission to visit Gabrielle, he almost ran along the corridor.

“Thank God you’re safe”, he said as he sat on the side of the bed.

“And you”, Gabrielle replied, tears not far away. “I was so worried. They told me you were unconscious when they got you out. I can’t remember anything. Not even this.” She raised her fingers to her face. “I don’t know how it happened. I didn’t feel it happen.”

“They say it was the broken window glass.”

“It wasn’t that. I know it wasn’t that.”

George touched her chin gently with his fingertips and turned the damaged side of her face towards him. The wound was long and ugly, made worse by the puckering stitches and the bruised flesh.

“Oh my dear”, he said. “It must be very painful.”

“It’s not. It’s so strange. I didn’t feel it happening, and it’s not painful now. There’s just a tightness. I’m terrified it won’t heal properly, but the doctor said that in three months it will be invisible under light make up.”

“I’m sure he’s right”, George said with an assurance he didn’t entirely feel. “They’ve done an excellent job.”

They sat and talked for some time, making plans for their immediate future, although neither mentioned the flat.

When George rose to leave, Gabrielle attempted to smile, but the pull of the scar caused the latent tears to well up in her troubled eyes.

Three days elapsed before a policeman handed George a set of grimy keys and told him he could return to the flat if he wished.

Investigations had been completed without finding an obvious cause for the gas explosion. In the meantime, George had contacted his bank and insurance company, had got Gabrielle back to the rooms she shared with a friend, and was living in a small hotel nearby.

He knew he had to return to his flat, if only, he told himself, to find out if anything was salvageable; but it took him another twenty-four hours to screw up the courage to go.

The key scraped painfully in the lock and he pushed the door open. He saw what he had expected to see. Blackened ceiling and walls; sodden, filthy carpets, charred furniture in the lounge and boarded up windows. Where the gas fire had been, there remained only a pile of rubble.

All of this he saw from the doorway.

He took a deep breath and stepped into the hall.

Of its own volition, the single naked light bulb came on, struggling to be seen through a thick layer of soot. George stopped and stared in disbelief. It shone for perhaps thirty seconds, then it flickered and dimmed, brightened for a moment, flickered again and went out. Transfixed, George watched three separate teardrops of water trickle down the sooty surface of the bulb, each leaving behind a clear glistening streak before falling to the floor.

A tremor passed through him. Then he turned his back on his disfigured flat and was never there again.

THE HOLE IN THE ROAD

Hello there. I see ye're working hard. Is this you diggin' a hole, then?

Whit gied ye that idea missus? Naw, ah'm buildin' a wall.

It may be small tae you, but it looks awfy big tae me. It's a nice day, isn't it? I'm just out fur a wee walk whilst it's nice. The weatherman says it's goin' tae rain tomorrow.

Thanks for tellin' me. Ah'll bring mah umbrella.

Bella? Don't tell me she's been by? I hope she didny keep ye back. Bella's an awfy blether. Once she starts, ye canny get her stopped.

Goad Almighty!

Naw, Naw, McPherson. It's Maisie Golightly. Don't tell me she's been round as well? She's worse than Bella. It's a wonder ye've got on as far, if ye've been talkin' tae them.

Missus! Ah doant want fur tae hurt yer feelins, but wid ye please stagger off. Ah've goat work tae dae!

Aye. Ah wis sayin' that tae somebody no' that long ago. It's a lovely day! The forecast says it's going tae rain tomorrow though. Whit dae ye do aboot the hole when it starts rainin'?

Ah take it intae the hoose tae keep it dry!

Good fur you son. That's what I always say. Ye've got tae try.

Ah couldny agree mair. Ye're very tryin'

Oh no son. I hope I didny give ye that impression. Ah wouldny like ye tae think I wis pryin'. No, ah just wanted a wee chat. With livin' on mah own, it's nice tae have a friendly face take talk to sometimes. I'm glad ye don't have one of they things that makes a lot of noise.

Ah didny; till you arrived.

Whit d'ye call them again? The things that jump up and down?

Kangaroos?

No, that's not the name. I'll think of it in a minute.

Pneumatic Hammers.

It's right annoyin'. The word's on the tip of mah tongue.

There'll no be much room fur it there.

That's the worst o' getting' on a bit. Ye begin tae forget things. What did you say your name was again?

Ah didny!

Sidney! That's a nice name. My husband's name was Robert. But he's gone now.

Gone but not forgotten!

Aye, it was rotten. He died real sudden, ye know.

Earache, wis it?

No, Robert, I told ye. Eric wis his brother. How did you know that?

Ah didny.

Here, your memory must be as bad as mine. Ye told me your name already.

Missus. If you don't stop talkin' and let me get oan wae mah work, ah'm never goin' tae get hame.

It's nice of you to ask. Margaret's mah name.

Beam me up Scotty!

O here son. I can see why Bella and Maisie's been speaking tae ye. Ye know fine ah'm mair than forty.

Aye missus; an ye're pittin years on me an all!

Ah wis jist thinkin that. Ye are quite small fur all that hard work.

Ah aye look small when ah'm staunin' in a hole!

There seems to be an awful lot o'them about just now.

Eh?

There's two in the next street an' one jist round the corner there. There's holes everywhere.

Aye it's an epidemic. We're tryin tae find an antidote.

I mind now. Electric Hammer. I knew I would remember. You've jist got a pick and shovel.

Please Goad, wid ye jist take this auld bampot oot o'mah sight!

Of course I'm right. That's one thing aboot me. I've aye had a good memory for names. Well, here, this is nice isn't it. So ye dig holes for a livin' do ye?

Naw missus. It's mah hoabby! Ah collect them. Ah keep them in a cupboard at hame!

A shame? It's nothing to be ashamed of. Somebody's got tae do it.

Missus! Ah'm no' ashamed o'anythin'. Ah jist said it was mah hoabby!

Ach don't worry about it. Ye were likely too wee tae be a boabby. But there's nothin; tae be ashamed of, diggin' holes.

Ah'm no the least bit ashamed missus. Ah like it!

That's good. I'm glad you like it.

Allah is merciful. Ah finally hit the right wavelength.

Aye, ah can see ye'd need a lot of strength... Oh here. Here this is awful. I can see yer lips movin' but I can't hear a word.

Ye're aw right missus. Ah wis jist havin' a wee silent prayer.

Oh that's better. I heard ye that time. But ye'll need to speak up. Maybe ye didn't notice, but I'm a wee bit deaf.

Ah canny believe that. Ye wid never know.

Ah'm glad it doesn't show, but it's no funny bein' deaf. No that I'm all that deaf. Some folks think if ye're deaf, ye're daft as well. Does your mother like ye diggin' holes fur a livin'?

She doesny mind me diggin' them, but she doesny like me takin' them intae the hoose.

That's nice. Huv ye found whit ye're looking' fur yet?

Naw, no really. Ah wis lookin' fur some peace and quiet, but you're still here.

Aye, quite clear. I'm not all that deaf, ye know. Are ye not feart ye pit yer pick intae somethin' ye don't mean to?

Naw, no really. But ah widny chance yer luck too long.

There's a lot o' holes aboot ye know. There's one round the corner there and two in the next street.

Ye tell't me that afore.

That's right, four. It jist seems an awfy lot of holes all at once. Ye wid think they wid space them oot a bit better. We havn't had any holes boot here for ages and now there's four all at once. Did ye dig them all?

Naw, jist this yin.

How dae ye know where to dig? Does somebody tell ye?

Naw. Ah jist made a cross oan a map wi mah pincil.

Aye, well, the council. Ah might've known. They're that busy diggin' holes in the road they canny find time tae fix mah roof. Mind, I'm no blamin' you son. It's no your fault.

Thanks very much. Ah'm awfy pleased.

Ah've had slates missin' for ages, but they don't seem tae be bothered.

There's nae answer tae that!

No. No' a flat. I've got up an' down stairs. Mind you, they're getting' a bit much for me now. I've been thinkin' about movin'.

Aye well missus, much as ah've enjoyed talking tae ye, ah wish ye wid. Anytime you like.

Oh hear, d'ye no' think ye should be more careful wi' that pick? Ye'll maybe hit a gas pipe, or something.

Missus! Ah don't suppose this'll get through tae ye, but: Wan – there's nae gas pipes aboot here. Two – ah know whit ah'm dain' and three – ah wish ye'd go away!

Stay? Aye well, maybe jist for a wee while. I'm glad ye're enjoyin' oor wee blether.

Enjoyin's no the word fur it.

Ye know, you remind me a bit o'mah sister Isa's youngest. Jist the way ye gie that sideways look. Aye... like that!

Ah think ah must've jined the wrang religion. She's a nice auld wumman, but Holy Moses, wid ye please move her tae some other hole? There's plenty aboot.

I wish ye wouldn't mumble like that son. I can't really hear ye. All you young folk seem tae mumble nooadays.

Ah huvny tried Buddah or Harry Krishna yet. All ah want is fur her feet tae start movin'. Any direction wid dae.

Aye it is a nice day, isn't it? But they say its goin' tae rain tomorrow.

Here ah wis, jist quietly diggin' a hole in the road, when along came this auld wife who started talkin' tae me, and then ah started talkin' tae masel, and prayin'! Withoot any luck!

Ye're mumblin' again son. Ach, but here, I'll just need to be getting' on. Ah've one or two messages tae get. Ah', goin to treat masel' tae a warm jumper.

Well there ye are ye see. Jist when ye've finally given up hope, Goad finally gets through tae St Michael.

Oh but here son, ah wish ye'd be more careful with that pick. Wid ye get yer books if ye hit a gas pipe?

Naw! Ah wid get a rise.

Size? D'ye mean if ye hit a wee one ye wouldny get yer books, but if ye hit a big one, ye would?

Please Goad! Protect me frae big gas pipes and deaf auld wimmen. Jesus Christ!!

Aw here son. Wid ye look at that! Wis that whit ye were lookin' fur? It's jist like a big fountain, isn't it? Ah think it's going tae fill yer hole up wae water.

Missus. Ye'd better get oot o' here quick. Ah've hit a watter main. Ah'm awa ower tae that café tae phone the watter board an' the police.

Away across the road tae hae yer piece? Here come back! We'll all be flooded in oor beds! Is that no awful! Young folk nooadays. Away tae hae his piece and all this water. I better away an' phone the police. I warned him tae watch what he wis doin'! Ach, that's the trouble wi' youngsters. They never listen to a word you're sayin'!

THE LETTER FROM HITLER

"Right then", said Archie McDougall to Andrew, his grandson. "You were wantin' me to tell ye about the soldier that got a letter from Hitler."

"Yes," said the boy. "The soldier with the funny name."

"Aye, Obadiah McElhose. Right," Archie said. "What d'ye think. Will we have our mug o'tea now, or wait till later?"

"Wait till later."

"Aye, well. You're maybe right enough. They say it doesny do to drink too much tea. Nowadays there's lots o'folk drink coffee. Never drink tea at all. Imagine never havin' a cup o'tea." The old man shook his head. "There's a lot o'queer folk about."

"I'll make the tea if you want," said his grandson

"Naw, naw. There's nae need for that. Don't you worry aboot it. Mind you, tellin' stories fair dries oot yer mooth, but I'll manage fine. Naw. Don't you worry. Ah mind once goin' nearly all day without a cup."

Andrew rose from his chair, went across to the sink by the window and filled the kettle.

"Have ye changed your mind then?" asked Archie. "Ah tell't ye. There's nae need for tea on my account.... Wis that Jaffa Cakes ye brought in?"

"Yes, Grandad. You said you like them."

"Oh, aye. Ah like Jaffa Cakes. Especially now ah've stopped smokin'."

He paused and then continued. "Ye didny notice, did ye?"

"Yes, I did," said Andrew

"Ye didn't say anything, then."

"I didn't want to make you think about it." The boy poured milk into the two mugs he had taken from the cupboard.

"It was the army started me smokin'," said Archie. They used to give ye fags for next tae nothin'. They must've thought it would make ye a better fighter."

When he had made the tea, Andrew filled the two mugs, handed one to his grandfather and settled down into the chair opposite. He waited patiently saying nothing.

The old man sipped his tea.

"Ye forgot the Jaffa Cakes," he said

"Sorry, Grandad." The boy fetched the biscuits and offered the opened packet.

"That's better," said Archie, taking a large bite out of his biscuit and a few more sips of tea. He looked thoughtfully at his grandson for some moments, then said. "Ye're a good lad, Andrew. There's no' many boys your age would bother comin' up to see an auld fogey like me once a week."

The boy looked up, surprised. "I like coming," he said simply. "I like hearing about the war. Anyway," he continued,

"There's nobody at home until Mum gets in after five. If I'm in when she gets home she sometimes sends me to get stuff for the tea."

"None o'yer pals about?"

"Not on a Wednesday."

Archie smiled. "Its good tae think I'm no' entirely useless. But I wouldny like you getting' the idea that the war was great fun. Wars mebbe seem awful excitin' hearin' stories. But it isny. War's a lot aboot bein' feart an' wantin' to run away. But mostly it's aboot bein' fed up and tryin' to make the best out o' it that ye can. So this story's no aboot shootin' people. It's just something daft that happened. A lot o' daft things happen in war."

He paused and took another biscuit before beginning the tale.

"There were one or two really hard men in oor lot, but most o'us were jist ordinary, no' all that interested in fightin.' Take big Oaby – that's what we called him. He was a great big bloke with a face that would frighten the life out o'Frankenstein, but he wouldny have hurt a fly. In fact, I mind not long after I met him, we were in our bunkhouse and there was a bluebottle buzzin' about, annoyin' us so we couldn't get to sleep. Oaby gets up out o' his bunk and goes to get rid of it. I thought he was going to splatter it all ower the windows, but he jist moved wan o' his big hands like lightnin' an' catches it. Then he opens the window an' flings it out. 'They don't like bein' inside.' he says. 'But they canny get the hang o' windaes.'

I never saw anybody like him for catching flies and bluebottles," Archie continued. "His hands moved that fast ye couldny see them. I always thought he could have been the heavyweight champion of the world, his hands moved that fast. The trouble was, he didny like violence."

"Why was he in the army then?" asked Andrew

"He didny have any choice, like the rest of us. Anyway, there was a war on and he wanted to fight for his country, even if it meant tryin' to do it without hurtin' anybody. But the thing about him was that he looked awful dangerous. He was like one o' they big dogs – what d'you call them again – Dobyman Pinchers – an' ye know what it's like with them. Ye're that busy lookin' at their teeth, it never occurs to ye that their tails might be waggin.' Oaby's tail was aye waggin', but he was fifteen stone an' six feet five in his soaks an' his face could turn milk sour at ten paces.

Ah mind once when we were on basic training we had to fix bayonets and charge at this sack filled with straw that was hanging on a rail. We were supposed tae take a run at it, howlin' like banshees, stick the bayonet in, and then run on like demented monkeys as if we were goin' to murder the hale German Army. When Oaby's turn came and he went chargin' doon the slope roarin' like a bull even the instructor turned white. Ah half expected the sack tae take its heels. He went tearin' doon, but when he reached the dummy, he missed it with the bayonet and hit it with his shoulder. It went flyin' about twenty yards an' burst open, its straw guts scattered a' ower the grass. If it had been a German soldier, it would have landed in Berlin."

'Very good, McElhose,' said the instructor after he got his breath back, 'But ye'll need tae aim better with the bayonet.'

Big Oaby told me later that at the last minute he hadny the heart tae stick the bayonet in the dummy, but he wasny quick enough to miss it with his shoulder. Ah think he felt sorry fur it… "Ye know," said Archie to his grandson, "Ah think I could manage another Jaffa Cake. An' while you're at it, ye could put a bit of hot intae mah tea."

As the boy went for the teapot, he asked: "Could his face really do that, Grandad?"

"Do what?"

"Turn milk sour."

"No' really. It's jist a thing ye say. Mind you, they never gave him canteen duties. Anyway like I said, he was real fearsome looking.. There was one time when we were in a pub havin' a wee drink and I wis arguin' with this soldier from an English regiment. The only part o' me that was violent was mah tongue, an' it sometimes got me into trouble. I mind o' saying to this lad that his mob should wear their uniforms back to front so that when they were runnin' away, everybody would think they were attackin.' Well, he went to hit me, but before he could hardly move, Oaby had grabbed him by the front o' the tunic and lifted him clear aff the ground. The bloke jist hung there, mooth hangin' open an' baith legs danglin'. 'Archie's mah pal.' Says Oaby. 'Don't hit him.'

The whole place went quiet and the only thing that was moving was the tobacco smoke. For a minute, ah thought there was goin' to be a riot, for the English lad had a lot o' his mates in with him, but they must have taken a good look at Oaby an' thought the better of it. Then Oaby lifts the fella a bit higher an' dumps his backside on the bar counter.

'Kin ah buy ye a drink?' he asks, as if nothin' had happened.

So you see," said Archie, "He got this reputation o' bein' Britain's secret weapon. Ah was practically the only person that knew he didny have a fuse. But he wisny very bright. He had an awful time getting' something into his heid. You could practically hear the wheels workin'. But once an idea got in, it couldny get out again, like a beetle in a bottle... How many Jaffa Cakes is that I've had?"

"Three, I think, Grandad."

"Ach well, I could probably go another one. Hae one yourself, Andrew. That the trouble with stoppin' smokin'. You start eatin' too much. I'll need to watch ah don't get too fat and end up like a barrage balloon."

The boy looked at the small skinny figure opposite and tried without success to imagine a fat grandfather.

"What's a barrage balloon?" he asked

"It was a great big balloon shaped kind o' like a whale. They filled it with gas and put it away up into the air with a wire attached. They were supposed to make Gerry aeroplanes keep away in case they flew intae the wire, but it didny work. The Gerries jist flew over them. It was a daft idea left over from the first world war."

"Why bother with them, then?" asked the boy.

"It wis in the regulations. 'When the Air Raid Siren goes, put up the barrage balloon.' And if it was in regulations, ye did it. Ye weren't allowed to argue, even if it was daft. There were lots o' strange things went on, and what I'm going to tell you next was one of the strangest."

Archie shifted position in his chair and stretched out his legs. "About eighteen months after the war started, and at a time when the Germans had occupied nearly the whole of Europe, a

Nazi called Rudolph Hess, who was one o'Hitler's right hand men, parachuted from an aeroplane into a field at Eaglesham, just south of Glasgow, no' that far from here. The first person he bumped into was a ploughman who took him home for a cup of tea and a blether."

Andrew gave a disbelieving snort of amusement.

"Well may ye laugh," said his Grandfather. "But it's perfectly true. Ye can read about it in books. When they got talking, he said that he had a letter from Hitler wantin' tae stop the war and for everybody tae be pals again. Ah'm tellin' you this,", the old man went on, "so that you'll understand how Oaby reacted when he got a letter from Hitler."

"Was it really a letter from Hitler?" asked Andrew.

"Not so fast," Archie countered, "Ah'll come ta that shortly. One day ah found Oaby sittin' on his bunk readin' a letter. It took him a awful time pointin' at each word in turn with his big finger, but when he was finished, he looked up and saw me and said:

"It's a letter from Herr Hitler," he said. "He's wantin‘ to speak to me aboot stoppin' the war."

"Is it now," says I. "Can I have a look?"

Oaby hesitated. "He says not to show it to anybody else, or even to tell anybody about it, or he'll no' come."

"Well," I said, "You've told me about it already, so you might as well let me read it as well."

Oaby looked surprised for a minute, then he said. "You'll no' count Archie. You're the only person I would trust." Which was true. He had learned that the hard way. He handed me the letter. It was on fancy headed papers with Swastikas and what looked like German words, but the actual letter was written in English (or as near as made no matter). It began 'Dear Private McElhose', and ended 'Yours Faithfully, Adolf Hitler.' Ah don't remember the exact words, but it more or less said that Hitler would like to meet Oaby down by the big Oak tree in the field beyond the camp the next evening, to see if they could succeed where Rudolph Hess had failed.

Oaby believed every word of it," the old man continued, holding out his mug as he spoke. He waited until his Grandson had 'topped him up' before continuing. "He maybe wouldn't believe absolutely everything he was told, but if it was printed on paper it was the Gospel Truth as far as he was concerned."

"And was it from Hitler?" Andrew asked

Archie smiled, "No, of course it wasn't. I bet you guessed that yourself. " The boy nodded and his Grandfather continued with the story. "I discovered that Sandy Anderson had sent it. Sandy was a man with a face like an angel who would sell his granny for sixpence the pound if he got the chance. He was aye thinkin' o' ways tae part people from their money, and I found out he was takin' bets with half the camp that he could get Oaby down to the field thinkin' he was going to meet Hitler, all bets being off if anyone let the cat out of the bag. Most o' the camp knew that Oaby wasny exactly an intellectual, but they thought he wouldn't be quite as soft as to fall for something like that, so Sandy stood to make a lot of money. The idea was for a crowd o'them to hide behind a wall beside the field with a dummy dressed like Hitler, wait till Oaby turned up (as Sandy was sure he would) and then run out and, as Sandy put it, introduce one dummy to another. That's the sort o' toerag he wis. I decided to put on a pound bet myself and got invited to be in the crowd behind the wall.

A hour before the appointed time, Archie came to our hut and asked Oaby and me down to the canteen for a drink. He did this to check that nobody had let on, and when Oaby said he couldn't come because he had an important business to attend to, he went away quite happy that his plan was going to work.

The whole camp was buzzing an hour later, when about twenty of us, picked to see fair play were hiding behind the wall just as darkness as falling.

Eventually, somebody said: 'Here he comes.'

A figure appeared at the camp end of the field and started to walk towards the tree. Then the man next to me says 'That's no' Oaby, it's.....' 'Hitler' Ah said, 'It's Hitler!'

All our heads were sticking up over the top of the hedge like coconuts at a shy, watching as the figure approached. It had a long black trench coat and a face with black hair plastered over its forehead and a wee black moustache. As it got to the tree, it raised its hand in a Nazi salute and shouts 'Heil me!'

'It's right enough,' someone shouted. 'It's Hitler right enough.'

'Don't be daft,' Andy Anderson shouted back, and with that, we were all running towards the tree and Adolf Hitler. The nearer we got, the more he looked like Hitler. Either him or his twin brother. Some o' them actually began to falter in their stride. Archie and I got there first. 'Are you Hitler?' I asked. The figure in the trench coat burst out laughing. He pushed his hair back from his forehead and whipped off the false moustache.

'Andy McPhee,' I gasped. 'You certainly fooled me.'

'It's Oaby that's fooled you all,' he said. 'He told me yesterday that some idiot had sent him a letter expecting that he would be daft enough to come here to meet Hitler and he asked me if I would dress up and come instead.'

As Archie paused to take another biscuit from the packet, Andrew asked "Why did Oaby change his mind? I thought you said he believed the letter."

"He didny change his mind," said Archie. "I had already made up the ploy with Andy and after Sandy Anderson left our Billet I told Oaby there was someone who wanted to give him and important message for Hitler. I took him to a store room behind the canteen and locked him in. He trusted me, ye see.

When I let him out later, I explained that Sandy had sent the letter and Oaby, by not turning up had made Sandy look foolish. It took me a long time, but I think he eventually began to believe me, although I think he always had a sneaking thought that he just might have missed the chance to stop the war.

Anyway, the good thing was that Sandy Anderson lost about three months' worth of ill-gotten gains and a lot of his reputation. Anyone who could be outsmarted by Oaby was personia ex gratia as far as sellin' his granny by the pound was concerned, and Oaby, no' for the first time was seen for what he wasny. He had to put up with me, with the war and with people thinking he wis King Kong with a PhD, but he managed it fine. He had a natural talent for it, a real sheep in wolf's clothing."

There was a long silence before the boy realized the story had ended. Then he asked: "Did you ever kill anybody, Grandad?"

"Me? No, I hope not."

"Why not?"

"Well, with me bein' in the catering corps, all the casualties would have been on our side."

Andrew smiled and stood up to go.

"There's a moral to that story," said Archie

"Is there?"

"Aye... Make sure you really know someone before you lend him a fiver."

Andrew looked at his grandfather in silence for some moments, then said

"I'll have to go now, Grandad."

"OK. Off ye go. Ah'll maybe manage a story with more violence in it next time."

"That would be good, Grandad. Bye."

"Cheerio, son."

As the door closed, Archie picked up the packet of Jaffa Cakes. "Only two left," he said in surprise. "That boy's appetite gets bigger all the time."

THE MAN WHO WASN'T HIMSELF

Percy Ponsonby of 15 Fork Street Fentham, looked at his face in the mirror as he poked his cheeks with a tentative finger. He was feeling out of sorts.

"I'm just not myself" he said to the reflection, which silently mouthed the words back.

But he didn't have time for reflection or introspection. He was a busy man. One of thousands of anonymous people who go to work each morning and, having put in eight hours of anonymous work, return each evening, with totally reliable and monotonous regularity. So after eating his breakfast cereal, he walked briskly to the railway station where he caught the 7.45, sharing a carriage with seven other anonymous commuters. At one time he had wondered why city gents always bought broadsheet newspapers, but after he started travelling by train he soon found the reason. You can't hide behind a tabloid nearly so well..

The tide of humanity carried him along the London streets and washed him into an office in a side alley, where, after the tide had passed, he was marooned for the day with several hundred others.

Nobody spoke much. They were all far too busy doing anonymous things on rows of identical computers. But one person did say "Morning, John. Feeling all right today?"

Percy raised his fingers to his cheek and replied. “I’m not quite myself, to be perfectly honest, Edward.” He didn’t know the man’s name, but he thought Edward was a good exchange for John.

By the time evening came, still out of sorts, Percy had an irresistible urge to do something different. So instead of going home on the train, he went to a pub. This was something he had never done before, but that evening it just felt absolutely right and proper. He seldom drank spirits, but he sat and drank one after another until his head began to droop.

“All right, pal?” asked an inebriated co-customer.

“Not really”, replied Percy. “I’m not myself today.” But the man had gone.

By now it was fairly late and as Percy was decanted on to the pavement, he joined a fairly large band of revellers, not all of whom were in a party spirit. Discussion abounded, which gradually descended into argument, then into argument with intent and finally argument of a fairly physical nature in which, much to his own surprise, and quite out of character, Percy was deeply involved.

He was, quite rightly, hauled off to a police station, where he was charged with affray.

“If you don’t mind me saying so, sir”, said a policeman. “You don’t seem the type to be mixed up in this sort of thing.”

“Mixed up is the word”, replied Percy. “I’ve been acting strangely all day. I’m just not myself.”

“Hardly a defence”, said the policeman.

“No, I suppose not”, Percy agreed.

But it was. Percy was released without a stain on his character. It turned out that just as he had been feeling all day, he really wasn't himself, but was a Mr. John Brown of Maximillian Crescent, Mumblesbury, who was rumoured to have a history of that kind of behaviour.

The whole episode may seem extremely far-fetched, but it's all there in the police records!

THE SALESMAN

The bell rang.

David looked across at Angela and said: "Don't answer it. They'll go away."

"I hadn't intended to answer it", she replied.

The doorbell rang again.

"Perhaps whoever it is saw us through the window", said Angela.

The bell rang for a third time.

David sighed and went to the window to peer out. "It looks like a salesman", he said. I'll go and get rid of him."

He went to the door and a few minutes later came back accompanied by a man in a dark blue suit.

"Fitted kitchens", said David. "He says he wants to give the lady of the house a large cheque."

The man smiled and asked if he might sit down.

"Of course," Angela said, indicating an easy chair.

Once sitting, he took some papers from his briefcase. "Now. Mr and Mrs Thomson."

Angela's eyes rose, and she directed a quizzical glance at David before asking of the salesman: "How did you know our name?"

"There are companies who supply that sort of information. Besides", he smiled. "There's a nameplate on the door."

Angela made a face and said: "Of course. Silly of me."

"We are operating a completely new scheme to reward customers for quick orders. If you sign up for a kitchen today, I will hand you a cheque for a thousand pounds, made out to cash."

"Pull the other one", said David. "What's the catch?"

"No catch", said the man, removing brochures from his briefcase. "All we ask is that you allow your kitchen to be used in our advertisements."

He handed a selection of brochures to Angela. In most of them a smiling couple figured prominently on the front page, all described as 'satisfied customers Mr and Mrs X'

"We *have* been thinking about doing something with the kitchen", said Angela. "But there are so many other things we need."

The salesman, seizing his opening, said "This is precisely why we are offering the cheque up front, allowing you to buy some of these other things, while still getting your kitchen, which of course can be paid up over five years."

"You add fifteen hundred to the price of the kitchen, then give us a cheque for a thousand", said David. "It's just a confidence trick."

"It's a discount with a difference", retorted the salesman, ignoring the remark. "The market is tight, so we look at innovative ways of helping customers to buy our product. I think this serves both the company and the customer equally well." He then went on to extol the virtues of their products. It became obvious that he considered anyone without one of their kitchens to be very much second class. Their kitchens were the envy of all who didn't possess one.

Angela wondered why, if they were that good, she hadn't heard of them before. But she wondered to herself. She didn't ask the question. The salesman was very convincing.

They moved into the kitchen, where the salesman made a number of measurements, then back into the lounge where he made various calculations, filled a two page form with figures and said: "With your size of kitchen, in the light oak, which you said you would prefer, the cost will be eight thousand, four hundred and forty-eight pounds."

"Is that all?" David asked with heavy irony.

"It's the very best quality you'll find anywhere", said the man.

"It would need to be, at that price", said Angela. "And that cheque for a thousand pounds. Like David said, I bet you just add that on to the cost of the kitchen."

"I assure you", the salesman said indignantly "We are a legitimate company, trading to the very highest standards of integrity. The thousand pounds is a genuine offer."

"And when would we get the thousand pounds?" David asked. "Before we get to be old age pensioners, I hope."

"Immediately", he said "You get a cheque for a thousand pounds, made out to cash, at the very moment the contract is signed."

"I still think there's a catch in this somewhere", Angela said.

"No, I assure you. This is absolutely genuine. We give you the cheque when you sign on the dotted line. We could do it now and you can cash the cheque later today. It's as simple as that. The customer gets cash for immediate use, we get an order, and you get a kitchen, payment to be made, as I say, over five years."

Discussion went on for some time, but eventually a deal was done. The contract was signed, and the salesman handed a cheque for £1000 to Angela.

"Just one thing I should make clear", he said. "Should you withdraw from the contract inside the specified period, the thousand pounds must be returned immediately. Delay beyond one week carries a penalty of £50 plus £50 for each week thereafter. "But don't worry," he went on as David appeared to be about to protest, "We haven't had a single case where we've had to invoke the law."

"I thought there would be a catch", said Angela.

"No really, there's no catch. It's all quite straightforward. As long as you honour the contract, the thousand pounds is yours. You won't regret it", he said, shaking each of them by the hand enthusiastically before taking his leave.

"These people are getting more and more desperate to sell", said Angela after he had gone. She waved the cheque gently in front of her. "I still think they've added a thousand to the price of the kitchen."

"More like two or three", said David. "But they use psychology well. They know few people can resist what appears to be money for nothing. And having cornered the victims in their own home, they know they can't run away."

“You’ve got to admire them”, said Angela. “Real con artists.”

“Aren’t they just”, replied David. “But not infallible. Here we are, having come in here to help ourselves to a few small trinkets while the owners are on holiday, and someone hands us a cheque for a thousand. Not a bad bonus, eh?”

They both laughed and went into the back room to finish filling the suitcase.

THE VICTORY

From where he stood on the trestle bridge high above the river, Tom had a panoramic view of the scrub covered hills and the blue sky beyond. The river was fast flowing, pulsing with life, taunting him as he stood breathing the fresh morning air, feeling the rough texture of the timber bridge rail through his fingertips.

The preparations were almost complete. Six planks had been removed from the surface of the bridge and one placed lengthways, at right angles across the gap, ready to be pushed out into the void. Two pairs of trestle legs rose from the river bed and stretched up to a point six feet above his head. From one of the crossties which connected the top ends of the trestles had been lashed a hanging noose.

The noose was for him.

A tremor shook his body as his eyes caught the movement of a small group of confederate troops advancing. The execution detachment.

His mind, attempting to blank out the reality of the situation, raced back to the beginning of the path that had led him here.

He was a Virginian. Born and raised in the state where the divisions that had torn America apart had affected communities and families, setting father against son and brother against brother. So it was in his case. He had believed passionately in the Union cause, while his younger brother Frank had taken the side of the confederacy. They had never been close and had often wondered if Frank had taken the opposite side merely because of him. Their mother had died giving birth to Frank, and subsequently their father had laid his feelings of guilt at her death on Frank and behaved almost as if his younger son did not exist. As he grew older and became aware of the situation, Tom tried to get close to Frank, but nothing he did created any lasting bond between them. Then their father died and left the small farm which was their livelihood to Tom. Although Tom told his brother that they would share the farm between them, within weeks Frank was gone, leaving without a word.

They saw nothing of each other after that, but it came as no surprise to Tom after the civil war had started, to hear that Frank was fighting on the side of the confederacy. It seemed a natural extension of the division between them.

Tom had earlier volunteered to fight for the Union and after some months had been persuaded, because he was a Virginian and would therefore be readily accepted by the enemy, to join the Confederate army and pass what useful information he could to the intelligence service of the Union.

In this he had been only moderately successful until recently, when on attachment to a headquarters unit, he had heard of a massive attack being prepared by the Confederate army. The importance of this had seemed to be him to be so great that he decided to desert immediately and make his way on horseback, as fast as possible towards the Union lines.

He had ridden hard, and at nightfall he had decided to snatch a few hours of sleep, so that he and his horse would be fresh to make the rest of the journey before daybreak, but he had scarcely tethered the horse and begun preparing a quick meal before he found himself surrounded by a Confederate patrol. Initial belligerence quickly evaporated when they saw his uniform and the Captain of the patrol readily believed his explanation that he was carrying despatches from headquarters to the front and had to be off again in two hours. The Captain had allowed him to carry on with his food and then he had lain down to sleep, only to be wakened almost immediately it seemed, by being dragged roughly to his feet.

The Captain was standing before him, this time far from friendly.

"I have information that you are a Union spy", he said. "I am about to have your saddlebags searched. You will remain here under guard until the search has been completed."

Tom was bewildered. He couldn't understand how his identity had been discovered, until looking round in the light of the various small camp fires that were now burning he realised that another two patrols had arrived as he slept; and standing some way off he saw his brother and an old neighbour speaking together. One or both must have recognised him and told of his Union sympathies.

For all the years that he had suffered his brother's dislike, even hatred, Tom prayed that it had not been Frank who had betrayed him, but Sam McBride, the neighbour.

As Tom watched a soldier handing the Captain a bundle of papers and a small Union flag that he had kept so that he could be identified as non-hostile by Union troops, he knew there would be no escape. His arms were pinioned by two hefty soldiers and another stood with a rifle at the ready.

"There is ample evidence of your guilt", said the Captain on his return. "You will be executed at seven in the morning."

He had then given orders for the bridge to be prepared and a hanging noose put in position before the troops, with the exception of those on sentry duty turned in for the night.

Tom was unable to sleep. He waited and hoped that Frank would come and speak to him, but he never did. And so he sat and watched the sunrise as if for the first time. He sat and gazed until full daylight flooded the camp and stirred the sleeping soldiers, watching them awaken to another day. And they were full of other days. Tom watched them go about their routine duties; refused the food that he was offered, watched and dreamed until he was led out on to the bridge.

As he saw the execution detachment approach, he felt a brief moment of relief when he noticed that Frank was not among them.

After the troops had taken their positions, he was led towards the edge of the space created by the missing boards. One of the detachment placed the noose round his neck, the loose plank was pushed across the gap and two soldiers stood by its inward end. He hoped, as he walked out, that the trembling in his legs was not apparent and as he stared, now unseeing, straight ahead, the order was given, and the two soldiers kicked the end of the plank away from its support.

The sudden searing pain as the noose tightened was agonising but mercifully brief before blackness engulfed him. Then he was falling, and a sudden shock of cold water brought him back to desperate awareness. He was in the river being swept along in the swift current, fighting to stay afloat. As he gasped for breath, the restriction in his throat reminded him that the noose was still tight about his neck. He clawed at it with his hand and managed to loosen it sufficiently to ease the tightness. As he fought to keep his head above water, and unaware of the bullets thudding around him, he was swept out of sight of the bridge and into an area where the river widened and the current slackened.

He struck out for the side and eventually managed to crawl on to a shingle bank where he lay for some time as his mind cleared and strength returned to his body. In time, he was able to sit up. He removed the noose from his neck and threw it on the shingle. He looked at it in a kind of fascination and as he did, he noticed that the end of the rope had been cut almost through, so that only a single strand remained to take his weight.

"Frank!", he thought. "Frank must have done this sometime during the night. It must have been difficult for him to avoid the sentries. Difficult and dangerous." But it had been done and he was free.

Free. But for how long. They must be searching for him. The thought spurred him into action. He pulled his bruised and aching body upright and made for the low brush covered hills rather than the wooded area he could see down river, where he thought the troops were likely to search first.

The sun was fully up now and before long his clothes were dry. He moved as fast as his bruised body would allow and as he climbed upward, he began to regret having refused the meal he had been offered.

Finally, he could walk no further. He staggered into the protection of a group of rocks and sank thankfully to the ground.

He did not know how long he had been there; he must have been asleep, but he became aware of the shadow of a man.

A Confederate soldier stood before him, rifle in hand. It was his brother.

"Frank!" he gasped, struggling to his fee.

"Hello, Tom."

"Frank", he said again. "Thank God it's you. It was McBride who turned me in." The statement was really a question.

"Yes", Frank replied. "It was McBride."

There was a silence between them, each looking at the other, Tom desperately seeking some warmth in his brother's eyes.

Tom spoke first. "And you cut the rope?"

Again, there was a silence.

"No. It was McBride He came to me after you had escaped. He said he couldn't bear the thought of seeing you hanging there, knowing that he was responsible. When they sent us out to look for you, I chose to come into the hills. You always used to go to the hills when you were in trouble. I knew I would find you here somewhere."

Tom took a step forward.

"You won't turn me in now, will you?"

"No, Tom. I won't turn you in."

The crack of the rifle echoed through the hills and down to the riverside, causing other searchers to turn their heads towards the sound.

Frank stepped forward and with his boot, gently turned the body of his brother onto its back. He looked down into the glazing eyes.

He had done what he had been trained to do. He had scored a victory over the enemy. And when the war was over, he would have a farm to go home to.

UNNECESSARY VIOLENCE

Mary Davidson locked the car and came wearily up the garden path, staggering slightly under the weight of two enormous shopping bags. She laid them on the doorstep, opened the door, picked them up again and went into the hall. Long practice enabled her to push the door shut with her left foot. As she passed the lounge on her way to the kitchen she called:

"I'm back, John."

The acknowledgement was made indistinct by the noise of the television set. A few moments later she signed with relief as the kitchen floor took the weight of the bags from her aching shoulders.

It took her some time to stow away the contents of the bags and after she did, the two floor-to-ceiling cupboards, the chest freezer and the refrigerator, which had been almost full before she started were stacked to overflowing. There were in fact a number of items for which she was unable to find a place. These she left in one of the bags, which she slid into a convenient space beside the back door. Although she was very tired, her face radiated pleasure as she considered the fruits of her evening's work.

She made a pot of tea and waited until it had infused before filling two mugs. Then she went to the lounge and handed one of the mugs to her husband.

"I seem to have some stuff left over again", she said.

"Again?" he echoed. "Surely not! I'm beginning to think you're doing it on purpose."

"Don't be such a grouch, John" said Mary. "I'll give it to old Mrs Martin. It must be hell trying to exist on the pension."

"For goodness sake, Mary", her husband replied. "We're not a charity. I don't see how we can possibly afford to be giving food parcels to the needy. Not on my wages."

"Oh come, on John", Mary coaxed. "Have I ever asked for more money so that I can give away an occasional tin of food?"

"That's just the point. It's not just an occasional tin, it's dozens of them and packets of frozen food and biscuits and goodness knows what. I mean, everything in moderation, eh?"

Mary just smiled. By tomorrow he'd have forgotten it, and she would take the groceries to Mrs Martin.

They drank their tea and watched a wildlife programme on television. It was about squirrels.

"Just like Mary, these creatures", thought John. But he really couldn't complain. He didn't know how she managed to cope so well, never mind being able to give stuff away. He couldn't do it, that was for sure.

Then, as Mary had predicted, he forgot about it.

The following Thursday evening after tea as John was sat in front of the TV, Mary said as usual:

"I'm off, then."

And he replied, as usual:

"OK dear, see you later." Adding. "And don't buy anything for the indigent of the neighbourhood."

She laughed.

"All right", she called. "I won't. I promise."

Three hours later, John was just beginning to wonder what was delaying her, when the doorbell rang. She had obviously forgotten her key.

He opened the door to two policemen.

"Mr Davidson?", one of them asked.

"Yes", he replied.

"Can we come in?"

"What? Yes. Come in."

"What's the matter?" he asked anxiously. "Is it Mary?"

"I'm sorry", was the reply. "I'm afraid your wife has had an accident."

"An accident? In the car? Is she all right?"

The taller of the two men looked down at his feet.

"It wasn't a car accident", he said. "Our information is that she was attacked."

"Attacked! My God! Where? How? Is it bad?"

The tall policeman was still avoiding John's eyes. The other one was looking round the room.

"I'm afraid it's pretty bad, Mr Davidson. I think she's got head injuries."

"For God's sake man!" John shouted. "You think! You're afraid! Don't you know?"

"We don't have all the facts, sir. We were sent to take you to hospital."

John didn't waste any more time. He went to the hall and pulled his coat from its hook.

"Let's go", he said.

On arrival at hospital they were shown into a private waiting room, where, very quickly, they were joined by a baby-faced doctor, who looked as if he should still have been at school. He didn't waste time with preliminaries.

"I'm sorry, Mr Davidson", he said. "I don't know how else to say this.... I'm afraid your wife is dead."

John couldn't believe what he was hearing. Dead was for other people. He went to work. Mary did the shopping and housework. Dead didn't come into it.

"What do you know about dead", he retorted angrily. "You're just a child."

"Quite a lot", the infant medic replied. "I've had to learn quickly."

"Let me see her! I want to see her", John said. He was quite certain that the whole thing was a mistake. Mary had gone shopping.

He was led along a seemingly endless corridor, then taken into a small, bare walled room. On a plain metal framed cot lay a body covered in a white sheet. The boy removed the sheet from the face and John saw waxen flesh that had once been his wife. His wife who had gone shopping after tea. The whiteness was counterpointed by an ugly black bloodstained cavity on the top of her skull.

"She just went to do the shopping", he said emptily. Then he began to weep deep body wracking sobs.

He was led gently away and was subsequently aware of being taken from the hospital and driven across town to some other place. The other place turned out to be a police station. He was given a hot sweet mug of tea and a seat in a small room smelling of sweat and furniture polish. There were three other chairs and a plain wooden table. Shortly afterwards two plain clothes police officers arrived and sat down opposite him.

"We're very sorry about your wife, Mr Davidson. It must be a dreadful shock for you..."

"Yes", replied John

"...But we have to ask you a few questions."

John wondered vaguely if it shouldn't be he who was asking the questions, but he was too numbed to think clearly.

"How often did your wife go shopping?"

"Shopping?" thought John. Yes, it was all to do with shopping. Mary had gone shopping.

"Just once a week", he said. "Every Thursday. That is unless she had forgotten something, which was very unusual."

"And you went with her?"

"Me? No, I never went. I hate shopping."

"Never? You never went with her?"

"No, I didn't." John had the uncomfortable feeling that he was being accused of neglect. "She preferred to go alone. What's wrong with that?"

"Nothing at all. It was just a question." Both of the men were looking at him intently. "Did she always go to the same supermarket?"

"I think so, the one at Cameron Toll."

"Cameron Toll." The man nearest him wrote this down in his notebook.

The other one asked:

"Was your wife good with the housekeeping money? Was she a good manager?"

"Yes', said John firmly. "She was absolutely marvellous. I don't understand how she does it...did it."

"And you never went with her?"

"You asked me that before."

"And she enjoyed shopping?"

"Oh yes", John almost smiled. "She lives...lived for Thursday evenings. You know how women are about shopping."

One of the policemen was tapping his fingers on the table.

"Surely", he remarked. "Women like shopping for clothes, jewellery, cosmetics, stuff like that. I didn't think they got excited about groceries."

John's eyes shone.

"Well, Mary did. Her life revolved around Thursday evenings. The nearer Thursday came, the happier she seemed."

The two men exchanged glances.

"Your wife's body was found in Marchmont", one of them said abruptly.

"Marchmont?" John echoed stupidly. "She couldn't have been in Marchmont."

"Has your wife been going to the Cameron Toll supermarket for about four years?"

"Yes, I suppose about that. How did you know that?" She started going not long after we moved here.

"Ah", said the nearest policeman, as if a mystery had been solved.

"I don't understand", John complained.

"Your wife was struck on the head with a hammer. The person involved has been charged with manslaughter."

"Womanslaughter", thought John in his haze. "I don't understand", he repeated. "Who would want to do that to Mary?"

"It fits in with the pattern, Mr Davidson. Every Thursday evening a lot of people go shopping and leave a lot of houses empty. There have been a lot of burglaries in that area over the last four years. Quite unusual. The thief only stole groceries – tinned stuff mostly." The two officers looked at each other again. "It was dark, you see", said one of them. "The house was in darkness, but it wasn't empty."

"Just a glimmer of light from the street lamps", added the other. "The householder, the assailant, was very frightened. She thought she was in danger, so she lashed out with the hammer."

"Perhaps you can understand", the first man went on. "You can become very afraid, terrified even, when you see someone moving in the darkness, near you in your own kitchen."

"So you lash out blindly", said the second one. "With what may seem to others to be unnecessary violence.... We are sorry, Mr Davidson."

BIOGRAPHY

Creative writing has always been an interest for Willie Miller who, whilst working as a mechanical engineer and perfecting his soup-making skills, would jot down ideas and plots in his spare time. He sees humour as his forte and having honed his creative writing skills in a local writer's group has produced the collected works contained herein.

Three of these short stories, 'Close Encounter of the Fourth Kind', 'Penny for the Guy' and 'Penalty' were broadcast by the BBC on Radio Four; as was the play 'Dance In The Old Fashioned Way', a recording of which still exists in the family archives. 'Andy's Trial' was previously published by Collins.

Willie has been a voracious reader all his life and has an extensive vocabulary. This has made him a formidable Scrabble player, often leaving him open to accusations of cheating by his thwarted opponents. He also enjoys painting watercolours and is an accomplished bridge player.

Now approaching his 90th birthday, Willie is still the font of all family knowledge on matters of grammar, punctuation and misuse of the English language; up with which he will not put.

Lightning Source UK Ltd.
Milton Keynes UK
UKHW01n1923210918
329320UK00001B/1/P

9 781786 233547